OLD WOUNDS

LOGAN-ASHLEY KISNER

DELACORTE PRESS

This is a work of fiction. All incidents and dialogue, and all characters with the exception of some well-known historical and public figures, are products of the author's imagination and are not to be construed as real. Where real-life historical or public figures appear, the situations, incidents, and dialogues concerning those persons are fictional and are not intended to depict actual events or to change the fictional nature of the work. In all other respects, any resemblance to persons living or dead is entirely coincidental.

Text copyright © 2024 by Logan-Ashley Kisner
Jacket art copyright © 2024 by Zoë van Dijk

All rights reserved. Published in the United States by Delacorte Press, an imprint of Random House Children's Books, a division of Penguin Random House LLC, New York.

Delacorte Press is a registered trademark and the colophon is a trademark of Penguin Random House LLC.

Visit us on the Web! GetUnderlined.com

Educators and librarians, for a variety of teaching tools, visit us at RHTeachersLibrarians.com

Library of Congress Cataloging-in-Publication Data is available upon request.
ISBN 978-0-593-81474-1 (trade) — ISBN 978-0-593-81475-8 (lib. bdg.) — ISBN 978-0-593-81476-5 (ebook)

The text of this book is set in 12.5-point Fournier MT Pro.
Interior design by Michelle Crowe

Printed in the United States of America
10 9 8 7 6 5 4 3 2 1
First Edition

Random House Children's Books supports the First Amendment and celebrates the right to read.

Penguin Random House LLC supports copyright. Copyright fuels creativity, encourages diverse voices, promotes free speech, and creates a vibrant culture. Thank you for buying an authorized edition of this book and for complying with copyright laws by not reproducing, scanning, or distributing any part in any form without permission. You are supporting writers and allowing Penguin Random House to publish books for every reader.

For Brandon Teena, Daniel Aston, Nora Prochaska, Nex Benedict. For everyone gone. For everyone still going.

Author's Note

Old Wounds does not solely exist for the sake of "representation." This is not a book where trans identity is mentioned, pushed aside, and forgotten about before the end of the first page. *Old Wounds* is intentionally about gender and trans identity, and the ways in which the horror genre has historically forgotten about us.

On that note, please be aware that this story contains many depictions of transphobia, references to suicidal thoughts and actions, and language that some readers may find upsetting. There are also several references to real murders and/or suicides of trans individuals. I do not invoke these names lightly. You are, of course, not required to finish this book, though I hope that you will see Max and Erin through to the end of their story. No matter how long the darkness seems to stretch for, know that the sun will come up again.

For more information on the content of this book, please visit loganashleykisner.com.

1

ERIN IS RUNNING AWAY TONIGHT. She's been soaking in the cold, soapy water of her tub for what feels like hours. Her chin rests atop her knees, arms hugging her legs. The tiles on the wall are a shade of blue so deep that it seems almost purple. It creates an effect that makes the room feel impossibly large and yet deeply constrictive. But maybe she's just looking for excuses as to why she feels so nauseated. The weird paint job seems as likely to be the offender as anything else.

Erin finally pulls the drain and grabs her towel, resting her face in it for two long, deep breaths. She wonders if anybody's ever died from anxiety before, or will she be the first?

The mirror is partially fogged up, but Erin can still catch her reflection when she approaches. Her hair is plastered to the sides of her face. Ordinarily, it hangs just above her shoulders, a near-white level of blond. Bluish-green eyes. Her mouth curves downward naturally, which makes it look like she's always fighting a pout. She definitely is *now*. A fraught expression keeps forming despite her best attempts to look normal.

The family photos that hang in the hall paint a strange portrait. Erin takes note of them as she treads past. There used to be more, before Erin complicated the adolescent boyhood depicted and her mother packed almost everything into storage boxes. What remains of Erin is a mix of genderless baby pictures and glossy senior pictures. It's rather funny. As if she were born at eighteen, fully conceived.

She knocks gently on her sister's half-open door before she steps inside. Hayley, already covered in summer freckles, lights up at the sight of her. She casts her book to the floor and pulls her covers up to her chin with a toothy, eager grin. Erin smiles and sits at her feet. Despite the decade between them, they get along just as well as if they were twins.

"Did you already brush your teeth?" Erin looks her sister up and down, reaching over and tucking a few wild strands of hair behind her ear.

"Uh-huh."

"*Uh-huh*. Let's see 'em."

They bare their teeth at each other. Hayley's teeth are tiny and perfect.

"Okay. You're good." Erin sighs and looks around the room. "I don't know, are you enjoying summer break?"

Hayley nods. "Are you?"

That depends entirely on how this next week will play out. Erin still pretends to think about it. "Well, it's not summer break for me anymore, it's just summer. Adults have to work."

"*You're* not gonna be—"

Erin shushes her. Downstairs, she can hear the sound of the front door closing: Mom is home. Hayley's blue eyes get big, and she nods knowingly.

"You remember what we talked about?" Erin whispers, as quiet as she can get. "You're gonna have to be the woman of the house. Can you handle that?"

Hayley nods with deadly seriousness. "Swear to God."

"Do you know what the woman of the house has to look out for?"

Hayley shakes her head.

Erin puts her feet on the ground and leans in. "Ghouls. Ghosts. And tickle monsters."

Hayley's eyes go wide again, but she's not fast enough to stop Erin's hands from rushing to her sides. She shrieks, and Erin takes a wild kick to the ribs, but they're both laughing so hard that they're out of breath within seconds. Tickle monsters don't often manage lasting attacks around this house.

The light above them turns off, then on again. Erin and Hayley look up to find their mother watching them. She's still in her scrubs, and most of her hair is poking out of its bun.

"Get some sleep, you two." She takes her hand off the switch.

"Good night, Mom!" Hayley grins, flopping back against her pillow, audibly out of breath.

Their mom lingers. Her eyes shift to Erin.

Erin smiles bashfully. "You might've just missed a tickle monster breach," she admits.

As quickly as it comes, her concern melts away. "I thought we agreed, no more tickle monsters at bedtime."

"That's why I said *breach*."

"Uh-huh. Hayley, if you can't sleep, I want you to bug your sister, not me. Got it?"

Hayley shoots her a thumbs-up.

Both girls listen as the footsteps grow softer and softer, until they're no longer able to be heard at all. Erin realizes that might've been the last thing she'll say to her mother for the foreseeable future. Her stomach rolls with too many emotions to neatly sort out.

"Are you ready?" Hayley's hands are cupped around her mouth.

Erin returns to the present moment and nods.

"Promise you'll be safe?" Hayley asks.

"Yeah. I'll send you guys a postcard."

"Promise?"

Erin sighs and puts her hand out, pinkie up. Hayley does the same and intertwines their fingers. She gives Erin a good, firm shake with her whole arm.

Then Hayley pulls herself out from under the covers and wraps her arms around Erin's neck. Erin's face twists up as she hugs her back, holding Hayley's tiny body against her own.

"I'm gonna miss you," Erin breathes.

"I'll have an extra good summer, just for you," Hayley whispers, "so when you come home, I can tell you and Max all about it."

Guilt knots up in Erin's throat. She forces a laugh.

Yes, Erin told Hayley that she's leaving. Hayley is good at keeping secrets. Even still, Erin omitted a few crucial details. Like where she's headed, and the fact that she's not coming back.

Erin hates the way lying weighs on her shoulders, pressing down on her until it feels like she can't breathe. She carefully takes Hayley's arms from around her neck and lays her back down. She tucks the covers snugly underneath her chin.

Eventually. Erin will tell her everything eventually. Now is just too fragile of a moment. Too many things could still go wrong. Erin only hopes that, unlike their father, she'll get the chance to explain herself to Hayley one day.

"Tell Max I said hi?" Hayley smiles with all of her teeth.

Erin tries to smile back, but it doesn't quite reach her eyes.

Downstairs is so quiet that it makes the whole house feel brittle. Erin tiptoes across the hardwood, as if the slightest noise will bring it all crashing down on top of her. This is a familiar routine. Like she does every night, she checks that the back door and all the windows are locked. The fire alarms are set. It's a nice neighborhood, and they're a careful family, and neither fact is related to why she does this. It's about feeling the control that comes with her fingers sliding against the dead bolt. The knowledge that *she* is responsible for this house. She needs that feeling of control on a normal day. It is especially vital tonight.

The front door comes last. On the wall beside the door are two things: a mounted rack, which holds a variety of lanyards, coats, and bags. And then there's the family photo.

Erin's always thought it was strange. Her parents divorced when she was twelve. The family that greets her at the door hasn't existed in six years. And yet it hangs there anyway, at her mother's insistence. It's supposed to be a reminder of what they've come from. Erin struggles to see it as anything more than a marker of what they've lost.

In the photo, Hayley is two, nothing but a head full of blond hair and their dad's smile crowded onto the left side of her face. Erin is twelve, wearing this horrible plaid shirt that makes it even worse that this is the only nongirl photo still hanging in the house. Mom is holding Hayley on her lap; Dad has his arm around Erin's shoulder. He looks like Franco Nero, face dominated by a thick mustache and a laid-back swagger that hangs in the air even now.

Her parents divorced only a few months after the photo was taken. Last fall, her dad died.

Erin stares at the photo for a long time before she jiggles the doorknob and turns away.

It's a contradictory thought, but as she looks, she can find all the spots where life was once lived so much. The corner of the couch where her dad used to fall asleep on Saturday afternoons, halfway through one of his Westerns. The patch of carpet that's still indented from Hayley's baby stroller. The half window in the front door; Erin can remember the sight of Max's hair through it, his eyes peering inside before his thumb jammed against the doorbell.

There's so much that isn't here anymore. Within a matter of hours, Erin won't be, either.

Back in her room, Erin gets dressed for real: a pair of jeans, a hoodie that goes over her tank top, and her most comfortable sneakers. Two half-packed suitcases take up her bed. Once she's sure that the rest of the house is asleep, she goes about filling the bags with whatever fits.

Inevitably, Erin finds herself at her desk. She put it together with her mom, one of those early efforts at bonding as mother and daughter. It's white and bubblegum pink, with a vanity mirror as its centerpiece, where several photos are taped around its rim. Her and Miranda, the day after graduation. Hayley's kindergarten portrait. In the corner, there's a photo of Max.

His face is obscured by windblown bangs, and he's not smiling so much as baring his teeth to the camera. It's been years since Erin has seen him look this happy.

Erin checks her phone. Max lives ten minutes away, and the *on my way* text illuminating her screen is already seven minutes old. So she tops off her suitcase with her bottle of estradiol, her Monday-through-Sunday premade pill case, and a disposable camera she bought for the hell of it, then zips both suitcases up and drags them across the room.

She opens the window and sticks her head out. There's a stretch of flat roof underneath, which is directly above the front porch. The perfect launching pad. Erin takes a deep breath before she ducks back inside and pushes her bags through the window.

It occurs to her, briefly, that this might be the dumbest thing she's ever done, though the night is still young. On her hands and knees, she crawls to the edge of the roof and looks out.

Her vision warbles with vertigo for a few scary seconds, and Erin shuts her eyes until the spinning feeling stops. When she can breathe again, she looks out, not down. The house across from hers is another two-story, with bushes along its porch. It's dark in the windows except for the upstairs bedroom, where, judging from the time, Martha and Jakob are ready to settle in for the night. Erin remembers going through the neighborhood with her dad to clear out driveways in the winter, how Martha would always reward her with five dollars and a candy cane. That all stopped once her dad left, but the couple was still very nice. Very Polish. They never fussed about Erin's whole *thing*.

Erin carefully drops each suitcase over the edge. They fall with firm, muted *thud*s. She turns and grips the edge of the roof and lowers herself as much as she can, until her fingers ache, but there's still a good five or six feet between her shoes and the ground.

She means to do a countdown, from three to zero to letting go, but her grip fails at *two*. Which means she falls silently and lands on her back. It knocks the wind out of her, but it also probably spares her one or two broken ankles.

Still. Erin lies there for a minute. Her breath comes back to her in gasps, each one less shallow than the last. Somehow this is all still easier than sneaking through the inside of the house. Her mom wakes if a pin falls on the carpet. The stairs creak and the front door squeals. Nobody, in all her years of being alive, has been able to sneak out like a normal human being. Nobody's really tried before, either, but that's beside the point.

She sits up. Her back hurts, but nothing seems broken. For a moment, while she's still getting her breath back, she looks around. It's eerily silent. So much so that her own breathing seems heavy and awkward to her ears. She seems so *loud*. She almost expects people to start poking their heads out from behind their curtains: *Just look at that girl disturbing the peace of their neighborhood. Again.*

Tires crunch on street gravel. She can hear it before she finally looks over her shoulder. At some point, the Impala may have been white. But now, in its age, its color has faded into a horrible-looking rust-tinted cream.

She takes a deep breath and, with a bag in each hand, pushes herself to her feet and walks up to the car. The passenger window is already down. Erin bends forward and looks inside.

Despite the fact that it's June, he's dressed in layers; a shirt over a shirt under a jacket. But Max might be the happiest he's ever been. His hair, dark brown, has been freshly cut, uneven ends hanging just past his jawline. His face is marked by acne and lingering baby fat. If they didn't know him, people might assume he was a tween boy. In reality, he turned eighteen last week. It's hardly passing, but Erin knows it's better than not passing at all.

Max beams up at her. "Hi! Are you ready?"

After a moment, Erin nods. "Uh-huh."

One lone suitcase sits in the back. Erin stares at it for a moment, the knot in her stomach twisting again, before she hoists her own bags inside.

After she settles in the passenger seat, Max sits there for a moment. His fingers drum against the wheel. "Sure you didn't forget anything?"

"Yeah, let's go," Erin answers tightly.

Despite the lingering awkward silence, a grin returns to Max's face before they peel out of the neighborhood.

Four days, Erin reminds herself. That was the amount of time Max told her it would take to drive from Columbus to Berkeley. Four days with a boy who broke up with her almost two years ago. A boy who hasn't really spoken to her since. Until now.

Although dread still clings to the back of her throat, Erin can't deny that it is tinted with some bit of exhilaration.

2

MAX'S EVENING BEGAN just after midnight, listening to his mom and stepdad move around their bedroom. As soon as the light went out, he started the stopwatch on his phone. Once twenty minutes had gone by without any sign of consciousness, Max got up, tiptoed to the bathroom, and sheared off most of his hair.

This only took a few minutes, first to hack away at the length that had built up over the last few months, then to clean up the edges so it looked a *little* less crazed. He could still feel some jagged edges at the back of his neck, but it was fine. It didn't need to look perfect, so long as he stopped looking so much like a girl. Once this was accomplished, it was packing time.

His first binder went missing from his dresser drawer way back when he was fifteen. The second had been openly disposed of in ribbons. And then he lost a whole lot more, shirts and underwear and the ability to get his own hair cut, but it was really the loss of the binder that started the snowball.

Not much had been rebuilt in the last eight months. Altogether, everything he was taking fit into one suitcase. Max had shelled out for his fourth binder (shipped to and from his friend Alex's house, an awkward exchange that marked the last time they'd spoken) and he slept with the damned thing shoved down his pants, or tucked into the side of his sports bra. He got good at lying about the things people seemed to want him to lie about.

Although his parents' room remained dark, Max took care to be especially quiet as he slipped out of his room and crept down the long, dark hallway to the kitchen. He imagined having to explain this, if he were to be caught—dressed in men's clothes, hair cut, grabbing the sack lunch he'd prepared for himself a few hours earlier under the guise of needing to bring lunch to work the next day.

Halfway back to his room, Max bumped his hip against a side table. The sound was brief, but so sudden that it felt like it should've brought the whole house down. Max froze and held his breath. His parents' room was still.

Max kept one hand on his dinner while he pulled his phone out with the other, revealing a houseplant he'd nudged to the very edge of the table, as well as a picture frame that was face up on the carpet. He carefully pushed the plant back into the center of the table before he looked down at the photo.

It was his graduation portrait. Still glossy and new. It was almost funny how little you could see the makeup, considering how it'd felt like his mother *caked* him with it. He would've put good money on it being bolder. Real overcompensation to make him worthy of his grandparents' fridge.

But he just looked like a normal girl.

It took a second for Max to realize he was grinding his molars. He reached out with his foot and turned the frame over, until his picture was no longer leering up at him. And then he stared at his parents' door as he slowly brought his foot down, pressing until the carpet muffled the sound of the glass cracking under his weight.

Harder still. He glared at the door and ground his heel. Something *snapped*.

Max looked down. The backing board was twisted off, and he could hear the jingle of broken glass as he moved his foot. Maybe now it wouldn't take so long for his parents to realize he was gone, but Max suddenly cared less. He wanted them to feel his absence. He wanted it to weigh on them. Even if he knew it wouldn't.

It was almost two in the morning when Max pushed his bag through his window and threw it into his car. He texted Erin—*on my way*—and then winced at the roar of the engine sputtering to life. But the car rolled down the street without incident, and Max took the long way out of the neighborhood. He devoured his sandwich before he hit the freeway.

He knew the clock was ticking now. In just a few hours, his parents would be awake, and they would check the apps on their phones to see where Max was. Life360 and OurPact, which were just the ones he knew about, would create a beat-by-beat map to his exact location, so long as his phone was in hand. It was imperative that he throw the trail cold as soon as he could.

3

ERIN'S EYES LINGER on the loose cigarettes rolling around in one of the cupholders. The stink of nicotine seems to have been baked into the carpet. A pop-punk cover of Kelly Clarkson's "Since U Been Gone" is playing on the radio, which is certainly a choice.

It's almost funny how little has changed. How familiar all of this feels, even though it really shouldn't.

There's no conversation to be had once they're rattling westbound on the I-70. No "How's it been?" or "What have you been up to?" Erin wouldn't even know how to answer those questions if they were asked. So she tries to enjoy the silence and scrolls numbly through Facebook instead. It doesn't help. She knows she's just wasting time.

Eventually, she opens up Google Maps and checks the route. The most direct path from Columbus, Ohio, to Berkeley, California, is thirty-seven hours. That's roughly three full days of driving, which is actually closer to five, when you consider the need for food and sleep and the like. Max assured her they could make it in four.

"You know I know where I'm going, right?" Max suddenly says. "We're on this highway until, like, Indianapolis."

Erin doesn't look up. "I'm sure you do."

"I do!"

She says nothing. She can tell there's a *but* at the end of that sentence.

A stretch of silence goes by. And, sure enough, Max flips on the blinker to move into the rightmost lane. "We have to make one stop first. But after that, you can be in charge of the map."

Erin finally comes up from her phone and gives him a pointed look. When the silence has gone a little long, Max looks over.

"What?" His voice rises slightly with indignation. "It'll be quick! Come on, I wouldn't be doing it if it weren't really important."

"It's gonna be a long enough drive without detours."

"Which is why we're only making one!"

Erin shuts her eyes and sighs. "Only one?"

"Only one, I swear. On my life."

She doesn't quite believe him, but she closes her phone anyway.

They're off the main highways within the first hour. As they drive, the buildings stacked on top of buildings erode into empty, abandoned fields. The moon hangs overhead, half-full, in a cloudless summer sky. Erin rolls her window down and lets her arm catch the breeze. Occasionally, she looks up at the moon, but she mostly just lets her eyes close and feels the breeze break over her face. It's quiet. Not calm, really, but it's something.

In the silence, Erin stews. This all feels like the setup to a very stupid joke: two trans kids pile into a car. She doesn't know the punch line yet.

The fact that he's asked her to do this means he can't hate her. That's not a lot, but it's also not *nothing*.

Her eyes snap open when the car suddenly pulls off the road and jostles on the unpaved dirt until they finally stop. The trees around them are tall and tightly condensed, so thick with unkempt foliage that it's near impossible to see through them. One or two cars zip by behind them, but even that soon fades away into silence.

Erin looks at the clock on the dash: 3:30 a.m. blinks back at her in tiny red numbers.

If Max drove her this far out just to kill her, she's going to be so mad about it.

Max pulls the keys out of the ignition. "All right, c'mon," he says, and leaves no room for argument as he steps out.

Ask her any time prior to these last few months, and Erin would swear that Max is simply *too stubborn* to die. Immortal through pure force of will.

But Max is also desperate. When he gets out of the car, Erin is close behind.

As she follows, Erin wonders how Max can walk so confidently, as if he knows the place. She imagines him driving down every back road in Ohio until he finds—whatever this is. They're on what seems to be a cyclists' road, uneven but straightforward, until they emerge at a bridge.

Erin hesitates at the edge, but Max marches onto it with that same unwavering confidence, so Erin forces herself forward. The wooden slats groan with every step. They get all the way out to the middle before Max finally stops.

He looks around and sighs. "Okay. This should work."

Erin looks for herself. Either side of the bridge is flanked by more thick foliage. Rusted beams tower over their heads, red and brown splotches eating away at the white paint. They hardly seem more stable than the wood. And although the river underneath them doesn't seem especially deep, it still gives her reason for concern.

There's also the fact that it's impossible to see through the trees. They're all so tightly bunched together that it feels like soon she won't be able to breathe. Each leaf is a pair of eyes, and there are thousands locked on them. They are alone out here, exposed like nerve endings.

"This is creepy," Erin finally says.

"Then I'll be quick!" Max steps up to the rail.

Erin's hand twitches with an instinctual urge to grab him and pull him back. Which is a stupid thought. Jumping from this height wouldn't kill him. Bones would certainly splinter and snap apart, but he wouldn't die. She thinks.

Either way, he doesn't jump, and he doesn't seem to notice her twitch. He just clutches his phone tightly in his hands as he stares out at the river beneath.

"Do you want to do it together?" Max suddenly asks.

Erin frowns. "What?"

"What?" Max makes a little throwing motion, as if Erin just doesn't understand what he's asking. "We've both gotta ditch the phones, otherwise what's the point?"

The wind whips around them. Erin just stares. "My mom wouldn't try to follow us," she finally says.

"You don't know that."

"She wouldn't do that to *you*."

"But you know my mom." Max takes a step closer. "You know *Brian*. And they *would* do that. They have."

"Max—"

"*The deal was* that if we do this, we go all the way with it. We go to California and we *do not* look back. I love your mom, but you think she wouldn't sell us out if she thought we were doing something stupid?"

Erin makes the decision to hold her tongue.

"If my parents know where I am," Max continues, "then they are gonna do everything they can to drag me back there themselves, or make me feel like such *shit* that I—that can't happen, okay?"

His face is gaunt. Erin's eyes drift down to the river, then to the railing. There are a few scattered carvings in the wood, but the one that draws her attention reads OLIVER + LUCY.

"How do we get to California without a map?" she finally asks.

"I've got plenty of maps, I know exactly how to get us there."

Erin gives him a skeptical look.

His shoulders slump. "C'mon, I wouldn't have asked you to do this if I didn't already think about all of it. I'm not going all the way across the country just to get dragged back to that shitty, evil town!"

He takes a breath before he quietly begs, "Please? For me?"

And there's the magic phrase.

Erin knows it's a mistake, but she takes her phone out anyway. She catches the way that Max's face brightens, although he says nothing as he readies alongside her. As if saying anything will make Erin reconsider. She's very close to doing so. This is a terrible idea, and yet her rising adrenaline does not yank her back.

"On three," Max finally says. "One, two—"

Both of their phones go spiraling into the darkness. Erin doesn't see where either of them land, although she hears two distant twin *plop*s when they hit the water. For a moment, they both just stand there, listening to the wind push against their backs. Max is almost solemn. Perhaps the seriousness of the situation has finally begun to weigh on him.

But then a smile quickly spreads across his face, and he's jumping up and down again, straining the boards underneath them with some terrible groans. "Okay! Let's go!"

He gleefully shakes Erin's shoulder before he takes off, back toward the car, and leaves her alone with the bridge. And the water.

Dread has taken root in her chest again. The bar is down

over her legs, the ride already in motion. Nobody lets you off once it's going. Not until it's over.

All around her, the trees rustle. Erin looks down to the far end of the bridge. There's nobody there; of course there isn't. Still, Erin swears the shadows encroach upon the beams above her, like gnarled fingers pulling themselves toward her. Pulling *something* toward her, even if it's only more shadows.

She realizes that even if she is being watched, as her gut so strongly insists that she is, there's no way for her to know. Not for certain. The phantom eyes are invisible while she stands as a beacon in the night. Naked, under the stage light of the moon, unable to see whatever is surely watching her every move.

The boards under her feet suddenly moan in the wind and Erin runs for the car, goose bumps up her arms and shadows at her heels.

4

BACK IN MARCH, when Max laid this whole thing out for her—Berkeley and everything—they were standing behind the C-1 convenience store where Max worked. When he finished, Erin had one question: "Why do you want me to come with you?"

Reasonable question, she figured. This was their first face-to-face conversation since they had broken up. It had been almost two years.

Max stared at the ground for a long time. "I figured it wouldn't hurt to ask," he finally said. "I'm not gonna be mad if you say no."

Erin watched him carefully. It was still Max. Although his name tag said otherwise, and long hair curled gently at his shoulders, Max was still shining through the cracks.

He put his cigarette out on the wall, completing a lopsided circle of ash marks. "But why not, y'know? I—look. Every single day, one of us gets murdered. Not literally. I mean, sometimes." He took a deep breath. "But every day, somebody decides that we aren't allowed to transition. That we can't use the bathroom. That we can't have our own names. Every day, whether it's in school or at work, or in some big-ass building full of old, white Republicans, they take away whatever they can until there's nothing left. If they can't *fix* us, then they just try and kill us."

"If you're trying to make me feel bad about everything, good job." Erin nodded along.

"*What I'm getting at* is that California is guaranteed. It guarantees that I get to transition, and it guarantees that you get to *keep* transitioning. 'Cause you see what they're doing. You *know* that's the endgame for them, making it impossible. Do you wanna be stuck here when they finally do it? Or do you wanna be in California, where nobody knows you're trans, let alone knows your deadname?"

Erin did not have an answer. What she said was: "I'll text you."

On the drive home, Erin thought about when Max first came out to her, only a couple of days before he broke up with her.

She'd tried, many times before, to find the definitive moment that marked the beginning of the end for them. She couldn't. At most, over the four years they were together, there was simply a collection of moments where things felt . . . *odd*. A hostility that would suddenly simmer in the air between them before it would fade away again. A hostility that Erin had ignored, because she never believed it was that serious, because it always went away on its own.

Then he came out to her, and Erin had even thought: *problem solved*. But Max still broke up with her before the week was over, barely giving her a reason why beyond some platitudes about how he just needed space and how they could still be friends. Erin believed him. She knew what an emotionally tumultuous thing it was to come out, especially as a teenager. She wanted to believe him.

Not only did Max completely stop talking to her, he stopped talking to their entire shared social circle. There one moment, gone the next, a horrible vacuum of absence where Max was supposed to be. Without explanation, without so much as a goodbye.

It didn't feel like the same Max who kissed her on their first date. The thirteen-year-old Max who, against the backdrop of the summer sunset, pinks and oranges blotting against the clouds over the state fair, managed to get Erin on the Ferris wheel, despite her horrible fear of heights.

"Just look at me," he'd said. "I'm not scary."

Erin was the first openly trans person in their graduating class; Max was the second. Although Erin's novelty had somewhat worn off by junior year, Max's coming out reinvigorated the side-eyes. Maybe it was just the strangeness of it, *both* of them being trans, dating each other and then breaking up. Everybody assumed there was some kind of drama. Even Miranda, who had been Erin's best friend since elementary school.

Miranda had once begun, "It just seems convenient that *he* breaks up with you, then *he* decides—"

"Yeah, that's not how it works." Erin didn't let her finish.

A few people did what Miranda did—tried to stir up drama under the guise of *just asking*—but Erin never gave them anything. Not because she couldn't. She knew she could. She could have easily vented her frustrations to them, might have happily ranted about how confused and humiliated and *hurt* she was that Max had cut her off so suddenly.

Erin remembered reading somewhere that, in 2015, there were at least 941 transgender people living in the whole state of Ohio. Nine hundred forty-one out of almost twelve million. She and Max were more than just relationship drama; they were anomalies. The girl who used to be a boy and the girl who was now a boy. They didn't even have each other to lean on anymore.

Nearly two years later, that pain was no longer quite so sharp, but it certainly hadn't gone away. Erin didn't know what made Max push her away the first time, and she didn't know what compelled him to ask her to ditch Columbus with him.

Ohio sucked, sure, and it was getting worse all the time. It was also the only home Erin had ever known. Just up and *leaving* was an entirely unworkable concept until Erin walked back inside her house and was greeted by the photo hanging on the wall. A very blunt reminder that leaving was more than possible.

The central focus of the portrait had always been her dad. His presence was still suffocating all these years later. Erin still wondered if he'd love her now, if he had ever really loved her to begin with, or if the attention he showered on her had just been an easy way to start a competition between a wife he was falling out of love with.

Even as an almost-adult, it was difficult for Erin to reconcile her memory (subjective, tainted, impossible to shake) with the facts of the man, which were: he never held a job for more than a few months, he needed to be the biggest man in the room, and you could almost never count on his word for anything. Erin knew that fact especially well.

For perhaps the first time, Erin's eyes drifted to her mother. She was smiling, although her mouth was closed and the smile didn't quite reach her eyes. Erin found herself wondering: *What about Mom?*

Erin realized she was probably a terrible person for questioning their love, but she questioned it anyway. All of the happy, treasured memories she had of her dad didn't stop him from completely leaving her behind. He left her with a mother he'd spent Erin's entire childhood villainizing, minimizing, belittling. Erin grew up thinking of her mother the same way her father did: as nobody much at all. Even with all the time she had with her mother without her father's shadow looming over them, that knee-jerk desire to treat her as an enemy still lingered.

Erin wondered how much of their relationship survived not out of love, but out of tolerance.

A little after four that afternoon, Mom came home from shopping with Hayley. Erin watched them come into the house from her spot on the couch, where she'd curled into the armrest to read and to ignore her phone; the text thread with Max still waiting for her to say *yes* or *no*. She watched them both for the few seconds where they didn't see her. Where, in a way, Erin was already not there. They were talking about Hayley's plans for the weekend: this included the mall and talking her best friend, Emma, into sneaking a net into the aquarium to finally acquire a koi fish.

They seemed happy.

Erin knew she was loved. But for several years, she'd been fighting against a suspicion that she was, perhaps, not necessarily liked. She didn't blame her mother. She had been a strange and decidedly unlikable son. It was hard to believe she was a very likable daughter. She knew that she wasn't. She was a never-ending argument. An embarrassment. A burden on the two *real* girls of the house.

It was all too easy to fall into that swamp of self-pity, internalized transmisogyny that Erin kept tucked away for those special moments where she *really* wanted to twist the knife on herself. A vat filled with every backhanded compliment she'd ever gotten. Every fight, every weird look, every implication that she was too young or too stupid to know what she was doing and who she was.

"Erin." Her mother poked her head into the living room. "If you're not doing anything, come and help."

Erin ripped herself out of her own head and set her book down with a sigh. "Yes, *ma'am*."

Mom was already going back to the kitchen when she

threw her response over her shoulder: "Hey, you're enough like your father without taking his attitude, miss."

Erin's slight smile slid from her face. Her mother didn't seem to think twice about such a comment. It was the final nudge, though. The gentlest slip of the blade that nicked the artery.

Her father's daughter. Erin was going to test exactly how far she could take that. And what did her father do better than leave?

5

THE FARTHER AWAY THEY GET from Columbus, the more the tension slowly, finally starts to unwind from around Max's throat. Even still, as soon as the sun breaks over the horizon and they switch drivers, he falls asleep like somebody hit a switch. He dreams in fragments. Caught in a fight where his blows don't land and his legs move like they're caught in molasses. Wearing a dress that sinks into his skin like tar.

When he wakes up, they're parked at a gas station. In rural Kentucky, according to Erin. "Go Your Own Way" is playing on the radio. It's an unremarkable little spot, just two pumps and a building with chipped paint and cracks in the window tint. The kind of place that looks like it was built in the 1970s and hasn't been touched since then. There's a smattering of half-dead trees off in the distance and a whole bunch of pitted, uneven asphalt.

A bell announces their arrival with a short, crisp ring. The overhead speakers are tuned to the same station as the car,

Fleetwood Mac softly echoing across the aisles. It's humid in here, too. Flytraps hang from the ceiling, each of them full and sagging with the weight of so many small corpses. Max watches Erin wrinkle her nose at the sight of them.

Max looks over at the guy behind the counter. He's tall and lean, probably in his early twenties. His hair is brown and shaggy, hanging slightly over his eyes as he scrolls through his phone. At the sound of the bell, he looks up, gives them both a once-over, and then goes back to whatever he was doing before.

Some of that tension has returned to Max's shoulders. He forces himself to try and relax. "Okay, I'm gonna get some directions."

Erin turns to him with her eyebrows slightly raised. "I thought you knew *exactly* where you were going?"

"Yeah, I know the highways. I don't know where in bum-fuck Kentucky to get a decent lunch."

He gently bumps her shoulder before he wanders toward the counter. On his way up, he stalls in front of the shelves of Red Bull and grabs a four-pack of the watermelon ones. He puts them down on the counter before he nods at the wall of cigarettes. "How much for a pack?"

The man behind the counter doesn't ask which kind. Doesn't even look up from his phone. "Eight. And I've gotta see some ID."

Max wonders what part of his driver's license would surprise this man the most: his legal name, or the giant *F* stamped right next to his face. "How about ten, and we say I left my ID in the car?"

The man's eyes finally fix on him. Max can at last read the name tag on his chest: Charlie.

Charlie grins. "Fifteen."

Max's expression shifts into something like a glare, even as he takes his wallet out of his jacket. "How about eight for the cigs, eight for the ID, and you tell us where we can get lunch around here?"

He takes out a twenty and holds it out. A long stretch of time passes. Max never breaks eye contact, and then Charlie finally takes the cash. The edge of a driver's tan pokes out from under his T-shirt.

"What direction are you headed?" he asks.

"West. Uh, so far we've been on the 65."

Charlie nods before pointing to the wall behind him.

"Newports. Please."

Erin comes up to Max's side as the man slides a pack (and his change) into Max's waiting hands. She sets down strawberry Pop-Tarts, with a five-dollar bill already on top of the box.

As Max sticks the cigarettes into his pocket, he watches Charlie's eyes. They stick to Erin. There's a moment of panic—*he's clocking her*—before Max realizes he's not. He's just leering. Like a caveman seeing a woman for the first time in his stupid life. Charlie smiles at her.

Max watches Erin smile back at him.

A wave of heat smacks Max in the face. Some of it's embarrassment. Some of it's indignation that that *worked*. And some of it's just equally simple jealousy. He almost doesn't hear Charlie start talking again.

"Just keep goin' down the 65," Charlie says, ringing up Erin as he does. "Eventually you'll be able to get off on the 61. Keep going down that and you'll get the best barbecue this side of Kentucky. Bright yellow building, can't miss it."

Max nods and looks away.

"And, uh, I'd be careful where you flash that thing."

Charlie makes a gesture to Max's wallet, and Max looks down at it, as if it's changed. It's just an old piece of junk leather, held together by a strip of curling duct tape, and it's bulging with cash. Max can see Erin staring at him out of the corner of his eye.

"You don't look like hard targets," Charlie adds, "if someone wanted to take that."

Max realizes it's not embarrassment burning underneath his skin. It's hatred. "Totally. Thanks."

It's not until he's already started to walk away that Max remembers the Impala, and he stops. Face still burning, he grabs a handful of bills, only checking to make sure they're not hundreds. He walks back just enough to slap them on the counter. "Fifty. For gas."

Charlie nods and takes the cash without a word, even though he's still smugly grinning. Max wants to punch that grin off his face. A worse part of him wants to bring him and Erin right back down to earth and ask, *Do you leer at all eighteen-year-old girls like that, or just the trans ones?*

Instead, he beelines for the door and pushes through it, so hot he feels like he's on fire.

6

AS THE RING OF THE BELL settles into silence, Erin turns back to Charlie. Max's Red Bull is still on the counter. She smiles apologetically, as if one look can make up for whatever Max's deal is at any given moment.

Charlie smiles. "Let me get you a bag."

He crouches down behind the counter. Erin relaxes slightly and looks at the flytrap hanging overhead. At least one of the bugs is still alive, making the whole thing jump around as it tries to break free.

She grimaces and looks away. She moves the box of Pop-Tarts aside and picks up the postcard she hid underneath. Embarrassment gives way to some degree of shame. She grabbed it impulsively. She hid it impulsively, too. A grinning red cardinal sits perched atop large bubble letters that spell out KENTUCKY, with one wing waving in welcome. For whatever reason, it makes her think of Hayley. Hoping, almost, that she is being missed.

Only now, staring at the cardinal's grinning face, it's not nearly as charming as it was before. It's smiling *at* her now. Laughing at her.

Erin starts to turn it in her hands, folding the corner between her fingers, when the bell at the door suddenly, sharply chimes again.

She startles. The edge of the paper slides across the pad of her finger.

Her hand reflexively pulls into a fist. Erin grimaces and turns to the door.

There's nobody. The door isn't even open, isn't swinging in the breeze. She can see the back of Max's head near the pumps; he hasn't moved. Erin frowns before she looks down at her hand. Blood bubbles up along an invisible line. She grimaces again, putting the tip of her finger into her mouth and briefly quelling the sting.

Charlie pops back up, sees this, and frowns. "Okay?"

Erin nods and takes her finger out. "Paper cut."

She wants to ask: *Didn't you hear that?* But she doesn't. He doesn't look as if he heard anything at all.

"Oh. Hang on." Charlie ducks down again and comes back with a mini first aid kit.

Erin smiles and shakes her head. "I'm fine—"

"No, it's no trouble." Charlie holds out his hand.

Erin uncertainly places her own inside of it.

Charlie smiles. It's a pleasant distraction from the sting that comes from the disinfecting wipe, which Charlie holds against the cut for only a moment before he sets it aside. A faint line of blood marks the fabric. Erin stares at him while he puts the Band-Aid on. His fingers are calloused, but warmer than she was expecting. She counts the freckles on his nose. His eyes are so brown that they're nearly black, but they're the furthest thing from threatening. In a word: he's cute.

Charlie smooths out the edge of the Band-Aid and holds his hands out in a *ta-da!* motion. "Good as new."

Erin carefully takes her hand back and flexes it. "Thanks."

He packs her things into a little plastic bag. "Don't mention it. It's nice to see a pretty face around here."

Erin laughs, even as a distinct sense of discomfort wraps around her lungs. He's cute, but he's also a stranger, and doesn't know that she's trans. "Uh, thanks. Thank you."

Charlie nods politely while a wry smile works its way up the left side of his face. "Have a safe drive, miss."

Outside, Max is leaning against the pumps with his arms crossed over his chest. He doesn't acknowledge Erin as she walks around, and Erin pretends she doesn't notice. She puts the bag on the floor and slips the postcard into her suitcase.

"Does it feel weird when dudes try to flirt with you?" Max asks suddenly.

Erin looks up at him before she frowns and shuts the door. "I don't think he was flirting."

"Beside the point. Does it?"

She shrugs and walks up to him. "I dunno. I guess. But he was just being nice."

Max gives her a look. "Come on. You're probably the best-looking girl to come through here in decades, and besides that, he'd *never* know." He kicks at the pebbles underfoot and perhaps misses the glare that Erin shoots him. "You look at *me* for more than five seconds and it's like Velma went butch."

"No, it's not."

He gives her the same look.

Erin's mouth quirks up. "Velma wears glasses."

A tense moment. Then Max's face breaks with a snort. "Asshole."

"Seriously, though, don't worry about shit like that."

"It just skeeves me out." He shakes his head and pushes off from the pump. "Dudes shouldn't be looking at either of us. 'Specially around here."

Erin opens her mouth before her eyes narrow. "When was the last time a dude flirted with *you*?"

Max stares at her for a second. "Recently," he says. Like he's not sure if that's supposed to be a good thing. He takes out his box of cigarettes. "He didn't know I was a dude, obviously, but he was still plenty into me. For your information."

Erin nods. She wonders if he's dated, *who* he's dated, since her, and she tells herself that the weird taste in the back of her mouth is not something as childish as jealousy.

"Well." Erin shrugs. "Maybe you shouldn't worry about random dudes at truck stops. Or just—keep your short guy syndrome in check."

"You don't get to talk. You were never a *short guy*."

Erin doesn't deny this (nor does she bring up that, at five feet nine, she's only three inches taller than he is), and simply slips back inside the car. She rolls the window down and rests her arms on the door. Something reeks, although it's hard to parse out between the smell of gasoline and the oppressive heat, which has a strange, musky smell of its own. Erin wonders if there's a dead animal somewhere near the road.

"Where'd you get all that money?" Erin finally asks.

Cigarette hanging from his lips, a look of offense crosses Max's face. "I didn't *steal* it."

"Yeah, I figured."

The nozzle lock clicks. Tank full.

Max reaches forward and takes it out. "Cops can track you through where you use your card. You can't track cash."

"And your mom didn't notice?"

"No." He laughs, as if her question was *so* ridiculous, and lights his cigarette. "I got my paychecks cashed at work. Most of it went in the bank, and I kept a little on the side. Then, y'know, once I update my bank stuff and take my mom off the account, I can go back to using my card. But right now, it's just one more way to lead 'em right to me."

Erin doesn't love this answer. It's paranoid. She's not convinced that Max is aware of this. She also knows that if she continues to question it, they're just going to keep spinning in circles, and Max is just going to keep acting like she's an idiot, so she brings her arms back into the car.

The field behind the building is full of dry and dead grass, which chitters whenever the breeze kicks up. A low billboard faces them. It reads: LOSING FAITH IN GOD? CALL (83)-THE-TRUTH

Something out there really *reeks*.

A motorcycle rips by on the road. Erin startles, although the fear is quickly replaced by irritation and embarrassment. She turns back to what's in front of her, and her focus lands on the glove compartment. There aren't words for how much she misses her phone. But real paper maps are better than no maps at all, and she needs something to do. She opens the latch.

The compartment pops open, and Erin jumps as a tidal wave of maps spills onto her lap. Her shoulders slump as soon as she realizes it's nothing more than paper, and she parses through a few of them. Max has got the legitimate, glossy maps right alongside instructions he printed from Google Maps. Most of them have their route marked with Sharpie, and they're all a little warped from being crammed into such a small space.

She looks up at him. "You couldn't condense some of this?"

"Could I make sure we'd have enough maps to know where we're going? Of course I could, Erin. You're so welcome."

Erin rolls her eyes. *Could you stop being a dick for five seconds?*

While Max takes his smoke break, Erin goes through the plan as she attempts to put the maps into some kind of order. By tonight, they should be in Memphis; Oklahoma City by day two; somewhere near New Mexico by day three; Berkeley on day four. Nearly 2,700 miles, cutting through the middle of the country, with a boy she's spoken to more in the last day than she has in the last two years.

By the time Max has put out his cigarette in the rocks and gotten back into the car, Erin's at the bottom of the map pile. That's when her fingers brush against something with a distinctly different texture. Uniquely smooth. Erin frowns and pulls it out.

Her eyes widen as she starts to laugh. "Oh my God, you kept this?"

Max is in the middle of finally taking his jacket off when he turns to look at the photo reel Erin holds out between them. It's old. Sophomore year homecoming. Erin's hair is short, still clearly in the process of growing out. But it's Max who looks strangest of all, in a black lace dress and long, straightened hair. Erin is literally sitting in the presence of both Maxes, and she finds it hard to believe that one used to be the other.

Max huffs more than laughs before he starts the car. "I don't know why I didn't clean this car out before. It needs it so bad."

Erin tilts her head. This implies a number of nonsensical things, chief among them being the fact that Max obviously and recently shoved the glove box full of maps. "You weren't old enough to drive when we were dating."

"All right, then I wasn't old enough to clean the car out, either!"

Max rolls his eyes and mutters something under his breath before he shifts into drive. Erin shuts the glove box with the photo reel still in her hand. She tries to fight the smile that spreads out across her face before she pulls down the sun visor and tucks the photo under the mirror cover. Max gives her a weird look, but she ignores it. This photo represents everything they are simultaneously driving toward and away from. Erin wants it up.

Plus, she misses that dress. She looks great in it.

7

THEY HAD SKIPPED THEIR FIRST homecoming, too. That was where Max's memories of the dresses began. They had a much better time sitting together at home and marathoning *The X-Files* than they would've had playing expensive dress-up. That's what Max thought, at least.

But then the next year came around, and suddenly social functions were all Erin could think about. The issue then was her mom. Maybe there were just too many articles out there about trans and gay kids being the butts of jokes at school functions, or maybe she'd just watched *Carrie* recently—*They're all gonna laugh at you*—but homecoming was the first hard line Max had ever seen Erin's mother draw. No homecoming.

Maybe rightfully so. While most people weren't outright ghoulish to Erin's face, all that meant was that they gawked and giggled behind her back. Max kind of feared the *Carrie* outcome, too. He didn't want to try to conform to the same crowd that shouted slurs at them from across the cafeteria.

Except cisgender girls all went to homecoming. They got to buy beautiful dresses and get their makeup done and post their photos all over Instagram. Erin wanted all of that.

Which was how Max ended up spending two hours of his life dress shopping with his own mom. Her barely disguised apathy toward Erin was apparently overridden by her joy that Max was deciding to wear a dress. It was hardly of his own volition. Rather, he knew that having his mother help him buy a dress for his trans girlfriend was already a big ask. No way would she agree to buying him a suit or dress shirt on top of it. It was not a bullet he wanted to bite, but one he felt compelled to bite, nevertheless.

His dress was stupid. And it was nothing special, just the first thing he grabbed from the Macy's clearance rack. Pure black, with a rounded neckline made of lace and no sleeves. It made him look like he was going to a funeral. His mom made him do a little spin, and then declared that it was *just perfect*.

The funny thing was, Max might've actually exploded if they had gone to the dance. He got tunnel vision just thinking about that many people seeing him in a dress, as unnatural and disgusting as he had ever felt. Thankfully, the point was not *really* the dance itself. The point was the dress and going through the motions. The point was Erin. And that was easily accomplished with a date night that just happened to fall on the same day as homecoming.

Max had always been rather horrified at the amount of effort that went into being a girl. He'd been horrified by his *own* relatively light upkeep of it. And yet the difference between him and Erin had been apparent for ages, and only seemed to become more stark by the day. Erin navigated her bathroom the same way computer scientists probably navigated the Apollo 11 launch. She explained everything she did, first as she did them on herself, and then as she did them on Max. Less was more when it came to foundation; a little bit of highlighter under the eyes would accentuate them (and draw focus away from the rest of your face); and *primer, primer, primer.* Max didn't retain a lick of it, but he nodded along and shut his eyes when he needed to.

It was weird, to be envious over a skill he'd never had any desire to possess before. And yet the ease with which Erin learned and mastered it made something in Max's brain twitch. She had that whole laboratory in which she'd already figured out all the perfect ways to help herself pass, and Max couldn't even get his voice to drop with the entire internet at his fingertips.

When Erin was done with him, Max examined his reflection in the mirror. They didn't look all that different since they'd shared the same lip gloss and stuff. But Max was also nothing like Erin. That should've been what he wanted, but it actually made him feel worse. He didn't pass as a boy, and he made for an unbearably ugly girl.

Even as he thought those things, the only indication of it on his face was his jaw, clenching ever so slightly. He disconnected. It was simple: that thing in the mirror was not Max.

He and Erin were playing dress-up, and none of this was real, and that girl was not him. That girl was only for tonight. No biggie.

While everybody else going to homecoming was shelling out for fancy Italian, or driving out of the way for one of the two Cheesecake Factories in town, Max and Erin positioned themselves in the back booth of a downtown pizza shop called Mikey's. They both looked ridiculously out of place, though not to the extent that it became an exercise in humiliation. Max remained vigilant, waiting for that one bigot to come in and ruin it all, but one never materialized. It was actually mostly okay. He just kept making eye contact with toddlers who didn't know not to stare.

"I can't believe you didn't have boobs and then you willingly gave yourself boobs," Max muttered after spending way too long trying to get a piece of cheese off the lace covering his own chest.

Erin just laughed at him. "Yeah. Boobs rock."

"Then you can have mine."

Erin gave him a strange look but said nothing.

After dinner, they drove over the freeway to the Grandview Theater. They bought the biggest sodas and their own separate bags of popcorn, and then they sat in the very back, under the projector, and put their feet up on the seats for a mostly empty screening of *The Wizard of Oz*. When the movie ended, rather than going straight back to the car, Max and Erin walked up Grandview Avenue, past all the little clothing boutiques that had already closed for the night. It was cold, but neither offered the option of going back. They were just two normal, cisgender teenage people. Doing whatever cisgender teenage people were supposed to do in dresses and tennis shoes.

Erin, under the spaced-out glow of the streetlights, was another level of ethereal. Her dress was a dark, basil-ish green, ruffled on the ends and around the neckline. While Max's dress stuck to him like plastic wrap, Erin's flowed and fluttered as she walked. Her hair had long ago grown out of its early-transition mullet and was now hovering at this half-kept bob stage. Less Billy Ray Cyrus, more of a looser, freer Daisy Buchanan. She was finishing off a hot dog she'd bought on the way out of the theater, and her hair was wind-whipped and knotted, and she was the most perfect girl that Max had ever seen.

On some level, he understood the importance of doing this, Erin's near-pathological insistence on normal teenage girldom when they both knew very well that it was impossible from every angle. And yet Max just didn't understand where any of that came from. She was beautiful now, and she was beautiful long before she had been Erin.

And there was Max, wrapped in plastic, like an unwanted little sister trying to look just as much of a woman as Erin did. There was Max and his dumb, stupid brain, ruining everything.

Erin drove Max home with the windows down, blaring Meat Loaf's *Bat Out of Hell* from her Hyundai's shitty speakers. This happened every couple of months. Not the Meat Loaf thing, obviously, but some new band. Usually from the '70s or '80s. Always from the box of vinyls that her dad had forgotten to take with him. Erin would pick out a new one, and it would become the only thing she'd listen to for a *long* time. Max didn't have all the words to "Paradise by the Dashboard Light" memorized yet, but it was so far the only song he could mostly sing along to. Erin took the female lines instinctively, which let Max do all the fun, weird dude voices that such a song like "Paradise by the Dashboard Light" necessitated.

Then Erin kissed him goodbye, and Max got out of the car, and real life resumed. While Erin went home to a five-year-old sister who knew her only as Erin, Max went inside to Brian, who almost instantly started cracking jokes at the sight of him. "Why do lesbians hate looking like women so much?" Max could hear his mother immediately snap that he was going to discourage Max from ever dressing like that again, and Max almost felt brave enough to walk back and inform her that Brian had no bearing on why Max hated himself in a dress. Instead, he just showered, scrubbed his face raw and clean, and decompressed alone inside his room.

Underneath his covers, wrapped in two shirts and one of his larger hoodies, Max almost felt something like comfort. He disappeared into his phone and kept listening to *Bat Out of Hell*, as if it could keep out the rotting taste of jealousy that kept rising up in the back of his throat.

8

ERIN'S FATHER HAD BEEN HER favorite. He was the fun one, who introduced her to Johnny Cash and Fleetwood Mac. Who let her stay home from school when she was "sick," and who taught her to shoot after her mom had already said *no*.

She could still remember the day. The sky was perfectly clear, the air just a *little* too cold. The trees hadn't started to die yet. The range was a thirty-minute drive outside of town, technically beautiful but terrifying to a kid like Erin. Her dad helped set her up with the others, all in a line against cement blocks. The ground on either side of the awning was slanted, creating this strange tunnel effect all the way down to the targets, which were arranged against a towering mound of dirt. Erin had to squint through the scope to get a good look at what was supposed to be hers.

"The longer you look through that scope, worse it'll be for your eyes," he'd told her before he moved the butt of the gun into the crease of her shoulder. "You want to protect yourself against the kickback. Wield that baby wrong, it's gonna knock you back on your ass *good*."

Erin listened to him. When he told her to take a deep breath, she did. Squeeze the trigger, don't pull it. "Anticipate that it's gonna hurt, accept it, and don't forget to breathe."

When they pulled down her target, Erin had exactly two "kill shots," neither of which were especially close to the bull's-eye. Nevertheless, her father had shaken her shoulders excitedly, like she'd outshot everybody else there. "A little more practice and you'll be giving *me* a run for my money," he'd said, which didn't exactly make him sound like the best marksman, but it didn't matter. Her dad was proud of her, and that was everything.

That was the dad who left her. Who left all of them, when the divorce finalized. In his absence, there was suddenly nobody for Erin to need to impress with her half-competent pantomime of masculinity.

Then Mom was suddenly the only parent Erin had left. By the time Erin turned fourteen, they almost had a functional dynamic going. Until Erin came out and it all went sideways again.

Erin came out only a few days after her fourteenth birthday, and it was a whole screaming fight of *why* and *since when*, as if her transness was something that needed to be justified. Then, for about two days after the fact, Mom barely spoke to her.

Despite how quickly her mom came back around and began work on Erin's transition, that initial response was laser-burned into Erin's memory. She could not comprehend why her mother needed to mourn a child who was not dead. Although she never vocalized this, Erin suspected that her resentment still hung in the air. She suspected her mother could still sense it. So, while her mother was as supportive as she could be, it never quite eliminated the tension between them.

Sometimes, after an argument, Mom would let her skip school so they could watch movies and eat ice cream together. Like Dad used to.

Erin found him again when she was fourteen, right after she came out. Thirty minutes of focused teenage angst and she had a ping. Brett Arlos. Hot Springs, Arkansas.

Being limited in options (couldn't drive, didn't want to Greyhound her way down, a little too cowardly to just *run away*), Erin wrote to him. Just one letter at first, then another, once a month for four years. She wrote about high school, about Mom and Max and the strains of each relationship as they happened. She wondered if he'd sensed it, the trans thing. If he had, why hadn't he said anything?

A few months after they had their homecoming fight, Mom turned forty. The gathering they held was the first time that a lot of Mom's friends and coworkers were going to see Erin. Freshly sixteen. New and improved.

Mom must have spent only half the time on herself that she spent on Erin. She did Erin's makeup for her, helped pick out the pink sweater that she wore, and then, protectively curled around her, (re)introduced her to everybody who came through the door. And though they smiled at her, it was obvious most of them didn't really know what to *do* with her. Certainly nobody knew what to do with Max, who had shown up for moral support.

The scripted nature of the night was strange. Erin drifted between groups, with Max tethered to her side, and played hostess. She smiled lots and kept her hands folded in front of her, trying to be small. Nonthreatening. The adults cycled through the same handful of questions, all shallow and impersonal.

How's school? Nobody's giving you trouble, right? Oh, that's good. You know, you look just like your mother. How long have you—two years already?

Oh, yes, you really look amazing.

I would never have guessed just from looking at you.

At first, she and Max found it funny. But as the night stretched on, Erin felt the room start to narrow. It was so easy to assume the worst. To translate *looking like her mother* as code for Looking Like A Real Girl. Maybe it shouldn't have gotten under her skin the way it did, but it made her want to throw her hands down and scream: *I'm my* father's *daughter, not hers*.

The only guy who deviated from the script was one of her mother's old college friends. He was one of the few brave souls to venture onto the back porch. His glasses were like Coke bottles and his scarf was checkered red and black. He said: "You're one brave kid, the way people are these days. That scare you? Or do you try not to think about it?"

Max had been swiping unattended beer bottles from the kitchen all night; it was only after that question that Erin finally joined him. They were quick and discreet little alcoholic vultures. As the night went on and the drinks continued, the novelty of the transgender daughter finally seemed to wear off, and the crowd finally left her alone.

It was just past midnight when it occurred to Erin that mixing her alcohol was a bad idea. She wasn't *nauseous*, exactly, but heavy somewhere deep inside of her. So she grabbed her winter jacket and fumbled her way through the front door. Max joined her on the front porch through the door she'd left open behind her. He sat between her legs, his back to her chest, holding her hands inside his own.

Erin could hear the oldies karaoke still going on the TV inside. She didn't know who had whipped out the machine (an anniversary present her mom had kept after the divorce) but a window must've been cracked because every song vibrated against her spine as if she were still inside. Meat Loaf's voice was literally shaking the walls.

"Hey, Er."

A warm numbness tingled under her face. "Mm."

"Do you think all that back there was a time loop, or body snatchers?"

Erin's face scrunched with laughter. "Shut up. My mom probably threatened to kill them if they said anything weird."

Max was laughing, too, little tufts of breath visible in the air. "You think so?"

"God, yeah. 'Cause if someone upset me, it'd ruin the whole night. For her, at least. She probably talked to everybody before. Tried to babyproof it. It's so embarrassing."

Max didn't answer, and then neither of them said anything for a long time. Erin dug her nails into her palms.

Then Max looked back at her, eyes dark and unfocused but still striking. His thumb worked its way between her fingers and her palm. Meat Loaf was still coming through the walls.

"What're you thinking about?" Max asked.

"How there are, like, a million of them, and there's only one of me."

"It's not just you, though."

"Might as well be."

He blinked. "Ouch."

"I mean—" Erin sighed and took her hands back. "I don't know. It just sucks. All of it. I can see them trying to find the cracks, whatever proves I'm not *real*, whatever that's supposed to mean. Whatever makes me less real than you, or Miranda. And it—it means a lot, you being here, but I don't know how to explain how any of this feels. How lonely it is."

Max was quiet for a minute. "High school's only two more years."

"And then what? *Life* like this? This, here, for the rest of my life?"

"Then—shit, I dunno, where do you wanna go? What do you wanna do?"

Erin laughed. "Anywhere. I don't care, as long as it isn't *here*."

"Okay. Bucket List."

Erin frowned. "What do you mean?"

Max shrugged, suddenly seeming so much more sober

than Erin felt. "I mean, let's do that. We graduate, then wherever you wanna go, I'll take you. Where do you wanna go?"

Erin started laughing again.

"What?"

"Nothing, that was just super butch of you."

Max pushed her knee and grumbled something, but Erin had already grabbed him and pulled him back in, innocent in the way that teenagers were. "No, that sounds all right," she mumbled into his hair. "I'll think of something. And then we'll go. Later, though."

Later, in the early morning after everybody had finally gone home, and Erin was finally more sober than not, she was laid out across the couch, scrolling through her phone and waiting to get tired. Mom had a trash bag and was trying to clean up quietly. Without any sort of easing into it, and maybe looking for a nerve, Erin put her phone down on her chest and asked, "Do you think I look like you?"

She did not look directly at her mother, but she could still see her stop and think about it. "Yeah," she finally answered. "Sometimes."

"Do you *want* me to look like you?"

Another pause. "Sometimes."

"What does *sometimes* mean?"

Erin finally looked to her mother, who she found standing at the edge of the entryway.

"You can't know, because—well, it's not like you're ever going to have kids. But you don't spend fourteen years raising a son and ever expect them to become your daughter."

Erin said nothing. Something like shame ran hot under her skin.

It only continued to burn as her mother finished the thought: "So yes, sometimes you do. Sometimes you remind me of your father. I don't know which is harder."

It would be two more years before Erin finally found out what happened to her dad. The only letter she ever got in return came in October, just a few months before her plans with Max were set into motion. Posted out of Little Rock by a woman named Kailee. She had been cleaning out Brett's things when she found a box of Erin's letters, all kept neatly inside of their opened envelopes, and that was how she'd gotten Erin's address, she explained.

It was a motorcycle crash. Kailee did not give many more details besides that, although the word *instantaneously* jumped from the page. Some loggers had found him within minutes of the crash, but the impact had killed him almost instantaneously. The cremation was done. He'd been scattered to the wind over some cliffs in the Ozarks.

Alongside all of the emotions that came crashing over her as she attempted to process this, Erin was tempted by the thought of writing back. But she recoiled from the idea just as quickly. She didn't want to know. She couldn't bear to. The only person she wanted to answer her questions had already settled into the cold Southern soil.

9

THE HIGHWAY THEY RETURN TO is desolate. The buildings they pass are similarly abandoned, overgrown with brush and covered in garbage. When Erin turns the radio on, it's mostly frat-country that haunts the margins of fire and brimstone. Without meaning to, she catches bits of the preaching: *"We are living in an age of sin! We are living among those who seek to disfigure the face of man and woman, who—"*

It's then that Max decides to mention the sleeve of CDs under Erin's seat. "You *hate* my music!" he says to justify himself, after Erin gives him a look of bewilderment.

"It's better than *that*," she answers.

She flips carefully through each sleeve. *For Those Who Have Heart. Collide with the Sky. A Lesson in Romantics. The Black Parade.* It's not an awful time capsule for the late 2000s, and Erin considers some Hawthorne Heights until she flips to the last sleeve and finds *Bat Out of Hell*. Just sitting there. She frowns, then smiles, then takes it out. Max looks over.

"What?" He shrugs. "It was, like, three bucks on eBay."

Erin says nothing, just smiles and pushes the disc into the player. She's never even owned a record player, but her walls back home are decorated with her dad's old record covers. The ones she likes, at least. *Bat Out of Hell* is still up on the wall beside her bed, right between *Rumours* and *American IV*. The title track starts, and the drums, piano, and electric guitars all hit the speakers at the same time. It's been years since she's listened to these songs; it sets a good mood.

Erin reaches back and pulls her bag close enough that she can rifle through it. Most of it is useless in terms of entertainment. Shampoo she double-wrapped in ziplock bags; an electric toothbrush; her pill case. The first interesting thing she manages to pull out is the disposable camera.

"Hey, smile."

Erin gets one photo of Max looking over at her before he's processed what she said. The second photo is likely to turn out all blurry, with Max's hand lunging toward the lens. Erin pulls back just in time to save the camera. The car swerves a little.

"Hands on the wheel," Erin warns him, even as she laughs.

"Uh-huh. No pictures. I'd literally rather kill us both."

"What am I gonna do, upload them to Facebook?"

She can hear Max mimic her under his breath, but he doesn't actually offer a rebuttal, so she drops it. She looks out at the trees instead. They're curling over themselves with age, leering down at the Impala as it cuts through the morning. Max got off the 65 and onto the 61, just like Charlie had suggested they do, and then he went even farther, speeding down the back roads that snaked directly through the woods and fields. The highways were not especially crowded, but it's a different kind of lonesome way out here.

Erin shuts one eye and raises the viewfinder to the other. All the trees blur together, a rush of greens and browns.

"Then I'm dying at—torn and twisted—torn and twisted—torn and—"

Erin frowns and turns to the stereo. The disc continues to skip.

"Oh, c'mon." Max smacks the slot a few times with the hard part of his palm.

"Three bucks on eBay," Erin echoes.

Max rolls his eyes and ejects the disc. Erin takes it for him. She looks it over but finds no visible scratches. In fact, for a three-dollar disc, it looks to be in pretty good shape.

"Okay." Max sighs dramatically, stretching until his arm pushes against the roof of the car. "We need to find something to do, 'cause at this point I'm gonna fall asleep and kill us both before we even get close to lunch."

"If I'd known we were gonna throw our phones into a creek, I would've rented an audiobook."

Erin pushes the disc back into the slot and skips ahead to "Two Out of Three Ain't Bad" before she fishes through her bag again. She threw a few books in at the bottom: *The Drowning Girl*, *Everyone on the Moon Is Essential Personnel*, *Tell Me I'm Worthless*. They're not all trans lit, though, and she's not sure she wants to start reading about suicidal trans girls and bodies tearing themselves apart right now anyway. Instead, she pulls out two of the less depressing paperbacks. "Okay. *Through the Looking-Glass*, or *White Fang*?"

Max raises an eyebrow. "Are you my AP English teacher?"

"And sass gets you literary nonsense." Erin tosses *White Fang* back into the bag and settles with *Through the Looking-Glass* on her lap.

Max groans.

Maybe it's just clinging to their clothes, but Erin catches another whiff of that smell that was lingering around the gas station. It doesn't smell like smoke, exactly, but like something burning. Erin grimaces and turns the air-conditioning up a notch.

"Okay. Fine. Hit me with Alice in Nowhere, USA. I don't even care, start anywhere." Max hangs one hand loosely off the wheel.

Erin glances over at him. It's rare to see him without sleeves. She's been consciously trying not to stare since they got back in the car, but it's hard to keep her eyes off of him. There are a few little cardboard cuts on his knuckles, and a bruise turning green on his elbow. There's also a scar running along the inside of his left arm. A few inches of raised, milky-white skin.

Erin turns back to the book. Flips through it for a moment. With her finger, she picks a spot and reads aloud:

"'Twas brillig, and the slithy toves did gyre and gimble in the wabe: all mimsy were the borogoves, and the mome raths outgrabe.

'Beware the Jabberwock, my son! The jaws that bite, the claws that catch!'"

To her right, something heavy *thwack*s against the door. Erin looks up.

Of course there's nothing there. Max tilts the wheel a little, so that the car pulls farther away from the side of the road. Erin watches the oaks and the sycamores. None of the branches seem close enough to have hit the door. Still, Erin frowns and keeps looking.

"Starting off with a nonsense poem? Harsh."

"You were the AP English student, you'll survive." Erin shakes her head and focuses back on the book. She's tired, she's a little overwhelmed, she'd do well not to start hallucinating. *"He took his vorpal sword in hand; long time the manxome foe he sought—so rested he by the Tumtum tree and stood awhile in thought."*

The disc skips. Erin looks up. The title track starts playing, halfway through, a little warbled and suddenly loud. But it doesn't skip again.

"Like a bat out of hell, I'll be gone when the morning comes—"

She clears her throat. *"And, as in uffish thought he stood, the Jabberwock, with eyes of flame, came whiffling through the tulgey wood, and burbled as it came!"*

Before she's even finished the final line, Erin looks up again.

She's just in time to catch a shadow.

Well, a void. It *casts* a shadow of its own over Erin's face as it moves across the road, fluid and jerking as if it were being yanked along on strings. Her eyes latch onto the one splotch of color that she can find: the faintest glimpse of what might be an *eye*, yellow and burning, as if the sun were streaking across the night sky.

Nobody screams.

Instead, the brakes *squeal*. Erin grabs Max's arm. She shuts her eyes. The car jolts, not just with the sudden attempt to stop but with running over *something*. Then comes the slow, heavy *creeeeaaak* of finally coming to a halt. And then it's quiet.

After the car has stopped, Erin brings her head up. Her heart beats so hard she can feel it reverberate in the farthest curves of her ribs. They're facing in the direction they were just coming from. Erin realizes that they're caught in a ditch halfway off the road, her side of the car elevated slightly above Max's. She still has Max's arm in her grip while her other hand is white-knuckled around her door handle. Her book is open, facedown, where it's landed at her feet.

Erin looks out her window. There's no body in the road, no trail of destruction. Just the same dense foliage, leaves fluttering gently in the natural breeze.

"Did you see that?" Erin's question comes out like an exhale as she finally turns to Max.

He's still staring at the road, his hands gripping the wheel tightly at ten and two. Only when Erin speaks does his head snap in her direction. Then the tension leaves his body like a deflating balloon. He kills the engine, and the radio finally goes quiet.

She can feel his pulse thumping under her fingers. After a moment, hesitantly, she lets him go.

Erin undoes her seat belt and gets out of the car on wobbly legs. The silence out here isn't much better. It's less echoey, but it's still her own breathing that's thrumming heavy and fast in her ears. And there's still no evidence of anything out here. Only their tire marks stain the road.

Behind her, she hears Max get out of the car. She waits a moment, continuing to scan the trees in a desperate hope for *something*, before she finally turns away. Max is standing at the front of the car with his hands on his hips. He stares at the tires, eyebrows knit together.

Erin walks up to his side. She doesn't understand what they're looking at until Max bends down and wraps his fingers around a long, rusted nail, and pulls it from the tire. That's when Erin sees the number of nails that are sticking out of their front tires. Some are stuck in all the way to the head while others flap loosely inside bits of torn rubber.

Max spins the nail. "All right. Ditching our phones might've been a little stupid."

Erin doesn't laugh. There's only the feeling of dread squeezing around her chest. Constricting around her.

Then Erin can hear the sound of gravel crunching under tires behind her. She turns to look. It takes a moment for the car to come around the bend: a marked cop cruiser. It goes wide, and the siren chirps in greeting. Erin watches the cop drive past them, U-turn, and pull up behind the Impala.

Erin looks to Max, whose face is still washed out like he's seen a ghost. The air around them suddenly seems tight with tension as the cop steps out of his car, and Erin supposes this is either where their day takes a turn for the better or for much, much worse.

10

CHIEF D. LASTER IS THE NAME pinned to the cop's chest, although he introduces himself as "just Dennis, please." From what Max can see of him, his face is wrinkled, like old leather, and the hair sticking out from under his giant cowboy hat is a mixture of earthy browns and grays. But most of his face is taken up by these giant cop shades, which reflect Max's face back to himself. It's a lot.

Chief Laster uses his radio to call for a tow truck while they're still on the side of the road. The quiet chatter of voices continues as background noise after they've gotten into the cruiser and begun to drive. Max can still see a portion of his face in the reflection of the cop's glasses and the rearview mirror: his flat, dead brown eyes staring back at himself. Glaring. To his right, Erin is staring out the window. She's been quiet ever since Chief Laster pulled up.

"So." Chief Laster's voice is suddenly directed at them,

cutting through the open partition. "Where are you two kids supposed to be goin'?"

"Washington," Max answers, staring at Chief Laster's eyes, even though he can't actually see them.

The cop whistles. "You two are a long way from home."

"We're from Cincinnati, actually. I'm just going to school in Washington."

"Oh? Your girlfriend, too?"

Erin finally turns her head to the conversation.

"She's helping me drive out," Max answers, as level as he can be.

"Smart. I've seen plenty of folks come through here on a drive by themselves, who fell asleep at the worst moment." Chief Laster imitates the sound of a crash—*pshhh*—and shakes his head. "Awful stuff."

It goes quiet. Max tries to relax back into his seat, reaching down and playing with one of the drawstrings of his jacket. He threw it back on before getting into the cruiser. That's the last thing he needs right now, to risk a *cop* staring down his chest while he's trying to keep his lie straight.

Washington. Cincinnati. Not his girlfriend.

Outside, a motorcycle rips past them, going in the opposite direction. Max watches it go, and when he turns back, he finds that Erin is suddenly sitting upright, rigid as a pole. "Are there bears out here?" she asks.

Chief Laster looks at her through the mirror. There's a toothpick between his teeth, where a slight gap allows it to rest almost perfectly. One eyebrow cocks up. "Come again?"

"Bears. Or, like, big animals."

"Not much. We don't hardly even see bucks 'round here no more. Why?"

Erin finally sits back and shrugs. "Just thought I saw something."

Max nods. *Something*. That's the only word for it. "That's why I swerved and—"

"Hit that spike strip," Chief Laster cuts him off. "Yeah, I thought we had one missing."

Max tilts his head. "You *thought*? How'd you figure that?"

Even without being able to see them, Max can tell that the cop's eyes shift to him. "This is a slow place for some folk. They get so bored, they'll do just about anything to stir up some excitement for themselves."

"They could've killed us."

"And thank Jesus they didn't," Chief Laster agrees before he turns the radio up. Conversation over.

Max can sense Erin staring at him, but he ignores her. He curls up against the door and looks out the window. He watches a tow truck sputter past them, and continues to watch until it vanishes around the bend.

As it turns out, they weren't all that far from the next town. Or the next closest thing. After several silent minutes, Chief Laster pulls off the highway into a large open lot. Although there is ample space for more, only a handful of semitrucks are scattered at the far end. Chief Laster parks in front of a white building with a thick, blue-trimmed roof. Three entry ports sit to the right of the front door. Max watches a lanky blond guy in a ball cap linger in one of them. He seems to briefly stare back at him before he turns and disappears inside.

To the right, Max can see where the highway picks back up again. The glowing yellow arches of a McDonald's sign tower above all else. And, if he squints, he can see the backs of a few houses hidden among the shadows. To his left, telephone poles frame an endless grove of dead, gnarled trees. There might be the hint of a larger city beyond that, but it's only the ghost of such a thing. This is a last stop.

Chief Laster looks back at them. "I'm gonna go inside and talk to the boys," he says. "They'll get you some new tires and have you out of here before sundown. Consider it an apology on behalf of whoever did this."

"Thanks," Max answers flatly.

"Just keep your eyes open. I'd hate to have to clean the two of you off the asphalt."

"Unless you're that bad at—"

Erin sharply kicks him in the ankle. "Thank you, sir, we'll be careful."

Max gives her a look. Chief Laster doesn't say anything. He's still grinning by the time Max turns to him again.

All these guys know how to do out here is *grin*. It makes his skin crawl.

Max is out the door as soon as the cop opens it for him, and he doesn't even mind how *sweltering* it still is outside. Erin climbs out, too, and they both watch Chief Laster take the steps up to the front door of the shop, where he disappears inside.

The moment they're alone, Erin speaks: "How about we *don't* antagonize the guy trying to help us?"

Max looks at her, and then scoffs. "Dude, he's a cop."

"And we're two transsexuals in the middle of Kentucky!" she hisses. "I don't care what he is, we should be focused on getting out of here!"

"I don't want to be stuck here, either! But he's a creep!"

Erin opens her mouth, and Max is ready to keep arguing, but her focus suddenly shifts to something behind him, and Max turns to follow her gaze. They watch as the tow truck pulls into the lot, dragging the Impala behind it like a corpse.

The sight of it lands in Max's stomach like a bowling ball. In another world, he killed both of them. That thought blocks up in his throat. Not even a quarter of the way there yet, and Max has already almost killed them.

The truck driver glances at them as he passes. He's blond. Looks like he spends his days baking in the sun and shooting beer cans off fence posts. Max makes it a point to hold eye contact with him until he disappears into one of the entry ports.

Erin sits down on the stairs leading up to the front door of the place. Max lingers for a moment before wandering over to her, crossing his arms over his chest, and leaning against the building. Immediately, he can feel where he's been sweating through his shirt.

There's a knot in his shoulders so tight that it's started to crawl down his spine. They have no phones. *His stupid idea.* He almost got Erin killed. *His stupid fault.* They have no way of leaving whatever part of Kentucky they're now stuck in. *Also his stupid fault*.

"Are you okay?" he breathes, shutting his eyes.

"Yeah," Erin answers. "You?"

He shrugs. "Eh."

Quiet again. Max's heel bounces off the asphalt incessantly. He might throw up.

"I know you saw it, too," Erin finally says.

Max's foot stops. He can't look at her.

Flat-out, he doesn't know. He doesn't know if he saw something before Erin grabbed him, or if he's just imagined the shadow to make it even partially *not* his fault. Could he be cowardly enough to throw up his hands and blame Bigfoot?

"Maybe," he finally says.

"Maybe? You said—"

"I don't know what I saw!" He turns to her. "It was over in, like, ten seconds! Maybe I saw something, maybe neither of us did. What's it matter?"

Erin looks back at the door, then to Max again. "Why did he act like he had no idea what I could be talking about?"

"Because he's a lazy cop who doesn't care. It's not sinister, most of 'em are like that."

"You know that's not it."

Max shrugs helplessly. "Okay. Sure. We almost hit a bear. What do you want him to do about it? Or *us*? Go back and try not to miss this time?"

Erin does not answer him. Before they can say anything

more about it, Chief Laster steps out. "You two are set," he declares.

He tips his hat toward Max. Max just stares at him. He's not consciously trying to glare, but he suspects he might be.

"Thank you, again," Erin speaks up, drawing his attention to her.

Chief Laster nods. "Just stay out of trouble. And keep your eyes on the road. Both of you."

He walks past them, back to the cruiser.

That should be the end of it. But Max can't help himself. The question is already out before he can think better of it: "You're sure there aren't any bears running around here?"

Immediately, Chief Laster stops and looks back at him. Erin looks up at him, too.

Max recrosses his arms. "We know we saw something," he adds.

Max does not know this. He certainly doesn't have the confidence he's trying so hard to project. But, well, he can't renege *now*.

Chief Laster looks them over for what feels like ages. Max can see Erin nervously shift where she sits, but she doesn't tell Max to shut up. Which is kinda nice. And then, finally, the man starts to laugh and walk back over. The high-noon sun casts him in shadow, creating this faceless giant to loom over them.

"You kids ever heard of the Bullitt Beast?" Chief Laster asks.

Max actually thinks he has. He frowns. "Isn't that just regional slang for Bigfoot?"

The cop chuckles. "That'd be the Bullitt *County* Beast. Bullitt Beast is more . . . local. Been around since—shoot, probably the forties. Old wartime story."

Max resists the urge to roll his eyes and ask if there's also a Beast of Bullitt County he should be aware of. He glances down at Erin, wondering if she's getting any of this. "Cool, I guess."

"I'm saying, most folks around here grew up on all sorts of stories about the things that live out here. Parents scaring kids, and kids trying to scare each other. We're a superstitious bunch."

Max cracks a grin. "So your local legend just runs in front of cars like *Frogger?* C'mon."

"I don't expect either of you kids to understand—"

"No, seriously," Max urges. "Give me a real answer. What's the *Bullitt Beast?*"

Chief Laster seems to consider this for a moment before a dark chuckle shakes his chest. "An old way of handling an old problem. See, we used to have some awful floods out here. About every five years, the water'd get so high you'd have folks displaced for a week. Sometimes more. Houses ruined, animals dead. Always *someone* drowned trying to go back for something they decided they just couldn't live without."

"Sounds like you picked a bad place to put a town."

Erin kicks the side of his shoe for this.

But Chief Laster nods in what seems like earnest agreement. "My dad used to tell me the same thing when I was a kid. This town came up to support the railroad, and God tried just about everything to punish us all for it. First, it was fires. Then, with the war, we started having the floods. That's where the Beast comes from, I think. The floods. It was a convenient way to blame something that wasn't God for all the people who drowned. Some giant black beast. Eyes like torchlights."

Erin noticeably straightens. Max glances at her, although he's less scared than he is just plain curious. A giant black beast: *how descriptive*.

"Then, toward the end of the eighties, I think, we stopped having floods, and kids suddenly stopped seeing the Beast on every street corner. *That* became a story of its own. People say—well, the floods stopped, and we stopped seeing the Beast; maybe one was controlling the other. Maybe the floods brought the Beast, or maybe the Beast brought the floods. Either way, that leaves only one question: What stopped it?"

Chief Laster pauses there. As if he's going for dramatic effect.

Max only barely resists the urge to roll his eyes. "What stopped it?"

Another grin. "Fun little fact 'bout this place: folks don't die here anymore. No more fires. No more floods. Shoot, we haven't had a proper murder in about as long. We get the occasional runaway, but we've only got one true missing person's case we ain't solved. Local girl. Disappeared on the last night of the floods. Just walked right out of her house and nobody ever saw her again. You put that all together—girl goes missing, floods stop, Beast stops—and a picture forms.

"Now the story of the Beast ain't about floods, it's about

what happens if girls wander out into the woods alone at night. It's about how the Beast still creeps around out here, because it knows it can find a meal. It knows"—with this, he jabs a finger at Erin—"there are more girls to find. Rip 'em apart, piece by piece, and leave the eyes behind for the birds to clean up."

He starts laughing, like he's just told the funniest joke in the world. Max looks down at Erin again, and they share a look of mutual horror before Chief Laster collects himself. "Now, can either of you kids tell me anything about what you saw?"

Erin, frustratingly, says nothing as she picks at the Band-Aid on her finger. Max grinds his teeth. When it comes down to it, he has nothing better than a giant black beast.

After enough time has passed in tense silence, Chief Laster nods. "Then I'd be willing to bet it was probably the same delinquents who swiped that spike strip. Kids who grew up on monsters in the woods, who don't have nothing better to do than scare tourists."

Max has a very hard time believing that it was only some random teenager running across the road. But what are his other options? A shared delusion? Total insanity?

"Look at it this way: now you've got one hell of a story to tell your friends about."

Erin's smile does not reach her eyes. "Well, thanks again."

He tips his hat to her. "You two be careful."

That seems to be the end of it. Max has just started to feel around for his cigarettes when the man suddenly stops again. Chief Laster turns back to them, grins, and adds:

"Don't get lost."

11

THE GOOD NEWS: the repair shop will be able to replace their tires and have them on the road again before sundown, just as Chief Laster promised.

The bad news: they'll be lucky to be on the road *before* sundown. That promise was pretty literal.

The blond mechanic lets them grab what they need from the car, and Erin deftly slips her pill case into her pocket. Max lights up another cigarette and wanders off in the direction of the highway. With nothing else to do, Erin follows.

At the edge of the lot, Erin realizes there's an old train car looking out over the road. It's poorly placed. Erin would never have seen it if Max hadn't. The gray paint has faded and chipped away into rust patches, and the body has mostly been covered with graffiti tags. Erin is fine with looking at it from a distance—wondering *who in the world put this* here?—but Max jumps right up onto the steps and climbs aboard. He's gone for about thirty seconds.

Then, just as Erin's getting ready to go in after him, he comes out on his own. "There's stuff on the front."

Sure enough, as they walk onto the grassy field between the lot and the highway, Erin sees the sign erected on the side of the train car. It reads:

THANK YOU FOR VISITING LEBANON JUNCTION

Then, in slightly smaller text beneath:

EST. 1858 POPULATION 1,500

Erin glances over her shoulder at the highway behind them. That's the audience for this: the folks driving out of town. Again, odd place for such a thing, but Max has already homed in on the placard posted beneath.

"Hey, look." Max nudges her, and starts to read aloud in an exaggerated Southern accent that quickly becomes a Dale Gribble impression. *"On March 8, 1858, the L&N Railroad erected a railroad switching point to split railroad traffic—"* Erin kicks him, and Max drops the accent "—uh, yada yada yada, *plaque placed by the Bullitt County Parks and Recreation in the year 2003, in recognition of the founding history of Lebanon Junction, near these historical tracks* . . . historical tracks?"

They both look around. Erin is the one who finds the tracks, hidden in the tall, wilting grass. That explains the ever-so-slight elevation of the highway, making way for the abandoned railroad that, at one point, was this town's entire reason for existing.

"Well," Max sighs, "that's fucking depressing."

Erin agrees. "Still hungry?"

Max snuffs out his cigarette on the rusted steel rail. "Starving."

On the far end of the parking lot is a diner. Erin saw it when they first drove in. By the time they get over there, it's well past the usual lunch hour, so the place is mostly empty.

They seat themselves in the booth closest to the entrance. A neon Open sign glares down at them from the window. All the natural light pouring in makes everything feel too bright, too focused, glaring off the dark linoleum floor. It's quiet. The jukebox in the corner is dark, and the televisions on the wall are all muted. A Black woman wearing a striped button-up shirt walks over with two menus; her name tag reads *Samantha*. Her hair, tightly coiled above her shoulders, appears to shimmer when the light hits it. Erin orders a coffee. Max, water.

Estrogen, progesterone, and Aldactone go down the hatch, chased by one horrible swig of still-black coffee. Erin grimaces before she relaxes into the booth. After almost four years of taking it, estrogen is no longer the magic, all-powerful key to the kingdom. It's just a pill. And yet, for the first time in a while, Erin feels a bit of relief with taking it.

She looks over at Max, who's started to build a house out of sugar packets. It collapses on the second story. She can hear his foot tapping against the floor.

Erin looks around the rest of the diner. An older white guy sits on the opposite end, alone and reading a paper through thick, rectangular glasses. He glances up, and they make one second of awkward eye contact before Erin quickly looks away.

Back to Max. His face is scrunched in concentration. His sugar tower topples again. He sighs.

"Hey." Erin nudges him with her foot. "Bucket list."

Max gives her a funny look.

"Yeah, really. I don't want us to be depressed for the rest of the day because of this," she says.

"Too late."

Erin takes her hoodie off and hangs it from the back of the booth. "Seriously. Berkeley Bucket List. Go."

Max maintains his skeptical look, but he seems to at least think about it. "Well, the beach first. Obviously."

"Obviously."

"I wanna go to a Five Guys that's not, like, an hour from my house."

Erin thinks about that and almost sighs. She could kill for a burger right now.

She looks around, hoping to see Samantha hanging near the kitchen window. Instead, her eyes land on the old man, who's still staring at her.

Max plays with the splintered plastic ends of his hoodie's drawstrings. "I don't know," he finally says, "might just pass out on the beach and die there."

Erin rolls her eyes. She takes a packet of sugar from the rubble of Max's house and shakes it out into her coffee. "What about moving in?"

"I think summer housing opened the week before my

birthday. When I talked to them on the phone, they said it's fine for us to come in later. We paid, so we have a spot."

Erin smiles.

The house was part of Max's pitch. Erin looked up pictures of it after the fact. It's a frat house, technically, populated entirely by queer kids. The roof is this gorgeous shade of forest green. There's a communal garden out back where they grow all sorts of flowers and fruits. In the video she watched, there's even a fridge with a giant googly eye on it. It's adorable. The cherry on top? Being a Berkeley student isn't required for admission.

Max identified that loophole, too. So Erin signed up for an introductory history class at Berkeley City College. Something easy. According to Max, the plan from there is to find an actual apartment somewhere in the city after they've found their footing.

There's a lot of vague *yada yada yada* in that plan, but Erin is trying to ignore it. Of course they'll find a place. Of course they'll make it there. Because there's no backup plan for if they don't.

She looks up. The man is still staring at her. This time, Erin nervously maintains eye contact. A cold burn of nerves ripples outward from under her skin, and she can't look away.

The problem is that she knows this stare. The stare of teenage boys as they whisper to each other *No, really, that used to be a guy.* The stare of scornful teenage girls, which wordlessly imparts that they share no sisterhood with Erin. A stare that makes her feel like she's been stripped completely down to the bones.

Erin imagines her face and rotates it in her mind; what's this guy clocking her on? Or is he clocking her at all? Mundane, misogynistic leering is far more common in spaces where she's a stranger, but that makes it no less stomach-churning. If anything, it's *more* dangerous.

She untucks her hair from behind her ear and lets it hang partially over her face. As if it will actually do anything to hide the features he's so surely deemed *incorrect*. Max finally seems to notice that something's wrong, and frowns.

"Four o'clock," Erin whispers.

Subtle as ever, Max fully turns around. The old man goes back to his newspaper without a flicker of shame. Max stares for a few seconds longer before he looks at Erin again.

"Wanna move?" he asks.

Erin shakes her head, although her face is still hot with embarrassment. "So, we'll have a place to live. What else?"

Almost reluctantly, Max turns fully back to her. Then he shrugs.

Erin gives him a look. "There is no way you haven't planned out every second of your first *week* there."

"Well, *sure*, I bounced around on Google a bunch, but—I dunno." Max sighs and slouches down. "I feel like if I plan anything, it's just gonna jinx us."

"You're not gonna jinx anything."

Max's smile is thin. "Right."

"I mean it." She bumps him with her foot. "Going back isn't an option, so we don't go back."

Max looks down at his fallen house and hums. Erin kicks him a little harder. He looks up.

"We're getting to Berkeley. I promise."

It's silent for a moment. When Max smiles again, it's real. Erin smiles back, takes a sip of coffee, and steals another sugar.

She looks past Max again. The old man is gone. His paper is left behind, folded up on the table, but the booth is empty.

A notch of tension leaves Erin's shoulders, although she continues to stare at the spot, as if he might suddenly reappear. "I'm guessing you already have something set up for you-know-what?"

Luckily, Max doesn't need her to say the buzzword out loud. "Yeah." He nods, and his mouth wavers. "I figured we'd get there on the tenth or something, so I set up a consultation for the thirteenth. Which, y'know, kinda sucks. To wait. But I'd rather get there early and have to wait a few days than get there late and miss it."

Erin nods along. It's the emotion of her first shot that's lingered stronger than anything else: a lot of nerves, followed by intense relief. Euphoria. The first graze against the stars.

Max pulls the menu out from behind the condiments stand and opens it. Only his eyes are visible over the top. "So, what's on *your* bucket list?"

"San Francisco's right across the bay."

"Ha. Yeah, I think if we go up onto the roof and jump, we could maybe see the Golden Gate Bridge from the house. That'd be cool."

Erin smiles at the image that comes to mind, even though something about it suddenly makes her sad. It is such a perfect image: her and Max, together, *not in Ohio*. Like nothing ever changed. She wants that.

And yet. It's at the tip of her fingers, not yet in the grip of her fist. Every joyful image is tinted with the memory of how quickly Max ripped himself away from her the first time. How easily.

"You all right?"

Erin looks up. Max is staring at her and seems like he has been for a minute. Erin wonders how long they've been sitting there like that.

She nods. "Yeah."

"You seem a little spacey."

"It's just jitters."

Max says nothing, bending the already creased corner of the menu between his fingers. His hairline is noticeably damp with sweat. Erin resists the urge to reach forward and wipe it away.

"How's your mom?" Max suddenly asks.

Erin smiles a little. Shrugs. "Fine. She keeps herself busy."

"Is she still dating that tax consultant? The one who kinda looked like Michael Douglas?"

Erin makes a face and laughs. "God, no, that lasted for, like, five minutes. She hasn't dated anybody in ages."

Max starts to laugh, too, and, for a brief moment, it feels so familiar. She can recall their hushed, childish giggles while they watched her mom and the Michael Douglas guy chat in the doorway. Once, they'd been watching *Misery* together when the second couple came home, Max's head resting on Erin's lap while James Caan wailed.

Then the laughter fades, and the moment's gone. Erin takes another sip of coffee. It burns at the back of her throat, as if it were suddenly acidic. She grimaces and pushes the cup aside.

Max abruptly puts down his menu and pulls out his wallet. He scrapes out a handful of quarters and pushes them across the table to Erin. "Here. You have better taste than me, anyway. I need to find the bathroom."

He scoots out of the booth and walks off before Erin can get a word in. She watches him go, haphazardly slapping his hands against empty chairs until he disappears behind a corner. And then Erin's alone, with $1.75 in quarters, and coffee she's not interested in anymore.

The jukebox sits dark when she approaches it, but with one touch it lights up in shades of red and blue. Erin stacks the quarters on top of the machine and flips through the songs. There's hardly anything from after 1999. She flips through it all once before she makes her way back to the top again.

To her left is the doorway to the kitchen, where two waitresses are laughing with each other. They're both blonds, faces covered in foundation that's a noticeable shade darker than their arms. One of them is vaping; the vapor gathers around the light on the ceiling before it dissipates.

A frigid hand comes to rest on her bicep. Erin nearly jumps out of her skin. She spins around. The old man isn't *gripping her*, but his face is scrunched, wrinkles on top of wrinkles, into a frown. It's not a look she likes being on the receiving end of.

"The lady's room is the last door," he states. "Your girlfriend got lost."

"Oh." Erin's voice comes out like a whisper. "Thank you."

The man nods, satisfied. "Ma'am."

There is almost relief as he walks away. Erin makes a point to watch him leave the building. She doesn't move again until the door shuts behind him. *Ma'am.*

Erin holds the word on her tongue for a moment. Then she does the same thing for *girlfriend*. An even stranger word. She's laughing by the time she turns back to the jukebox.

12

THE DAY HAS BEEN BAD enough, but having to wait in the women's room makes Max the angriest he's been all day.

"I think you're in the wrong bathroom, hon," the creepy old guy said, like he was trying to be helpful. It was a crock of shit.

But Max forces himself to be the bigger man and waits it out in the girls' room, taking deep breaths until the constriction of his binder makes him lightheaded and it's harder to focus on the anger between his teeth. Then he hears a *flush* through the wall. He waits a few more seconds before he pokes his head out and watches the old man walk away. Then, at last, he runs and locks himself inside the men's room stall, where it reeks of piss and trucker sweat from floor to ceiling.

When Max comes back, Erin is at the jukebox. She's turned away from him, one arm folded against the base of the box while her other hand flips steadily through each track. An Elvis song is already almost over. Max doesn't draw any attention to himself and just wanders back toward their booth. He's hungry. And hot.

"Oh, Pretty Woman" starts when Elvis stops. It echoes across a few speakers, slightly out of sync and creating a weird vortex of guitars and drums as it bounces off the walls. Max almost starts laughing at the corniness of it. For all his love of pop-punk garbage, Erin has continued to cling to Dad Rock.

She doesn't exactly dance, but her head nods to the beat of the drums. Her shoulders start to move, followed by her hips. Erin slowly sways her way upright, unselfconscious and completely unobserved as far as she's concerned. Max lingers next to their booth and watches her for a minute. Or, rather, he stares.

She's not even trying. That's the thing that gets him. She's not wearing any sort of makeup, there are visible pit stains on her tank top, and her bangs are stuck to her forehead. Then she finally notices Max out of the corner of her eye, and her entire face scrunches up as she starts to laugh at herself.

Max hates the feeling that spreads in his chest. The static that constricts and expands, explodes and implodes. He hates how much he wants to chase that feeling, to start the song over and to watch her dance again.

Erin hurries back across the room in a few long strides. Then the song ends, and the Cure starts playing, and it's "Boys Don't Cry." Max's life is a punch line again.

He knows that Erin starts saying something, but he doesn't hear it. The static becomes a black hole inside of his ribs.

"You know, in 2006, this band called Pet Shop Boys made

a song based off *Boys Don't Cry*. The Brandon Teena movie." He plops down into the booth and sighs. "Y'know what they called it?"

Erin frowns. "What?"

"*Girls* Don't Cry."

He grins tightly. Erin grimaces. Max knows then that he's spoiled the mood, and he knows he should feel bad, but he doesn't. This isn't a vacation. Erin is beautiful, and he finds that he still hates her for it.

13

COLUMBUS WAS AN HOUR'S DRIVE from Kings Mills. That was what scared Max. Not necessarily the death itself, nor the manner of death (though these were, of course, still almost unbearably scary), but the fact that Leelah was killed in what was basically Max's own backyard. They killed Leelah eighty-three miles away from him. That wasn't the other side of the country, that wasn't twenty years ago or another continent, that was home.

In retrospect, that difference in language was probably one of the defining moments when his parents knew that something wasn't normal with Max. Because Leelah killed her*self*. That was the whole tragedy of it. A trans girl killed herself in Ohio, and national news stations picked up the story, and they put her deadname out from coast to coast, and a few of the especially stupid even offered up defense of her parents. She killed herself and it was sad. Even Max's parents could acknowledge such a fact.

But Max didn't talk about it like that. When his mom would mention it, Max would correct her: Leelah was *killed*. And then they'd argue about it, go back and forth about why Max was biased (obviously; his boyfriend had pretty much *just* become his girlfriend) and how he couldn't understand all the tough decisions parents had to make with their kids.

When Max came out to them, some years after that very strange period of time where enough people cared to make trans suicide national news, Brian just laughed at him. It was kind of a sad laugh, pitiful and disbelieving. Max had never seen his mom look so morose in her life.

For reasons he never quite understood himself, Max hoped that his mom would be his entry point. Maybe it was just because Brian was so cartoonish in how much he hated Max. Maybe it was because, compared to him, Mom seemed so much more reasonable. She didn't hate gay people! That was a starting point. Max just had to find where the armor was soft, had to convince her in whatever way he could that this was right, and maybe he'd be transitioning before he turned eighteen.

He was careful. He made a very conscious, serious effort to give her time and space to *process*. And it almost seemed like it was starting to pay off. She referred to Max as *her child* sometimes, which was pointedly different language than *her daughter*. And then, one day, she asked if Max wanted to watch a trans movie with her. Max thought that was it. Mother and son finally reaching an understanding.

Brandon Teena was not an unfamiliar name to Max. Much

like Leelah, Brandon was almost impossible to *not* know. Max knew about *Boys Don't Cry*. He knew, broadly, what it was all about, but there, sitting in the recliner next to his mom in the cold, tense silence of his living room, was the first time he'd ever actually watched it.

When it finally ended, the only thing his mom asked him was if he understood the life he was *choosing*. "I don't care if you're gay, honey, but if you go around lying to people . . ."

Later that night, Max walked down to Alex's house. The guys he'd started hanging around in those post-Erin times were varying levels of decent, but Alex was perhaps the only *good* one of the bunch. He was tall, one of the few Black biracial kids that Max knew, and he always answered his phone when Max called.

Together, they walked out to the unkempt baseball diamond a mile or so down from Alex's house, where grass and weeds had overtaken most of the infield. It was a good thing that Alex was a good listener, because Max didn't stop talking from almost the moment they were alone.

"It's bullshit, y'know?" Max said as he paced back and forth. "After they killed him, this guy wrote an article about Brandon for *Playboy*, and you know what he called it? 'Death of a Deceiver.' And he interviewed all Brandon's old girlfriends, and all he writes about is how they didn't know he was a boy, 'cause he was so good to have sex with. 'Cause all those girls were stupid and didn't know how sex worked, so they couldn't tell that Brandon was just a—freak liar. And

Brandon's mom *followed* him places, and she outed him to some of these girlfriends. They tried to institutionalize him.

"And you know? Nobody ever asked, like, what Brandon wanted to do when he was thirty? Did he care about football? If he could learn any language in the world, what would it be? Pepsi or Coke? Nobody cared about any of that. They just walked up to all these strangers in this crummy little town and they said, 'Excuse me, but did you know that Brandon was *really* a girl? He's dead now, but we just thought that maybe you should know that.' They made his whole memory that he was raped and shot in the head and that he had it coming because he lied about being a boy. And then they made a movie about how much he lied. And the movie doesn't ask none of those questions, either. It's this two-hour lesbian *Romeo and Juliet* shit, and it acts like Brandon being murdered was this tragedy predestined by God. Not just because he was a liar, but because all those small-town hicks didn't like lesbians. That's how most of the world remembers him now. A lesbian. Someone who wanted to *be* a boy but who was really just a girl. I don't know anything about Brandon except for how much he hurt. Except for what other people did to him. And that's not a human being. That wasn't his life."

He finally stopped, out of breath and out of energy. His hands were shaking.

Alex, sitting where home plate should've been, was quiet for a minute. "So," he finally said, and cleared his throat, "Brandon was a chick? Or, a dude who wanted to be a chick?"

Max just stared at him. Disbelief. "No," he said. "He was just a guy."

Two years after Leelah's death, Rae'Lynn was killed. In Columbus. Ten minutes away from where Max slept at night. He didn't even know any of these people, all these girls and boys who just kept getting killed, and yet the ghosts kept getting closer and closer to him, until Max could feel them breathing down his neck, weighing on him for the fact that he wasn't one of them, and it all just made him feel so, so hopeless.

14

AFTER MAX'S OWN ATTEMPT, his parents gave him an ultimatum:

Let go of the delusion of being a boy.

Or, spend the next six months going from mental institution to mental institution, with the risk that it might keep going even after he turned eighteen. However long it took to finally fix him.

Max chose the former.

15

THE GLARE OF THE SETTING SUN has only just begun to merge with the horizon when the mechanic finally drives their car out. "Brand-new tires," he explains to them, tongue heavy with regional drawl, "plus a quick lookover on everything else. You're all set."

They barely hang around long enough to get their seat belts on. Then Max's foot is on the gas, and that little blip of civilization shrinks and shrinks, until it finally disappears behind them. Max rolls the window down and cruises with one hand on the wheel. His jittery smile nearly reaches his ears.

Internally, Erin is less optimistic. But they're leaving Lebanon Junction behind them, and, she hopes, leaving the monster-obsessed, spike strip–stealing teenagers behind, too. She holds the map down with both hands to keep it from flapping around in the wind.

They leave the radio off. And they find themselves back on the topic of monsters.

"I'm just wondering, would monsters acknowledge trans'ed genders?" Max has started smoking again, and the cigarette does not help him look any less deranged when he asks this. "Do they even know what gender is? *How* do they know what gender is?"

Erin shakes her head. "If Bigfoot attacks us, that'll be the last thing I ask."

"Not Bigfoot, *Bullitt Beast*. Which sounds like some knockoff Tamagotchi crap, or something they'd sell at Spencer's next to the novelty dicks."

Erin cracks up because she can visualize both things so, *so* well.

"Anyway, the logistics of that are just insane. First of all, real cryptids almost never attack people. They won't. They might chase you, but they're not gonna *kill you*."

"Well, what about, like, Mothman? I thought—"

"What? No, Mothman's a big baby."

"I thought that was his whole thing, that he showed up and a bridge collapsed and a whole bunch of people died."

"Yeah, but nobody thinks that Mothman was up there chewing on the cables." Max snuffs out his cigarette in an ashtray shoved into the side of his door. "I mean—okay, sure, some people think that the presence of Mothman caused a bridge collapse in the sixties. That version of events is technically accurate. But then there are people who say that

Mothman showed up as a warning. That's the answer I like better. It's not that he brings disasters, he's just trying to warn you. If cryptids *wanted* to hurt people, I'm sure they could, but they don't."

Erin blinks. "Right."

Max shakes his head, like Erin's the weirdo for not having extensive thoughts about *what motivates Mothman*. "Anyway, the gender thing is even dumber. First, you'd have to try to introduce this thing to the concept of *binary* gender. And this thing probably has a brain that's the size of a walnut."

"First, you'd have to find a cryptid," Erin counters.

He waves her off. "That's the easy part. But after you get a cryptid through Gender 101, then you have to introduce trans people! And I know that trans people have always existed, but does *nature* know that? Like, intrinsically?"

Erin has been stoned exactly once. But suddenly, she feels like she's been transported to the back of Miranda's Honda Civic, the night before they walked the graduation stage. What steps did she take in her life to be here now, philosophizing about whether or not cryptids are capable of having gender ideology? *Bigoted* ideology, at that?

"That cop said they have a monster that goes after girls," Max continues. "So if we ran into it, would it go after me? Or you? Are cryptids transphobic, or aren't they?"

"He was just trying to scare us."

"Yeah, well, he sucked at it. Now I can't stop thinking about the gender politics of some backwoods monster that doesn't even exist. What if Nessie's a TERF, right?"

"Then some monster-fuckers are gonna need a whole bunch of therapy to get over it."

Max laughs so hard that the car swerves. Erin lets herself smile a little before she returns to the map. She smooths it out and traces her finger along their route.

"So, uh, anything weird-lookin' coming up?" Max asks once he's caught his breath. He cranes his neck to try to look at the map. "Anything cool?"

"No, nothing cool. Keep your eyes on the road." Erin gently pushes his face away. His skin is soft and warm to the touch.

The mechanic's shop isn't even marked on the map. But after a minute, she's able to pin where she thinks it *should* be. Just a bit north of Elizabethtown, the only marked town in the whole area. Erin drags her finger down along the little highway line.

"If I'm reading this right, I think there are a few rivers out here. But right now it's probably just going to be trees and churches."

"Dude, what?" Max groans.

Erin looks up. She's ready to tell him *We're in the South, you're just gonna have to deal with that for a while,* before she realizes that he's not reacting to what she said.

Up ahead, the road is blocked off. Reflective orange traffic cones are packed tightly, side by side, guarding more barricades and ROAD CLOSED signs. Max drives all the way up to the cones until the front bumper gently *thunk*s against one.

He puts the car into park. "Did you see anything back there about this?"

Erin shakes her head and sticks herself partially out the window. She can't see anything ahead. The road curves, obscuring whatever must be blocking it. But then, after a moment, the smell hits her.

Take whatever distant but unpleasant stink has been following them all day and magnify it by ten. Erin immediately folds herself back inside the car and rolls her window up. The smell settles on her tongue, as hot and heavy as the air. She puts a hand over her nose and mouth and still almost gags. It takes an extra moment for it to reach Max, and then he reacts in the exact same way.

"*Jesus.*" His voice is muffled behind his hands, and he turns to Erin with a bewildered expression. "What—"

"Don't care. Turn around."

Reverse, reorient, right back in the direction they just came from. Max rolls his window up, too, but the smell seems to have already caked itself into the seats. It makes Erin's head hurt. She holds her tank top over her nose and traces her other hand across the map. "We don't have to go all the way back," she finally says. "Just a couple of miles, get on the turnpike. It'll take us a little farther south, but not too far out of the way."

They aren't driving for more than five minutes before Max apparently decides they aren't taking the turnpike. Erin missed the side road on their first pass, but it's much more obvious coming from this direction. There's an old sign, full of rust-rotted holes, that says ONE-WAY ROAD, bolted to a tree.

Max turns onto the road and for a moment, Erin can still

see the highway. Then the road curves, and the foliage stays tight, and they're alone. Erin watches the trees, breathing in the powdery musk of her deodorant, waiting to see that fire streak across the green again. But there's nothing. Just trees.

She wonders if somebody actually hit that thing, whatever it was that ran across the road. Maybe that's what they're smelling. Death baking under the summer sun.

Max eventually takes his foot off the gas. The car slows, arduously, before Max pulls to the side of the road and puts them into park.

"Here, let me look at that again." Max leans over, bringing a wall of cigarette stench with him. "Aw, man, we shoulda stopped in Louisville."

"Why?"

"I think they have a goatman. I want a second opinion on the transphobic cryptid thing."

Erin gives him a look.

"You're no fun." Max sighs and shifts back into his seat. "Look, the way we're going, we probably couldn't make it to Missouri before the sun goes down. And I don't think I want to be driving at night anymore."

His finger jabs into the map. "Nashville's not far from here. Two hours, maybe three if we keep hitting dead ends. That's still pretty far south but—hell, we could stop anywhere, as long as we can find somewhere to spend the night. And tomorrow, we start early and get back on track. We could maybe make Texas!"

Erin opens her mouth, but Max just keeps going.

"Anyway, today's garbage. My head hurts. Everything smells like shit. And according to that"—he jabs his finger into the map again, just below Erin's kneecap—"there should be a river just to the left of us. That sounds almost nice, right? We can just, like, stick our feet in the water and cool down and not think about anything for five minutes."

Erin doesn't disagree. Her head hurts, too. But sitting here, in the flat, heightened silence of the car, there's a dread that starts to tickle the back of her neck. A touch, featherlight, about to grab her at any moment. Like how being watched feels. "Max..."

He's not listening. He takes the keys. "Unless you want heatstroke, you'll come with me!"

Max pushes his door open and jumps out. And then he's gone, disappearing into the trees on the far side of the road. Irritation simmers in the back of Erin's throat. She has half a mind to remain here out of spite. But that would mean sitting here. Alone. So she begrudgingly unbuckles her seat belt, grabs the disposable camera, and goes after him.

Leaves of all shades, green and yellow and brown, crunch underfoot. Erin can still catch a faint whiff of that horrible smell, but it's no longer so *immediate*. And then the trees open up and Erin emerges in an overgrown field. Wildflowers brush up against her thighs. In a movie, maybe, this place would be beautiful. But the open expanse doesn't exactly make Erin feel like frolicking. It just makes her feel spotlighted for everything around her to observe.

Max is still going up ahead. Erin crosses her arms over her

chest and follows. A few sun-bleached wrappers flutter where they've been caught in the brush. That's the only implication of humankind out here, old and ghostlike. Unseen crickets and bees hum around her, and when a faint breeze snakes its way through, it almost sounds like laughter.

She comes to a stop where the ground begins to dip into a slope, leveling off at a body of what might, by the dictionary definition, be a river. It seems only knee-deep at most, and one could easily cross it in just three or four long strides. The water is filthy. More trash is washed up on the banks.

Max has his back to her, and Erin takes the moment to look him over. His jacket and shoes are abandoned on the bank while Max stands in the water, facing the rapidly setting sun. His shoulders are still heaving. He probably ran the whole way here.

"That water looks disgusting," Erin states.

Max doesn't give her any response. Eventually, Erin sighs and carefully makes her way down to the edge of the river.

She raises the camera and snaps a picture of him before he can turn around and notice. She catches just the slightest angle of his face, lit red and orange. Then, for variety's sake, she takes a quick photo of the sunset itself. She sits down against the slope of the hill. If they don't want to risk getting eaten alive by mosquitoes and ticks, they probably shouldn't stay for long. But the little sunlight that's left, nearly devoid of all its scorching heat, feels like heaven.

Erin shuts her eyes. She imagines how the California beach must feel. Sand between her toes. The cold bite of the water.

The inescapable smell of salt and sunscreen. Max beside her. Warm skin pressed against warm skin.

Droplets splash against her legs. She opens one eye.

Max trudges over to the bank, kicking up water with every step, before he lies down next to Erin with a heavy *thud*. His feet linger in the water. The hair on his legs is stubbly, just enough to be noticeable. It's such a dumb detail to catch, but Erin can't help it. It used to be such a point of pride that he never shaved.

He splays one arm out, twisting blades of grass between his fingers. Erin watches him, observes the scar, and then forces herself to look away. Her own knuckles glisten with sweat. With each breath, she can feel where her shirt clings to her skin.

"Thanks for coming with me." Max's voice startles Erin out of her own head. She looks over at him; he is not looking at her. "I don't remember if I already said that, but, thanks. Seriously."

Erin nods. "Don't mention it."

Max nods, too, and an air of nervous tension suddenly settles. It doesn't seem like he heard her. "I mean, I almost got us killed—"

"Hey." Erin bumps the side of his leg with her own. "Don't. If I'd been driving, then *I* would've almost gotten us killed. Wasn't anybody's fault."

"It's just not the best start to this, and it's not what you signed up for. And I'm worried, like, what if it's a sign?" Max sits up. "What if California was the wrong choice? What if bad stuff keeps happening, and what if we make it all the way out there and I end up having to go back anyway?"

Erin frowns. "Why would you have to—"

"I don't *know*, okay? Maybe California flips overnight and it's open season on trans people like it is in half the goddamn country right now! Maybe a million things!"

Erin grinds her teeth. Of course *she's* the idiot for asking. "There's no chance of that."

"I mean, how many *artists* are in California? How many actually do something with that, and how many end up going back home to their little house on the prairie, working for minimum wage in some shitty burger joint for the rest of their lives?"

"And how many millions of people live in California because they figured it out?"

Max, at last, looks at her. He's almost smiling. But there's no joy. "What if I need them? My parents?"

Erin hoists herself upright. "You don't."

Max doesn't say anything.

Erin crosses her legs and rests her arms on them. "If we go, we go all the way. Right?"

She watches Max's eyes narrow with a glint of something; disbelief, perhaps. Behind him, the sun fights its own weight as it sinks on the horizon. Pulling against the inevitable. "Yeah?"

"Yeah. California doesn't have to be forever. It just has to be right now. And if it doesn't work out, then we figure out something else. We keep going. But you're not going back. You said it: that's not an option."

At last, some kind of real smile creeps across Max's face. "I knew I brought you for a reason."

He laughs, like it's supposed to be a joke, but Erin doesn't laugh back. She suddenly feels like she's just been given a test and passed it blindly. She realizes that the crickets have stopped. All of them, gone dead silent.

"Is that actually why you asked me to come with you?" she asks before she can think better of it.

A beat. Max, who's started to take his feet out of the water, stops and looks up at Erin. He's already frowning. "What do you mean?"

Erin holds his gaze, although something nervous ignites under her skin and begins to burn. "I mean, why did you want me to do this with you? California, all of this."

"Because you're my friend," he answers. Immediately. As if it were obvious.

Erin nearly starts laughing. "Okay, did you just forget the part where we didn't talk to each other for, like, two years? And the only reason we started talking again was to put together this insane escape plan?"

"I thought you wanted to come."

"Of course I did! I *do*! I—"

"Okay, so then what's the issue?" Max's eyes narrow. "We want this together, why does anything else matter?"

Maybe the reason Max wants her around is because she won't call him on his bullshit.

Erin sets her jaw. "We haven't talked about it," she says flatly. "About any of it."

Max stares at her as if she just spat on him. "Because it doesn't matter."

"It does to me!" Erin snaps, harder than she maybe means to. "For *two years*, you act like I don't exist, and then all of a sudden I'm your best friend again? It's that easy for you?"

Out in the distance, something *howls*.

It's not close. But at the end, the noise twists into something that Erin would swear sounds *human*. Deep, rough, and throaty. A scream. And then it keeps going, longer and more guttural than Erin has ever heard, and her surprise curdles into something closer to dread.

They both look. Blessedly, the noise finally tapers out, but it lingers in Erin's ears. Her heart jackhammers at the base of her throat. Even Max looks unnerved. Surely there are a few wild dogs roaming around the backwoods of Kentucky. That must be all it is. But what sort of thing makes such a noise?

Erin opens her mouth, but before she can think of what she wants to say, Max shakes himself out of it. He exhales. He grabs his jacket and quickly pulls his shoes back on, all without even glancing in Erin's direction.

"We can talk in the car," he mutters. "It's cold."

Max stands and pulls himself back up the slope. And then he's gone again.

Erin sighs and stands up. But instead of following close behind, she lingers. Uneasily, she casts one more look in the direction of that—*sound*. It doesn't happen again. Nothing bursts forth from the tree line. Not even the buzz of insects.

She looks out at the sunset. In the slight spaces between the leaves, she can see the solar flames licking at the sky. The horizon line is a light purple now, and the rest of the sky is only getting darker. One last breath. Erin finally climbs the slope and hurries after Max, who broods on ahead. She catches up without much issue, but she makes a point to stay a few steps back, until they've found the dirt road again.

"I'm not mad at you," Erin finally says as she comes up beside him. "I just—I don't know how to talk to you when you act like nothing happened."

"Because I didn't want to spend this whole drive fighting with you!" he answers tightly.

"We aren't fighting! This isn't—I want us to be on the same page. Before we get too far."

Too far to go back isn't what she's trying to imply, but Erin realizes that's probably how it comes across. Max still has that look on his face, like he's trying not to scowl. Even though he's absolutely scowling. His hands are pushed so far inside his jacket pockets that Erin starts to worry he'll break through the stitching.

"What's to understand?" he asks. "We're going to California. Columbus is gone, nuked, never existed. We're gonna blend in with the thousand other queers out there, and there'll be so many hormones going around, we'll drown in 'em. Am I missing anything?"

They stop at the car. Erin stands there while Max gets into the driver's seat. He leaves the door open, at least giving her the dignity of not having it slammed in her face.

"I just need to know that you're okay," Erin breathes.

Max looks up at her. His mouth is a tight white line. "Right. Well, I'm fine, because I'm finally about to have a normal life, and nothing else is gonna happen that's gonna stop that."

He puts the key in the ignition and turns it. The engine grinds, sputters—sounds Erin has never heard it make—then stalls and dies completely.

Max sharply turns and stares at the wheel. He twists the key again. As if the noise were a fluke and not a warning. This time, the engine can't even manage a death rattle. Somehow, the silence is worse. Erin just stands there, unable to move.

Max makes a noise in the back of his throat, somewhere between a groan and a closed-mouth scream, and punches the wheel. That sets off the horn for a fraction of a second, a *yelp* that makes Erin jump. Despite its brevity, that little noise echoes. It seems to bounce off the trees around them, carrying the sound of dread far into the darkening sky.

16

MAX TRIED TO KILL HIMSELF back in October. Erin pieced the events of the night together on her own. Slowly. Because although she was running away with Max, they were not talking about anything other than running away. Erin's picture was, therefore, more of an impressionist painting than a definitive narrative, but it was something. She needed *something*.

She got the gist of it from Miranda, and from her coworker Nancy. Nancy went to the same school as the kid who threw the party. That's all it was, some stupid party. According to Nancy, Max had spent most of the night talking with a blond girl named Heather, unaware that her on-again, off-again boyfriend, Jake, was less off-again than had been implied. It was a pretty uneventful night until Jake showed up. The argument that ensued was initially only between him and Heather. Max seemingly got sucked into it for the crime of sticking around.

The argument eventually shifted to Max's transness, if

what happened next was anything to go by. Erin didn't know how, but the *how* didn't really matter so much. It happened. Miranda had been just close enough to catch the end of it. She relayed the events, as follows:

Heather shouted something at Max, ending with "you fucking dyke."

Max responded by punching her in the nose.

Jake responded by punching Max.

Miranda recalled that a few people tried to break it up right away. But the crowd that converged upon them was too much to push through. Drunk teenagers egging it on and screaming for blood. To call it a fight would imply that Max ever had a chance at winning it.

Thankfully, sober heads prevailed, and the only serious injury would turn out to be Heather's broken nose. That should have been the end of it. But at some point, either from the fight or from the general noise of the party, somebody had called the cops. That was what got Brian involved.

That's the last solid detail Erin had. That Brian showed up. Took Max home. Something happened. Erin didn't know what.

Before she knew about any of this, though, Erin had known that something was wrong. She'd gone to look at his Twitter only to find it deactivated. Same with Instagram. Tumblr, user not found. She didn't notice his absence at school—they shared no classes and no longer shared a friend group; it was surprisingly easy to go for days without catching a glimpse of him—and it was Miranda who told her that Max had missed the entire week of school.

When he came back, allegedly, he was still sporting a ghost of a seafoam bruise on his cheek. Erin wasn't sure whether she should believe the more sensational details that Miranda told her: that Max was having weekly meetings with a guidance counselor, and that he stopped putting *Max* at the top of his papers. Miranda wasn't exactly an unbiased source. And perhaps Erin just didn't want to believe that something deeply, truly horrible had indeed happened to him.

Then she finally saw him. By then, it was close to Christmas; Erin was shopping with Hayley, stocking up on hot chocolate mix and candy canes supposedly meant for the tree but destined to become snacks for themselves later. The store was busy, as everywhere seemed to be in those two weeks leading up to Christmas. Erin let Hayley scan the contents of their basket at the self-checkout stand, and it was during that brief moment that she saw Max again. He was standing in one of the regular checkout lanes. The back of his mother's head was engaged in passionate conversation with the cashier ringing them up.

His hair was longer, which wasn't unusual on its face, but it was blown out and styled the way that girls would do. Maybe he wasn't Dressed Like A Girl, because that insinuated a whole lot about the gendering of clothes and gendered presentation that Erin emphatically did not believe, but Max was not dressed like *himself*. That was not his winter jacket. He was wearing form-fitting jeans instead of cargo pants, and his sweater was brown with little white hearts knitted all over. He was definitely wearing a real bra. Erin stared until Max happened to look in her direction, and he saw her.

Almost instantly, he spun away. Then Hayley tugged on Erin's sleeve and distracted her. In the time it took for Erin to take out her card and punch her PIN into the pad, Max was already walking toward the exit, in lockstep with his mom. It was so antithetical to everything Erin knew, that if she hadn't seen his face, she never would have guessed that *that* was Max. Hearing about it was one thing, but finally seeing it was something else.

Erin tried to reach out after that. She kept it simple: *Are you okay?* When no answer came, she sent another text. Then another. Then she began to seriously consider what the consequences would be if she marched up to Mrs. McCoy and asked what the hell she was doing to her son? Then she stopped sending texts altogether, angry and embarrassed that she was trying to beat down a door Max had locked her out of to begin with. She stopped looking out for him at school. Every day she felt something different, anger and grief and frustration and nothing she could feasibly do anything about.

Max remained silent until March.

Erin had just gotten off work, and was sitting in her car, waiting for the vents to start blowing hot air. She was in the middle of texting her mom when her phone buzzed.

max:)

hey. sorry i just got my phone back. would you want to talk?

There was no real acknowledgment of Erin's concern. But this was quickly lost to the weight of relief that pushed into Erin's throat. At once, the world fell away, except for that slight crack in the door, suddenly letting in the light.

Her response was immediate: *When and where?*

17

IT TURNS OUT THAT THE SOURCE of their problem is a bad spark plug.

In no time at all, the purple haze on the horizon snuffs out, and the only light they have is from a flashlight found rolling around in Max's trunk. Erin lingers at the front of the car, hovering over the guts of it for a minute. Max tries to calm down in the back seat. He pulls out one of his older hoodies, a navy blue zip-up that's worn so thin it has holes in the pockets, and puts it on.

He wants to cry. He's angry. He tries to cling to that, focusing so hard on the anger constricting his chest that it pushes everything else out.

It's not until he joins Erin at the front of the car that he remembers the hoodie is hers. One of the first things she ever gave him, even though, with the power of retrospect, it was probably just a way to shrink the amount of *boy clothes* in her closet. Like Max didn't start funneling his *girl clothes* into her closet toward the end, too.

Max just hopes she doesn't notice it. His face is red because he's hot, not embarrassed. It's maybe the first time he's been thankful for the hood lift being broken. Erin's focused on holding the hood up, and Max is focused on going through the engine, and nobody's talking to each other.

It's not as bad as whatever the smell was earlier—that hot, heavy stench of *rot*—but the engine still reeks of something burnt. Max knows something is wrong as soon as he starts going through the spark plugs. It's a V-6 engine, so there are only six plugs to sort through. He holds the flashlight in between his teeth as he unscrews them; each one is already stained with grease fingerprints. Then, when he lifts the sixth plug out and holds it up to the light, it catches the rust that flakes off.

It's ancient. Completely rotted through.

He falters, still holding it under the beam of light. Eventually, though, he sighs and takes the flashlight out of his mouth. He chucks the bad plug into the trees, then unscrews one of the better plugs and shoves it into the pocket with the least amount of holes. Erin finally sets the hood down and exhales.

"I got this car checked last week, and nothing was wrong with it," Max mutters. "Nothing was wrong when *I* checked it yesterday. But yeah, sure, why not?"

"This doesn't make sense," Erin whispers.

"You don't need to tell me!" Max snaps.

Just as quickly as it comes, though, the anger sputters out. It's pointless. Max just rolls his eyes and walks to the back of the car again, intentionally kicking up rocks as he goes.

The Impala is a piece of junk. Max has known this. It's *shit*. But it's shit that should have gotten them to California. It should have at least done that. Max grinds his teeth until his jaw aches, trying to think rationally. But all he can think is that this is *exactly* what he gets for trying to relax for five minutes.

He rifles through his suitcase until he finally finds what he's looking for: a tactical knife he bought last week with his graduation money. The blade is a matte black, same as the handle, which is molded for a grip. Max holds it for a moment, tries to find any sort of comfort from it, then tucks the flashlight under his arm and walks back to the front, where Erin is, anxiously drumming her fingers against the hood.

When her eyes land on the knife, she startles. "What is *that*?"

Max looks between her and the knife. "What?"

"Why do you have that?"

He shrugs. "In case we had to set up camp?"

"*Camp?*"

"Well, *first of all*, I wasn't about to try to buy a gun. But—y'know, in case something like this happened! In case we couldn't find a place to stay, or in case we *did* find a place and it was creepy. I didn't think there was room for us both to sleep in the car, so—"

"Okay, fine. Not important." Erin waves it off.

Max chews on the inside of his cheek, shifting from foot to foot. "Look, one of us should stay here with our stuff, and one of us should go get help. Or, find somebody who has a spare plug lying around, at least."

Erin's quiet for a second. Then her expression changes, and Max knows that she understands what he's talking about. "You can't seriously think you're going to *walk* back to that truck stop."

"Out of the two of us, I think I'm the least likely to get kidnapped, raped, and murdered."

"You?" she asks.

He glares. "Out of the two of us, you are the most visibly feminine. Better?"

Erin's frown only deepens. "That's still a terrible idea."

Max sighs. "Well, it's that, or we sleep *here*. Which also sounds terrible. Then we'd walk back together—under the *whole sun*, in *June*—and lose another day to more car bullshit."

He shouldn't need to explain this. This is not a vacation. They are on a deadline. If they lose the car now, then that's all hope of making it to California obliterated in an instant. Max can't bear to think about it.

He holds the knife out to her, handle first. Erin doesn't take it. She looks at something behind him. When Max looks back over his shoulder, all he sees are trees.

"The car was fine before it went into that shop," Erin finally says.

Max looks at her again. He understands what she's saying, between the lines, but he doesn't know what Erin's actually asking of him. "What reason would they have to mess up the engine?"

"How else do you explain the plug?"

"I can't! I don't want to explain it, I just want to fix it and get out of here!"

Max extends the knife out to her again, more firmly. Finally, Erin takes it. It's barely a relief, but it's something. "Just wait in the car and stab anybody that isn't me," he says, holding his flashlight in both hands. "I'll go get the part, and we'll be in Tennessee by tomorrow. If we're lucky, or something."

He shrugs, trying to feign a lightheartedness that he doesn't truly feel, and starts walking.

"Max!" Erin calls after him.

For a moment, Max stops, at the edge of the road, and looks back at her. Even though he can't really see her face, already mostly obscured by the darkness that the moonlight barely does a thing to break up, he starts to hear the little voice in the back of his head. The doubter. The little bundle of anxiety that knows splitting up is, like, literally always what gets people killed in movies.

Max still quells the voice. It's not like she'd be any safer with him, walking down the side of the road in the middle of the night, risking that they run into more freaks like the guy at the gas station. Girls are the ones who are supposed to be in danger out here. Boys just walk, get their car part, and go about their merry way.

So he responds, "I'll be fast!" and just keeps on going.

18

FOR A MOMENT, Erin has a half-cocked intent to follow Max. If they aren't going to wait for daylight, then they should stick together. But she doesn't. For some unknowable reason, she stays.

She watches Max go, until all that's visible of him is the distant beam of light that forges his path. Then that, too, is swallowed up by the trees. Another gust of wind blows through them. Every cluster of leaves looks like disorganized, blinking eyes. Fixating. Narrowing in.

Erin takes a step back and adjusts her grip on the handle of the knife. She knows that there's nothing there. She's alone. But that doesn't alleviate her fear. In fact, the more she tells herself this, the worse she feels. She's *alone*.

Thankfully, the overhead lights in the car work despite the state of the engine. Erin pushes the suitcases to one side, which gives her just enough space to sit comfortably in the back. She locks the doors, then cracks the windows. And then she simply . . . sits there, twirling the knife between her fingers. Waiting.

It's impossible to know how much time *really* passes, which is both a blessing and a curse. Time passes differently when you're bored, or when you're waiting around on someone. When you have no conceivable way of getting the actual time, even if you wanted it. The time is night. The time is *dark*. Erin can hear the wind push up against the body of the car, which softly groans each time in weak protest.

She looks out at the sky. Cloudless and empty. Comparatively, the interior lights must make the Impala the brightest thing around for miles. Erin can't imagine turning them off. It makes her feel stupid, but there she is. Afraid of the dark. Afraid of whatever might be carried in on that hot breeze.

She shuts her eyes and forces herself to take a deep breath. *Think about anything else.*

So she thinks of Max. *Because it doesn't matter.*

Erin grinds her teeth. She should've never let him go off without getting a straight answer. *What* didn't matter? The years Erin has spent convinced that Max hates her? The way he refuses to talk about any of this and just pushes her back every time she tries to broach the topic?

She takes another deep breath.

Erin hasn't been perfect. She knows. She's probably *still* piling up mistakes. Max hasn't talked about October, not even once, but neither has Erin. She's seen the scar tearing down his left arm, and she hasn't said a word about it. How would either of them bring it up, anyway?

So, Max, you're gonna want to get off the highway at the next exit, but before you do that, would you mind explaining why you tried to kill yourself?

Deep down, she shares what she thinks is Max's hope: that the balance of things will just naturally right themselves. That they will arrive in California, and everything will be fine, and they will never have to talk about the bad stuff ever again.

Erin sighs and sits up, putting her feet on the floor. Outside, the wind has died down into almost nothing. She pulls one of her suitcases over to her and opens it up, beholding the postcard that sits at the top. She almost feels guilty, now, for taking it. All Max is asking of her is trust—except that he's also asking her to trust in his paranoia. His paranoia is the reason she's stuck in this stupid car, bored out of her mind in sweat-stained, disgusting clothes.

The only writing utensil Erin can find is a pencil underneath the passenger seat, incredibly dull but still usable. On the back of the card, she writes:

Missing you two. Hope all is well. Will write more soon.
—Erin

Then, after a minute to think:

—Erin + Max

Erin sticks it back into her suitcase. Mom always liked Max. Whenever she gets this, Erin hopes it'll be something of a comfort to know that Erin didn't just run off on her own. Even if she is alone, and even if things with Max are still fluctuating between *okay* and *terrible*.

It's frustrating. They both put so much time and effort into each other, and it shouldn't be so nerve-racking to try and express that, the love that still lingers. Erin wants to know what went wrong so that she can try to fix it. Max doesn't seem willing to acknowledge that anything went wrong at all. The way he's acting, Erin almost wonders if she's blowing the whole situation out of proportion. Is *she* the asshole?

No. She's pretty confident she's not.

She doesn't think Max would still be wearing her clothes if he thought that, too. She wasn't able to react to it earlier, but realizing that he kept her hoodie all this time almost made her want to cry. *Still* makes her want to cry, if she's being honest.

Erin sinks lower into her seat. She can recognize that they were kids before. They were both the first trans person that the other had ever known. That has to be why this still matters so much. Max would still matter to her even if things hadn't fallen apart like they did, because nobody else in her life compares to Max.

Erin thinks about how, a few months before they broke up, she had gotten breast augmentation. For two weeks following the procedure, in which she was often functionally armless, Max lived in her room. Even during the first few days, in which Erin spent most of her time asleep. He was the one who got her water and ice cream and smoothies. Together, they played go fish and attempted to teach themselves other card games, to varying levels of success. They watched the original *Django* and a bunch of her dad's spaghetti Westerns that she had lying around, and she only started crying during a few of them.

Max was supposed to have slept on the air mattress that Erin's mother set up at the foot of the bed. And he did, for the first two nights. But after that, he crawled into bed with Erin once the lights went out. They'd lain there, in silence, holding hands. Listening to the warble of the fan overhead. In that moment, so close to the end she told herself would never come, Erin felt so much love that she could've sworn it was tangible inside her jaw, pooling into the back of her throat. It pushed open her rib cage so gently that it didn't even really feel like dying. And then she'd wake up, with her head on Max's chest. The only rational explanation seemed to be that this love, which was taking her apart in the first place, was just as readily putting her back together again.

It was probably a kid's understanding of the term, but Erin knows that she once loved Max. She believes that she still might.

Erin sighs and squeezes herself into the corner between the door and the seat. Her own reflection stares back at her from the opposite window. The worry lines have taken up a permanent residence on her face.

She pulls her suitcase over and unzips it. She takes out an old gray hoodie, the Michigan State logo half-faded in the center. Erin swaps her jacket for it and eyeballs a pair of black sweatpants she inadvertently pulled to the top. She doesn't know the last time she's been in jeans for this long.

As she places her hand on the fabric, the smell hits her.

Erin stops, only because she's sure the returning scent of burning fertilizer is new. It's not her and it's not the car. Which means that something has brought it toward her. Erin wrinkles her nose—it's muted, but still too strong to be ignored—and glances around, as if she might've disturbed something. As if it might just be one of Max's cigarettes, not quite put out.

That's when the darkness outside shifts.

Erin freezes, staring at her reflection in the window.

Her brain quickly jumps to the most rational explanation: she's only seen herself move. Her own eyes are staring back at her, even now. But the harder she peers into the darkness, the more it suddenly seems *too* dark.

As Erin brings her hand up to the roof of the car, she swallows. The back of her mouth tastes like rot. Then her fingers finally brush the overhead light switch, and her thumb pushes the button. Her reflection in the window vanishes. All that's left is the blackness, and a pair of grapefruit-sized yellow eyes, suddenly staring back at her.

19

ERIN DOESN'T SCREAM. Although a scream swells at the back of her throat and her mouth drops open, she doesn't scream. She *can't*. She scrambles backward, pressing herself against the door until there's nowhere for her to go.

Its lower jaw drops, as if in perverse mockery of Erin's own horrified expression. The faint sound of a deep, throaty *growl* cuts through the air. Saliva hangs from giant, pointed canines, each one crowded on top of the other, practically spilling out of its maw. Then it starts to *wail*.

Up close, it's like hearing metal scream as it twists and snaps. Guttural and, most upsettingly of all, *human*. The sound is so sharp that it seems like it should shatter the windows. Erin feels her own scream finally jostle loose from inside of her chest, but she can't hear it.

The creature moves faster than Erin can process, but the car unmistakably jolts with the impact of its body ramming into the vehicle. Survival instinct finally overrides dumbstruck terror as Erin frantically grabs for the door handle.

It rams the car again. The window shatters as the door crumples in on itself.

Erin screams again as she finally finds the handle. The door flies open and she falls onto the ground with a heavy *thud*. The back of her head bounces off the dirt. But despite the shock of pain, Erin scrambles to her feet. There's no moment to reconcile with the realization that she was right about what she saw. It's just: *run*.

She can hear the sound of it chasing after her. The weight of its paws slamming into the ground, the crunching and snapping of branches coming apart like toothpicks. Erin never turns around to see how close it's getting. She just runs, as fast as she can push herself, straight forward. She can see enough that she doesn't trip, by some miracle, though her face stings where the lower-hanging branches snap across her cheeks.

Ahead of her, for a split second, the moonlight reflects off the road tar. The trees part. And there's no time to react. As soon as Erin's brain begins the thought of *Maybe slow down just a little*, her foot hits the edge of the elevated asphalt. She goes down hard enough to knock the whole world off its axis.

Everything spins. The moon, the ground, the trees. Erin tumbles to a sliding stop on the far end of the road. She catches herself there, halfway on her side and half on her knees, already-blackened hands gripping at the road. As soon as she's stopped, she whips around, fully expecting that the last thing she'll ever see are those teeth, inside that gaping black hole.

There's nothing. The branches bob gently, in the wake of her warpath through them, but there is no monster.

Erin holds herself there until her arms start to tremble. The pain leaks in slowly, beginning with a *throb* that starts in the back of her head. Erin drops onto her butt.

A gentle breeze snakes through the air. The leaves gasp in time with her breath, shuddering and whispering. Her palms start to burn, as does her cheek. But she continues to stare at the woods from which she just emerged. As if this will force that creature to appear again.

It does not. Rather, a new source of light suddenly casts down the road from around the bend. It takes Erin a moment to recognize it as headlights. She doesn't move. She's safe where she sits, so she just continues to stare into the dark, picking apart every inch of warbling, consuming blackness. It's a white pickup truck that cruises by, right in front of her, and keeps going as if it didn't see her.

But then, out of the corner of her eye, Erin catches the red glow of brake lights. The truck slows, turns, and then its headlights are bearing down on her again. Erin winces a little, but she still doesn't move. If she tears herself away from the woods, what's keeping *it* from reappearing?

A door opens and shuts. Erin finally closes her eyes and tries to breathe. She needs to be calm. She can't come out of the gate raving about monsters in the woods.

"Hey—Jesus, are you okay?"

A warm palm presses against her left cheek. Erin jerks and opens her eyes.

It's Charlie. The beam of his headlights casts a soft glow around his head. An actual guardian angel, crouching in front of her.

"You didn't see it." Erin's voice is bent with this realization, and the subsequent disappointment.

Charlie gives her a funny look. "Uh, no? I see *you*, though, and you look like you just lost a fight. You all right?"

He turns her face, gently, and the burning sensation on Erin's cheek floats to the front of her mind again. She doesn't remember scraping it specifically, but all of a sudden she can find all the parts of her that took the brunt of the tumble. Her bloody knees have already begun to stick to the inside of her jeans.

"You are not all right," Charlie observes.

Erin shakes her head. "I'm fine. I just fell."

It's hard to tell if Charlie believes her, but he doesn't question her. He helps her to her feet, and only then does he finally let go of her.

Erin stares at him, wondering for a moment if she and Max got turned around. She thought they left Charlie behind hours ago. What is he doing out here?

Then, suddenly grinning, Charlie asks, "How's your finger?"

Erin laughs and looks down at her hand. "I mean, I lost the Band-Aid. But, uh, it's fine."

"If I'd known I was gonna run into you again, I would've

taken some from the store. You seem like you're gonna keep needing 'em."

They both laugh at themselves, their dumb little joke, and for a moment, Erin isn't bleeding and nauseous with dread on a highway with a stranger.

"All right." Charlie glances up and down the road. "Where's your buddy? And what the hell are you guys still doing out here?"

"He's walking back to town. We stopped out here, and now the car won't start."

Charlie stares at her, and a small smile begins to form. "He's *walking*?"

Erin rolls her eyes. "Yeah, I know. He insisted. Someone had to keep an eye on the car, which is what I was supposed to be doing."

"Well, we were just coming from that way, and we didn't see him."

In an instant, the mood plummets. So does Erin's stomach. Suddenly, all she can visualize is every terrible thing that could've happened to Max while she's been sitting around and uselessly killing time. Hit-and-run. Lost in the dark. Murdered. *Monster.*

The panic must be visible on her face, as Charlie quickly adds, "But, hey, it's dark, and we weren't exactly looking for nobody, anyway. We probably just missed him. How about we make sure you're okay, and then we'll go look for your friend. What's his name?"

"Max," Erin answers. Her tongue feels heavy.

"All right. Reckon I should ask for your name now."

He's trying to be cute. Only Erin feels like she wants to throw up, so it doesn't land as well as it should. "Erin."

"All right, Erin, we'll go and we'll look for Max, but after we take care of you."

Erin finally makes eye contact with him. In the back of her mind, a little alarm bell cuts through the noise. "I don't think I should—"

"We're just going a few more minutes up the road. It's not far, I promise."

For the first time since Charlie got here, Erin looks out into the woods. Still nothing.

This is still a very bad idea. Charlie is nice, but nice in a way that *most* men are nice to women they don't know. And there are a few things he doesn't know about Erin. Things that would immediately put her into a serious level of danger. But while every rational part of her brain screams at the idea of going off with Charlie, a man she ultimately does not know, it's the choice between a *possible* threat and one she's now sure to be very, very real.

So, reluctantly, she nods. Charlie smiles and gives her what's meant to be a reassuring pat on the back. All it does is make Erin feel worse.

Her shoulders are rigid with tension as Charlie guides her over to the pickup truck. He opens up the back door for her before climbing into the passenger seat. And it's the first time that Erin really registers Charlie's continued use of *we*.

The first person she sees inside the truck is another man

sitting in the back seat. His face is a little sunburned, and he seems to be unintentionally cultivating a mullet. He's nowhere near the Midwestern Kyle Gallner that Charlie is, although he gives her a very genuine smile and wave in greeting, which makes Erin immediately feel guilty as she waves back.

"Erin, that's my buddy, Tommy. Tommy, this is Erin." Charlie turns halfway around and slings his arm casually over the seat. "Aiden's our driver. Aiden, Erin."

Erin looks up at the rearview mirror. The most she can see of Aiden is his eyes, which seem to have a natural shadow to them. He *seems* tall, though, just from the way he holds himself. He has one pale, thin hand on the wheel, and holds a lit cigarette that's nearly burned down to his knuckles. He nods curtly but does not speak.

"Hi," Erin says simply, attempting to relax in her seat before she shuts the door.

Every inch of her skin itches with nerves. She tries to shake it off. She's safer in here than she is out there.

Aiden turns the wheel until they're once again driving away from town. Nobody says a word, which doesn't exactly make the time fly by.

Erin forces herself, anxious knot by anxious knot, to try and relax. She walks herself through a deep breath in, then out. She rests her head against the window and watches the trees fly by in opaque, endless silhouettes. Her mind returns to Max, and every minute spent driving farther away is another minute that the dread can pool back into her stomach, despite her best efforts to gather it up in pails and chuck it out.

She thinks about what an awful last conversation they had. How easily they separated. How easy it seems to be for people to vanish from her life. She thinks about her dad, everything that was left unresolved and unanswerable in his absence, and she wishes she'd just stop thinking entirely.

But then she also thinks about that *thing* that sent her screaming through the woods. That cloud of darkness with a mouth that vanished in an instant, back into the void.

Fact: she's not crazy. Something is out there. Not some teenage weirdo. It's real.

Follow-up question: what the fuck is she supposed to do with that information?

"You lookin' for something?"

Erin comes back to the car. The guy next to her, Tommy, is staring.

"No," she answers. "Just looking."

The car slows as they turn off the main road, but still jostles as it goes from the paved asphalt and onto the dirt trail. Erin looks out the back and watches as the highway vanishes behind the sagging branches of the tight-knit trees. Like another mouth closing behind her.

Charlie's voice floats in from the front seat. "You said you saw something before, though, right? Out on the road there?"

"Yeah. No. I mean—" Erin shakes her head and turns back around. "I *thought* I saw something, but I probably just freaked myself out."

"That's why you were running?"

"Yeah."

He chuckles, as if she said something funny. Erin smiles to be polite, even though it doesn't come close to reaching her eyes. Her foot starts to bounce. She imagines Max's face, getting grayer with every passing minute, out there alone.

She leans forward. "Hey, uh, how much farther? Because if Max gets back to the car and I'm not there—"

"Relax," Charlie smoothly cuts her off. "If he walked, he'll hardly be getting to the mechanic's by now."

Erin wonders how in the world he can know this with such certainty. Or, at least, with such false confidence. She sits back and looks at Tommy again. He's still watching her.

At last, the endless legion of trees breaks up ahead. The car pulls into a field of beaten, dry grass, which surrounds a dilapidated one-story house. The headlights illuminate a body of white slats, dirtied by mud and peeling from sun damage. There are two little wooden steps that lead up to the front screen door. One large tree grows close to it, but the house otherwise stands alone in the field, with all the other trees forming a circle around it. A protective little barrier.

It is not until she's inside that Erin realizes with certainty that it is an abandoned house. Despite the ease with which Tommy and Aiden settle onto the couch in the living room, it is clear this is not *their* house. The walls are dull, off-white and unvarnished and peeling where they're not sagging from water damage. Erin sticks to Charlie's heels as he leads her into the hallway. Perhaps, she thinks, if she pretends she notices nothing wrong, nothing bad will happen. She goes along, heart fluttering in her chest like a butterfly caught in netting.

She is a normal girl. Nothing is wrong. Nothing bad will happen if she doesn't cause it to happen.

Charlie turns left into the kitchen; Erin lingers in the entryway. It's a tiny kitchen, decades old and unkempt. There are giant, cavernous spaces where a stove and refrigerator are clearly meant to be. The linoleum floor does not appear to have been cleaned maybe ever. Its stains, of which there are *many*, are completely unknowable.

Erin's focus snaps back to Charlie when he turns on the sink and the sound of running water fills the room. For the first time, she wonders what in the world he's doing out here, so far from that little gas station.

"Hey," she begins, wincing at the sound of her own voice. Charlie looks back over his shoulder at her. "Is there a bathroom I can use?"

He nods. "Sure. Down the hall, first door."

Once he's gone back to the sink, Erin quickly walks to the end of the hall. The first door she finds leads back outside, as the window beside it showcases. To the right, as promised, the bathroom is already open to her, revealing a toilet that is more gray than white and a mirror with a massive chunk missing from its bottom left corner.

Erin, still standing at the other end of the hall, stares at her distant reflection. Her hair looks like it's been through a wind tunnel. She looks exactly how she feels: strange and out of place. Nevertheless, she begins to walk forward, only to stop halfway there when the wall beside her suddenly curves to the right.

Stairs. Erin looks up at them, and the darkened second floor they lead up to.

Despite the fact that she was outside mere minutes ago, she suddenly cannot remember what the outside of the house looked like. She would swear that it appeared to only be one story tall. And yet here are stairs.

Erin glances back from where she came, as if Charlie might be watching. However, the sound of running water continues faintly from the kitchen. Driven by something between curiosity and fear, Erin races up the stairs as quietly as she can.

The second floor is one long dark tunnel, illuminated only by a single window at the far end of the hall. The wallpaper is peeling off in massive chunks, and every step Erin takes echoes with a *crunch*. Half a dozen doors, all closed, line the walls. Erin's heart beats violently against the base of her throat. What is she looking for up here?

A phone, maybe. A small, easily hidden can of pepper spray. Maybe she finds a brand-new box of spark plugs, thanks Charlie for his time, and runs out like her hair's on fire.

Erin pushes open the first door to her right. It's dark, and the light switch on the wall doesn't work. It seems to be empty, anyway, and smells like molding, wet carpet.

In the next room, at least the lights work. Erin leaves the door open behind her, just a crack, and looks around. It's completely empty except for a bare bed frame and the dresser beside it. Erin approaches the wire skeleton and observes it for a moment, wondering why it gives her such a feeling of unease. Then she focuses on the dresser.

The first drawer has a few shirts inside, crinkled and shoved against the back. Some are plaid button-ups, others tank tops and V-neck shirts. Strange, perhaps, but Erin shuts the drawer and moves on.

She crouches down and pulls open the one underneath. It is full of wallets.

Erin falters again. It's not just one, not even a handful, though it's hard to say exactly how many wallets are *too many*. Erin starts looking through them and quickly discovers that none of them are empty. Most of them still have credit cards and punch cards for shops that Erin has never heard of. They're all out of state: Tennessee, Arkansas, Florida. The faces on the ID cards are all young. They are all girls.

As her hand scrapes the bottom, Erin finds something different. A single loose photo. Erin takes it.

She recognizes Charlie's face instantly. He's several years younger, but there's no doubt about it. Same cluster of freckles, same bright smile. It's the girl beside him—the slow realization of what all of these photos and personal effects together must indicate—that makes Erin nauseous. The girl is lovely. Her smile pulls her mouth to the right, and her long brown hair is parted slightly off-center. She looks young. Incredibly young.

Erin flips the photo, where she finds one small scribbling, already faded to near illegibility:

Charlie + Cassie, May 2014

"Erin."

Erin slams the drawer shut. The photo crumples in her fist. Her stomach is already all knotted up when she recognizes Charlie's voice. It still takes her a moment to move her head, to slowly turn and look at him.

Charlie leans against the doorframe. Just watching her. Neither of them move for a moment. Erin knows that he knows: she's caught.

"Get back downstairs," Charlie tells her. His voice is unaffected.

Erin turns back to the drawers. She pulls open the last one. It's mostly empty, but its contents are nearly the worst: cans of pepper spray and stun guns in shades of pink and purple. A few key rings. She recognizes the round bit of plastic that rolls around in the corner of the drawer. It's the same panic alarm she has attached to her own car keys. Car keys that are still hanging on the hook next to her bed, however many hundreds of miles away.

Charlie's hand comes down on her shoulder. He doesn't need to tell her twice.

20

THE WALK BACK to the repair shop is long and tiring, but, more than anything, it is *boring*. Nobody comes driving by, in either direction, even accidentally. Max can't think of another time he's ever seen a place so devoid of life. And he grew up in Ohio.

Max is his own solitary companion for what feels like ages, cursing his car, his parents, that stupid cop and his stupid buddies who looked over the car but who *didn't* notice the spark plug was on life support. Cursing every name his brain provides. So when he finally comes over the hill and sees the blue brick building in the distance, it's almost enough to make him cheer.

He doesn't figure that anybody's going to be inside, but he gives a courtesy knock on the front door before he steps back and waits. Unsurprisingly, a very long minute passes in silence. Max eventually clicks the flashlight off and shoves his free hand back inside his pocket while he takes another look around.

He doesn't have anything on him that he could use to pick a lock with. The doors on the entry ports are probably too heavy for him to try and lift. Hunting for a window and hurling a rock through it is an option, but one that might trip a security system and get Cowboy Hat Chief Laster hunting him for breaking and entering. And he never wants to see that guy again.

That leaves him with Occam's razor. Start simple. Max reaches out and twists the doorknob, just to see.

He pushes the door open with ease.

Weird, but all right. Now feeling appropriately stupid, Max steps inside. The light switch is on the wall to his right, although the room isn't any less creepy when he can see it. There's one door, down a small hallway to his left, and another two doors to his right, which probably lead to the garage. Besides the counter, which is stocked with all the various bulbs and parts, that's pretty much it.

"Hello?" His voice is high and pitchy to his own ears. Max winces.

No answer.

Max climbs over to the other side of the service counter. The layout isn't dissimilar to the repair shop he was in last week, back in Columbus. The biggest difference is that he's doing a bit of unauthorized self-checkout here. No big deal. It's not like he's gonna raid the place for all it's worth. He just needs one lousy plug.

Cars are a hobby that he and Brian share, fortunately or otherwise. Brian works on his fleet so much that probably every repair and body shop in a forty-mile radius is familiar with the McCoy name. If Max were to try this back home, he'd be found out so fast that his head would be spinning from the ass-whooping days before it was even delivered. The thought actually makes him smile a little. He will never again have to ride home in the back seat of Brian's cruiser. He will fix this car with parts and tools his stepfather has never touched.

After a little bit of poking around, Max finds the spark plugs in a drawer close to the floor. He pockets them, then stands and looks around until he finds the security camera he's looking for. It hangs over the front door and is pointed directly at the counter. Max stares back at it while he fishes his wallet out of his pants. He pulls two twenties out and holds the bills up in the air, so there's no chance the camera misses it.

"I'm paying for this, okay?" he practically shouts. "Not stealing. I am not stealing these."

He waits for a moment, until the tips of his fingers get that staticky feeling. Only then does he put the money on the counter. It's more money than any reasonable person would ever sell spark plugs for. Max considers it a preemptive apology. Hopefully, if the people who run this place still decide to consider this stealing, Max and Erin will already be long gone.

Nothing's changed outside. Max shuts the door behind him and then turns his flashlight back on. What few streetlights there are have been placed too far apart to illuminate the roads in any meaningful way. Half of them are weakly flickering on and off. Max looks in the direction he came from, and that he'll have to go back through. It's even darker out there, the trees an indistinguishable sea of inky blackness.

He could start walking back now, maybe get to the car before sunrise and hope that Erin's slept enough to drive them out of here. His feet ache at the thought.

Or, he considers, as he looks back over his shoulder, at the faint glow of the town in the distance, *you try and hitch a ride.*

It's a very stupid and ill-conceived idea for a number of reasons. But his feet hurt and he's tired and he *hates* the thought of that long walk back. Max figures he can at least try his luck. There must be somebody in this good Christian wasteland who's willing to give a kid a ride.

He turns and walks around the back of the building, in the direction of those distant lights, and tries to be optimistic. It doesn't matter that he hasn't seen any cars since before he left Erin, even though that's something that probably should influence this decision. Do people just not drive out here?

But Max doesn't really care about how many cars are or aren't out on the road. And he doesn't care about why the repair shop was just left unlocked, for anybody to walk into. He doesn't care why the Impala stopped working. He doesn't care why Erin has started giving him those concerned looks out of the corner of her eye, like he's going to slit his throat the moment she turns her back on him.

Well. He does care a little.

But right now, he only has the ability to focus on the fire licking his heels. The longer they stay in one place, the longer it takes them to get to Berkeley, and the greater chance there is that *more* goes wrong. The greater chance there is that Max gets sucked back into the gaping black hole he's only just managed to crawl out of.

Max sighs and waves the beam of light around. He crosses over the abandoned train tracks, shoes crunching against the wilting grass growing over them. This is what he's always disliked the most about Ohio, and Kentucky's not all that different: the way it feels like everything is abandoned. Everything is decaying and nobody cares and the earth is slowly trying to reclaim it all. Max can't wait for the urban white noise of California to replace the cicadas.

Although, the cicadas have actually been quiet for a while now. Max can't remember the last time he heard anything trilling at his feet.

He comes up on the road going into town and looks again in both directions. No cars. Not even the suggestion of one. Max keeps the flashlight pointed ahead and starts to walk.

Halfway across the road, headlight beams suddenly expand over the ground. Max looks over his shoulder. There's a dark red pickup truck leaving the lot behind him.

Which, *shit*. That means there's a non-zero chance they watched him walk out of the repair shop, which also means he doesn't want to be anywhere *near* here. But running would immediately make him look suspicious, no matter what they saw or didn't see.

He's overthinking this. Max faces forward and switches the flashlight off. It feels like his shoulders have hunched up to his ears. He rushes across the road and then just keeps walking. He can hear the truck pull out onto the road, and the headlights continuing to shine down on his back confirm this. It rolls to a stop on the far side of the road.

The truck engine never turns off, but Max can hear the sound of two doors opening behind him. Both close. His grip around the flashlight tightens. He just keeps walking.

"Hey!" a man's voice calls out to him. It's not exactly hostile (as Max would assume it would be, if they watched him break and enter) but it's enough to make him jump.

Max's stride slows, a hot wave of embarrassment and nerves crashing over his face. He flips back and forth between engaging and running. Acting normal versus saying *screw this* and trying to disappear into the grove of trees to his right.

The owner of the voice doesn't seem bothered by Max ignoring him. He sounds closer when he speaks again. "Hey, kid, you need a ride or something?"

Max takes a look over his shoulder. Sure enough, there are two dudes following behind him, but he can't discern much about either of them. Their headlights are still on, blindingly bright, obscuring almost everything besides the fact that they're men, and that there are only fifteen or twenty feet between them and Max.

"No," he calls back, shaking his head. "I'm good."

The second man speaks up. "Where you goin'?"

His voice is scratchy, smaller than the first man's. He sounds younger. Max squints. The farther they get from the truck, the better he can see. The second man seems a hair shorter, too.

"Forward," Max finally answers before he turns around.

"And you ain't driving?"

Max smiles. "Look, you two seem like you got your own thing goin' on, and I got mine. Thanks, though."

The first man finally starts to sound irritated by this back and forth. "Come on, dude."

The second chimes in: "Yeah, come on, *faggot*, slow down."

Max stops before the slur even fully registers. He can, distantly, recognize the provocation. But that's not enough to keep him from bristling.

He turns around completely. Both men have stopped a few feet back. They're out of the glare of the headlights, but not quite obscured by darkness. The first man is a lanky guy in sun-bleached overalls, with straw-colored hair and a baseball cap that hides his eyes. Max imagines them beady and small. The second man is indeed shorter, and his only defining feature is the star-spangled wifebeater he's wearing.

"Look." The first guy sighs. "Let this be easy and let us give you a ride."

He drops his hand to his waist, and Max's eyes follow. First, he notices that he's wearing a belt, hooked on the fourth or fifth hole. Skinny guy. More importantly, there's what's on the belt. Holster and handgun. Hard to tell exactly what kind just from the grip, but that detail hardly seems significant.

Max looks up at the man's face, what little of it he can see.

He seems fairly young, somewhere in his early twenties. He'd still probably be the oldest man Max has ever tried to fight. Besides Brian. But those fights never lasted long.

"Fuck off," Max snaps.

He's barely said *off* when the second man suddenly lunges for him. Max moves entirely on impulse, and from a little experience with getting his ass kicked before. He swings the flashlight. The feeling of impact against the man's face reverberates through Max's entire arm. In his mind's eye, he imagines teeth flying, clattering onto the road.

In reality, the guy's head snaps back bloodlessly, and he starts screaming and swearing.

The first guy moves faster than Max can recover, and he doesn't make the same mistake his buddy did. By the time Max is rearing to swing again, the guy's already on him. He grabs Max by the arms and pulls him in, back to chest, hard enough to lift his feet off the ground. He starts to drag Max backward toward the truck.

Max writhes as hard as he can, kicking and squirming, while Star-Spangled Wifebeater recovers from taking a flashlight to the face. He runs up and tries to grab Max's legs. It's an all right plan—Max is trying to throw Overalls off-balance. Solution: stop Max from doing that—but it's not *smart*. As soon as Wifebeater manages to get his big, sweaty hands around Max's ankles, Max yanks his legs into his chest. Everybody stumbles with the sudden movement. Max can feel the grip on his right leg slip.

His parents once dragged him through the house like this,

his mom's arms under his own and Brian suppressing Max's efforts to kick him in the face. He might've been ten at the time. He has *no* idea what the context of the memory is. He doesn't remember why his parents decided to drag him through the house like a sack of potatoes, but none of that matters. What matters is that this guy in front of him is a whole lot smaller than Brian, and Max's legs have gotten stronger since then.

Max pushes his legs out so hard that it tears a noise from his throat, too primal to be anything but a scream. Both men holding him fall back in different directions. Wifebeater falls on his ass, and being forced to suddenly carry Max's full weight makes Overalls stumble. Another few steps, and Max catches a glimpse of the sky as they fall to the ground.

The second they hit the dirt, Max pulls himself free and scrambles to his feet. Wifebeater grabs blindly for Max's ankles as he sprints past, and it must only be through divine intervention that he misses. Hell of a time for a guardian angel to show up. Better to be eighteen years late than forever absent, though.

Max runs as fast as he can. Which, considering he just spent the last few hours on his feet, is not *that* fast. But he's got a decent head start by the time he hears the men give chase. If he's lucky, he might make it halfway to town before he runs out of breath. If he's lucky.

Briefly, he wonders what kind of freaks wait in an empty parking lot in the middle of Actual Nowhere, USA, to try and kidnap people. But Max doesn't really care to seriously consider the question. It won't make him run any faster, nor will it wipe out the men who are, by now, gaining on him. So he shucks the thought and just tries to ignore the burn in his calves.

The lights of a Family Dollar twinkle up ahead, in the too-far distance. It's bound to be closed, but the sight of civilization gives Max something to run to. He wonders if his momentum would let him crash through the glass windows, or if he'd just bounce off and kill himself. So many different ways he can die just on this one stretch of road.

But then his eyes fix on something much closer. A car, parked on the far side of the road. A police cruiser. Its headlights are on.

Max puts the brakes on, skidding to a stop just in time to slam his hands against the driver's window. It's too dark to see much, but he scares the shit out of whoever's in there. He sees them jump. Max doesn't care. He slams his hands frantically against the window until the cop finally takes the hint and rolls it down.

It's Chief Laster. Because of course it is. He's the only cop in the entire goddamn state. But Max will never be happier to see a cop again.

"What the hell are you doing?" Chief Laster snaps. "I—"

Max doesn't have the time or the patience to entertain the *I-could-have-just-shot-you* lecture. "Help me!"

"What?"

Max throws his arm out and points. "They're trying to kill me!"

The cop frowns and twists his body to look. Max does,

too, for the first time realizing that he hasn't been tackled. The men actually stopped quite a ways back.

They're not running away, though. They're just standing there. Watching. Like Chief Laster is nothing more than an obstacle to wait out. The sight of them, outlined by moonlight and the fuzziest edge of an LED glow, makes Max's stomach pitch with nausea.

With a heavy sigh, Chief Laster barely gives him time to get out of the way before he steps out of the car. Max switches his flashlight to his other hand and wipes the first off on his pants. He's drenched in sweat. The layers of clothes on top of the binder aren't helping.

After shutting the door, Chief Laster seems to notice the flashlight for the first time. He double-takes. "Jesus, kid."

Then he tries to grab it. Max jerks it away before he can and glares at him.

Chief Laster, very wisely, must decide it's not worth it to make this a point of contention. He just sighs and waves his hand, *whatever*, before he undoes the safety strap on his gun holster. They both check back on the two men. Still just standing there.

Chief Laster looks between them and Max, with an expression that reads more suspicious than concerned. Like he's trying to figure out what *Max* must've done to bring this on.

"All right, you wait here." He opens up the back door and gestures within.

For the briefest moment, Max hesitates. This is not a man he *likes*, let alone *trusts*. But between his two choices, Max kinda has to go with the guy who hasn't tried to murder him. He climbs into the back and grips his flashlight as tightly as he's clenching his teeth.

"Just sit tight. I'll be right back," Chief Laster says before he shuts the door.

Max doesn't feel any better sitting there, alone, in ear-ringing silence. His arms are shaking, either from how hard he's gripping the flashlight or from simple terror. He's no stranger to fights. But those were usually in contained settings, and usually maxed out at one or two swings before an adult came in to drag Max away. This is a first for him.

He looks down at the flashlight. He's probably imagining it, but he swears he can see blood speckled on its head. For a second, knowing that he hurt the guy feels good. But the feeling doesn't last. It just turns back into dread. Max sets the flashlight down and turns to watch the scene through the back window as Chief Laster approaches the two men.

He stops in front of them with his hands on his belt, like a cheap imitation of a Western standoff. Max wishes he could hear any of what's being said. He imagines that little warbling flute. The trumpet comes up from underneath.

Now listen here, that there queer is under my *protection.*

And then Overalls would say, *There ain't room on this road for the both of us.*

And then Chief Laster would blow them both away. And Max would call dibs on the pickup truck. Oh, God, he wants this dumb cop to blow them away so badly.

But they just keep on talking, and talking, and Max quickly

loses hope that they're going to face any real consequences. It's just going to be a *lecture*.

He wishes he landed a few more hits. He wonders, if he ran at them right now, how many he could get in before Chief Laster pulled him off.

Overalls seems to say something to Chief Laster, who visibly shakes with—laughter? He claps Overalls on the shoulder.

Max recoils. *What?*

Chief Laster waves the two men off, and then they just start walking back the way they came, as if none of this was a big deal. Chief Laster walks back toward the cruiser.

That feeling of anxious dread returns to Max's stomach. Those men are the only things between him and Erin, and Chief Laster sent them off with a pat on the ass for the trouble. He's exactly as worthless as Max thought he was. It's actually incredible.

All right. Screw this. He'll cut through the trees, hide out for a bit, and take the long way back. Erin'll just have to wait an extra hour. This is what he gets for thinking that simply walking back would've been too boring.

Max pulls the door latch. It doesn't budge.

He frowns and looks up at Chief Laster, who's getting closer, and tries again. Still locked.

He's close to freaking out, but it's not until the man walks *past* his door that Max feels his heels slip off the edge, and the panicked feeling of plummeting completely grips him. Max frantically slams his weight against the door and pulls at the latch so hard it feels like it should snap off. Chief Laster gets behind the wheel as if Max were not even there.

"What the *fuck*?" Max's voice breaks as he screams.

Chief Laster turns the key in the ignition, and the car comes back to life. He cranks the radio up and floods the car with schmaltzy drums and bass. Unmistakable '80s country. Max winces before his ears adjust to the volume. Then he starts whaling on the partition with his hands, as if it might do anything, until the car whips onto the road and throws Max back into his seat. The car keeps turning, until they're driving away from town. In the direction he needed to be going this whole time, but under the worst imaginable circumstances.

Then Max realizes he knows this song. Restless Heart. "The Bluest Eyes in Texas." The tragic love song for the lesbian that *Boys Don't Cry* canonized.

They cruise right past the men still walking to their truck. The guy in the wifebeater waves at him.

Max picks up the flashlight and swings it at the partition, which is smudged with blood and oil from his hands. His knuckles sting. And the flashlight bounces off the plastic just as his hands did. Chief Laster's mouth is pursed; he's whistling along to the song.

Escaped from the frying pan, and immediately swallowed up by the fire. Max screams until his throat goes raw. Chief Laster never once looks back.

21

THE RAG IS ICE-COLD WHEN Charlie presses it into the road rash on Erin's face.

It burns, and Erin winces, but she is silent. They've both been silent since they came back downstairs and sat down. Erin is at the head of the table, while Charlie has taken the seat to her right. She's not restrained, which is somehow almost worse than if she were tied to the chair. It tells her that Charlie has no fear of her trying to run away from him. She's expected to just *sit there*—and she does.

Erin follows Charlie with her eyes. He's so close that their knees are nearly touching. The casualness is what unnerves her. Like this is just another Tuesday for him. He's watching Erin as if she were a rat under glass, waiting to see what she's going to do and if it's going to be of any interest.

She shifts and feels the photo crinkle against the inside of her jeans pocket. She doesn't know why she kept it, why she shoved it there before being led downstairs again. Only that it feels like it's burning a hole in her thigh, and she doesn't want anyone to know she has it. Least of all Charlie.

"What do you want?" Erin finally asks him.

Charlie makes a face, the ghost of what might be a smile. "If it makes you feel better, it's nothin' you did."

Erin's shoulders are so stiff that her back has begun to ache. "What did you do to Max?"

"Nothing yet."

Before she can ask what the hell that means, Aiden walks in. He slows when he comes upon the scene, of Charlie gently cleaning the blood from Erin's face. He gives them both a funny look. Erin isn't sure it's a comfort that he's just as weirded out by this as she is, this strange softness.

"They're on the way," he says flatly.

"Great," Charlie mumbles, not looking away from Erin's face. "Thanks."

Aiden's gaze shifts to Erin, and she stares back at him. She's not expecting him to help her or anything, but some of that desperation for *something* probably bleeds into her expression.

He does nothing but glare at her. And, just like that, gone again.

"Max'll be here soon," Charlie promises, once they're alone. As if she wasn't present for what Aiden said. "They're on the way."

He stands up and walks over to the sink, where he drops the rag with a heavy, wet *plop*. Erin blinks; a pair of hot tears betray her and escape down the swell of her cheeks. She's scrambling for rationale, for an explanation of *whatever* this is, and there's nothing for her to grab onto. She's just sitting there, knowing she can't leave, and knowing that *they* have Max. Whoever *they* consist of.

Charlie walks back over and hovers at her side. Erin stares at the table. There is a splatter stain in front of her, dark and faded, streaking to the right. She wonders if she's deluding herself if she tries to tell herself that it's anything other than blood.

She isn't expecting to feel Charlie's thumb suddenly press against her face, wiping away the tear trail. A full-body shiver of revulsion snaps through her and she jerks, raising an arm to swat him away. Charlie grabs her by the wrist and stops her. Squeezes. Erin's heart skips a beat. She tugs against his grip several times before he finally lets her go.

He clicks his tongue, as if disappointed in her, and sits back down again. Erin shrinks into her seat, watching the skin of her wrist slowly turn from white to pink. She stares at the table, digging her fingernails into her palms until her joints ache.

"Look." Charlie sighs. "We're gonna be spending the next few hours together. No reason to make it unpleasant for yourself. So just . . . try and relax. Please?"

Erin looks up at him. She hopes, whatever is happening to Max at this moment, that he's making things miserable for them. "What do you want?" she asks again.

Charlie shakes his head. "Explaining it never helps."

"No, if you're gonna kill me, I want to know *why*."

Charlie doesn't answer. He doesn't correct her, either.

Which makes her guts rise up into the back of her throat. But in the silence, as Charlie leans back and studies her again with that removed fascination, Erin forces them down. Another pair of tears breaks down her cheeks.

At last, he sighs. "That thing you were running from is real."

Erin exhales, a mix of relief and horror. She's not crazy. But she knew that already. "Bullitt Beast."

He smiles and nods.

"What is it?"

A shrug. "Beats me."

"*Bullshit,* you don't—"

"Hey, there ain't no reason for me to lie to you," Charlie cuts her off. "Why the hell would I waste my time lying to you?"

Erin clenches her jaw until her teeth ache. Every part of her feels ready to blow.

Charlie sighs and slips back into his casual demeanor. "Look, nobody's ever sat down and studied the thing. I couldn't tell you if it lays eggs or if it's—warm-blooded or whatever. All we know for sure is what it eats."

That final sentence hangs in the air for a long time. Understanding dawns on Erin quickly. But it takes her a little longer to be able to acknowledge it, to lift the heavy phrase from her tongue and speak it. "You're gonna feed us to it?"

Charlie thinks about it before he holds his hand out and tilts it from side to side. "Sort of. *You,* certainly, but your friend is . . . he's an unavoidable casualty."

"*Unavoidable?* We didn't do anything! What are you talking about?"

Before Charlie can do more than open his mouth, a third voice enters the conversation:

"It eats girls."

Erin and Charlie turn at the same time. Aiden is standing in the doorway. As if he's been there the whole time.

It takes a moment for what he's said to hit. Even when it does, Erin's brain rejects it outright. "What?"

"Hey." Charlie shoots him a look. "I'm handling this."

"I don't know what this idiot's been telling you," Aiden continues, ignoring Charlie and speaking directly to Erin, "but it eats girls. It seems to like girls, so we give it girls."

The room falls silent again. Erin absorbs this all in waves.

The first thing to hit her is the concept of her own death. Which—she's trans. The concept isn't exactly foreign to her.

Then comes the weight of the fact that they are looking for *girls*, and that might become very complicated very fast. Suddenly, she wishes they spent more time talking about the gender essentialist ideology of cryptids in the woods, because all of a sudden it's *real*.

Concurrent to all of this, Charlie only sighs. "How far out is Dennis?"

"I dunno. Less than an hour. I guess the kid managed to get pretty far."

"Cool. Would you go wait with Tommy?"

Aiden looks between him and Erin. But, just like before,

he nods and leaves. Erin is still reeling by the time Charlie turns back to her.

He shakes his head and smiles sympathetically. "It's not as backwoods as it sounds."

Erin glares up at him. "Sure it's not."

"I told you, explaining this never helps."

"If you only feed it women, why does Max even matter? Why can't you just—"

"Hey. You're not negotiating your way out of this," he cuts her off again. "And believe me, this ain't the conversation you wanna end on."

Erin forces herself to take a deep breath, and she pushes anyway. "Why women?"

Charlie gives her an odd look. Then he starts to laugh, as if she asked him why the grass grows green. "Because that's how it works. That's how it's always worked. You could guess anything and have just as good a chance of being right."

Erin says nothing.

"Seriously. Shot in the dark," Charlie prods. "There are no stupid answers."

"I don't know. People used to sacrifice virgins. Maybe you're just really unoriginal."

Charlie smiles. "There are plenty of male virgins, too. But I like where your head's at."

"Then what's *your* answer?"

He takes a moment to think about it. Or, at least, he pretends to. "Because girls are just easier," he finally says. "Men don't want to take orders. Men make things a *thousand* times more complicated. Always gotta be the hero. Whatever makes up a man ain't meant to be consumed."

Erin watches his face. "What happens when it eats a *man*?"

When Charlie smiles again, it's less amused. "It won't."

"How do you *know* it won't?"

A beat of silence goes by. "You ever watch those videos of killer whales in captivity? The orcas? The ones that try and kill their handlers? There could be a pile of dead fish, a mile high, but that whale sees that human and it wants what it wants. Right?"

Erin nods. Slowly.

"Let's just say it wasn't always such a guys' club 'round here. But we figured out that the best way to control the whale was to stay out of the tank."

That little bit of information is all she gets. It still makes the metallic taste in her mouth heavy on her tongue. It makes the photo in her pocket once again feel like it's caught on fire. The monster eats *girls*, not *men*, which Erin would call out as some seriously misogynistic bullshit were she not more occupied with the whole human sacrifice thing. Charlie's sexist phrasing is, like, way at the bottom of her list of concerns.

In the lingering silence, Charlie seems to have a thought. He stands abruptly, and Erin follows him with her eyes as he walks to the sink. The water runs murky for a moment before it turns clear. Charlie picks up a glass from the windowsill and fills it, almost to the lip. Then he turns the water off, turns back to Erin, and holds it out to her. "You want some?"

She eyes the glass uncertainly. Dust sticks to the bottom

rim. Like it seems to stick to everything else in this room. She doesn't answer.

As the silence drags, Charlie suddenly smiles. He holds eye contact with her as he lifts the cup to his mouth and drinks from it. Repulsion wraps around Erin's lungs, but she refuses to break eye contact.

"I drank out of this cup earlier," he assures her, wiping his mouth with the back of his hand. "The pipes don't always run pretty at first, but water's water."

And, it's implied, dirty water is better than nothing if you're gonna be dead soon anyway.

Charlie fills the glass up again. When he sits, he sets the glass down in front of him. Erin tries to grab it and Charlie pulls it out of reach.

"So." He leans back in his chair. "Where were you two headed?"

Erin shoots him a look. She's not interested in whatever this is. But, despite the headache that's begun to throb behind her eyes, she hasn't completely lost her mind. She's hungry, she's thirsty, and if she wants to take her first chance at escape, she'll need water. She's not going to get very far if she's delirious from dehydration.

"California," she answers.

"Why?"

"Max is starting college in the fall."

Charlie seems surprised by this. "Really? Jesus, kid looks like he's twelve."

He moves the glass an inch closer. Water sloshes toward the rim. Answers get rewards.

"And that's a long drive," he goes on, "considering the plates on your car. Ohio, right?"

A beat. Erin nods.

"Right. Why not fly?"

Erin shrugs. "Lots of reasons, I guess. But . . . I don't know, we just wanted to go. A road trip seemed fun. Something we could do together."

"You two fall out?"

"We used to date."

Charlie's shoulders shake with laughter. "No kidding?"

He pushes the glass a little closer. Erin stares at it. If she lunged for it now, maybe there's a chance of grabbing it. Her mouth tastes like rot.

"Why'd you two break up?" he asks.

Erin glares at him again. "If I'm just gonna die, does it matter?"

"Not really," he readily admits. "But you're pretty. Good sense of humor. Sharp. I'm tryin' to figure out if you broke his heart, or if he broke yours."

It's incredible how disgusting Charlie's gaze makes Erin feel, and so quickly. She shuts her eyes for a moment and tries to wash herself of it. "I don't know," she finally answers, swallowing the lump in her throat. "We just broke up. And we didn't really talk to each other for a long time. And I thought that was it, but then one day he shows back up, and . . . here we are."

She leaves it there for a moment. It occurs to her she's probably gonna die without ever knowing *why*. She's had all this time to speculate, and it's culminated into one great, big nothing.

"So, you and him are split, and you still haul ass with him across the country?" Charlie's eyebrows rise teasingly. "I don't think half of my exes would spit on me if I were on fire."

"Well, if they were dead, I don't imagine they would."

Charlie's grin sharpens at the edges. He drags the cup back a few inches. Erin chews on the inside of her lip.

"He broke up with me." She clears her throat, staring intently at the table in front of her rather than looking anywhere near Charlie. "It sucked. And then, a few months ago, I think he tried to kill himself. I don't know. But it'd been, like, *years* since we last talked to each other, and I was still the only person he trusted. He was the only person I trusted, too, about a whole lot of things. So I said yes when he asked me to go with him, because I knew he was gonna go with or without me, and if I just let him go, I was gonna spend every day of the rest of my life regretting it. And I think a part of me just wanted to know that he didn't hate me. That whatever happened wasn't my fault. Whatever that even means."

Erin stops. Swallows. Her mouth is dry.

"But then we actually left," she continues, "and I keep trying to ask myself why *I'm* doing this, and nothing I can come up with sounds right. I sound selfish and stupid, and I'm scared that I might've just—done something selfish and stupid."

At last, Charlie pushes the glass into Erin's hands.

Relief. The water tastes like sand. She doesn't care. She's grateful for it, and for the fact that she has mostly stopped crying, even if her hands still tremble.

Eventually, Erin comes up for air. She looks at Charlie over the rim of the glass. "How often do you do this?"

"The first week of June and the first week of December. Every six months."

"Is it always you?"

A smile pulls at the edge of his mouth. "No. One of us finds an easy target, and someone else makes sure they stay in town. It's all luck of the draw, who does what."

"Do you kill them before you—" Erin falters. The word *feed* sticks to her mouth.

"No."

"Why not?"

Another smile. "It likes the chase."

The imagery makes the hairs on the back of Erin's neck stand up. It emboldens her to ask her final question: "Who's Cassie?"

For the first time, Erin knows she's struck a nerve. She watches Charlie's face harden, a curtain over whatever his reaction was about to be. *There*. A way under his skin.

She wishes she could get both hands on it and rip it open. Poke at his wounds as easily as he pokes at hers.

"Tell you what," Charlie finally says, "I'm gonna give you a minute to yourself. Then we can wait for Max together. How's that sound?"

He smiles at her, but it's a statement, not a suggestion. He stands and leaves without another word, and then Erin is suddenly alone.

It's not completely silent, as the voices of all three men soon become audible from the front of the house. An occasional gust of wind pushes a branch against the window, scratching back and forth. Erin thinks about how it'll sound when Max is here, and fear pools in the back of her mouth.

Erin lets go of the cup and puts her head in her hands; she can't stop shaking. Her teeth ache down to their roots. She tries to think about anything else, but it all brings her back to death.

She wonders if there's going to be anything left of her to find, or if her face will survive only on Facebook pages. Survived in her young sister's memories, which will fade and blur the same way that their father's face already has. She imagines the headstone that Max's mother will erect, a monument to the daughter she could only have in death.

They can't die here. Not here. Not now. Not after everything.

Erin grabs the closest thing to her—the glass—and hurls it. It shatters against the lower cabinets with a sharp crash. Then she gets up, sending the chair toppling backward, and runs.

She isn't thinking, but the plan is, vaguely, to get outside. Run and don't look back. Or to get upstairs. There's a drawer full of pepper spray and keys, and even if Erin can only get her hands on one of these things, that'll be enough.

There's no chance to do either. Erin whips through the entryway and runs right into Tommy's waiting arms.

She yelps, and although she attempts to squirm and kick her way out of it, Tommy's grip locks down on her like a vise. He spins her around and bars his arm across her chest. That's when she sees Charlie, waiting just a few feet away near the other entryway. In case she bolted for the front door.

"Go ahead and get ready," Charlie says to Tommy. "We'll meet you out there in a second."

Tommy drags her toward the back door, and Erin loses whatever composure she might've had. She starts screaming—just noises at first, then shrill cries of *stop!*—before she's suddenly outside.

The air is heavy with humidity. The grass underneath them crunches with every step, dead and brown and brittle. For a brief moment of lucidity, Erin looks around and sees the circle the dead grass forms around the house. The way it stops at the tree line, heavy and lush in comparison. Surrounding the house, or perhaps growing outward from it. Then the panic floods back into her.

"Please, you don't want to do this," Erin begs, trying to dig her heels in.

"Don't start." Tommy sighs like he's been doing this all night and he's already sick of it.

"No, listen, please—"

"I don't care, just—"

"I'm trans!" Erin blurts.

It's out before she can think better of it. Tommy, in the

process of finally pushing Erin in front of him, pauses with his fingers still wrapped around her wrist.

Then he starts to smile. "Right. So you *don't identify* as—"

"I mean I'm *trans*," Erin doubles down. "You guys need a girl, right? Aiden said you need girls?"

Tommy doesn't say anything. But he gets that look. That same goddamn look. Checking her for an Adam's apple, for stubble. Attempting to superimpose male features on top of her. Still less than an arm's length away, Erin can see the microexpressions forming on his face as he has his internal debate.

Erin drops her voice to a near whisper. As if either of the men still inside might hear her. "I swear to God, if you let us go, we won't say anything."

"No way."

"No! Seriously!"

"No, no way. You're not a dude."

Erin shuts her mouth so hard her teeth clack. If there's a hell, then this is it. But Erin's not going to find that out, because she's going to *live*. She is going to live, no matter what that entails.

"I'm trans," Erin presses. Her voice warbles. "Okay? I am a transgender woman. Male to female. I was born a boy. I started living as a girl when I was fourteen. I take estrogen"—her hands fly to her pockets until she remembers that her estrogen is in her hoodie, back in the Impala—"I'm not the *girl* you need. Neither of us are, okay?"

As she goes on, she starts walking *toward* Tommy, who, in

turn, takes a few steps back. Maybe he believes her, maybe he doesn't, but he's definitely not certain. Erin is breathing so fast it almost doesn't feel like she's breathing at all.

"You don't believe me?" she keeps pressing. "Check me. Look at me! *Listen* to me!"

Erin suddenly realizes, throughout this rant, she's been letting her voice go. Not much. There's not really anywhere for it to go, either. That's the thing about her midpuberty transition: her voice hadn't been dragged *that* far into the male tenor. She doesn't have to try very hard to avoid sounding like she did when she was fifteen. She's seen videos of other trans women online, bouncing from one end of the spectrum to the other, a skill which she almost envied simply due to the fact that she did not possess it.

But there's still enough of that old voice left to drag it out from under the proverbial bed, and it's the moment where she sees the expression on Tommy's face go from uneasy to *horrified*.

"*Charlie!*" he calls back toward the house.

Erin leaps at her chance. She rips her arm back and successfully pulls it free from Tommy's grip. As he spins around, grasping for her, Erin swings. It's not a great punch, but it does the job. She hits him in the throat and feels the Adam's apple against her knuckles. Tommy stumbles back and starts to cough, gasping for breath, and that's her window.

She turns and sprints into the trees. Behind her, she hears Tommy finally catch his breath and scream for his friends again. Although she runs as fast as she can, Erin doesn't get far. Her foot catches on something and she goes straight to the ground. Her forearms take the brunt of the fall. But in the dark, she's out of sight. As far as they know, she's long gone.

Dead leaves crunch and crumble in Erin's fingers as they curl before she pulls herself up and crawls to the closest tree. Some broken bits stick to her face when she puts her hands over her mouth. No matter how hard she tries, even behind her hands, her breathing still sounds too loud. But Tommy's voice remains distant. He's not running after her.

Carefully, slowly, Erin twists around the side of the tree, just enough to take a peek.

It's not a great vantage point, but she can see Tommy pacing back and forth where she left him. A moment later, Charlie and Aiden finally come running. Charlie, curiously, has a broom in one hand. Aiden is brandishing a rifle. Erin presses herself against the tree, wincing at the edges of bark that dig into her arm.

"What the hell happened?" Charlie snaps.

"She's a dude!" Tommy screams back. He wipes his hands on his shirt over and over again, almost compulsively.

Charlie pauses. "What?"

"She's a dude, man! We screwed up!"

The next thing she sees is Aiden, beginning to walk up toward the tree line, raising the scope to his eye. Erin goes rigid. But Charlie puts his arm out and stops him. They don't see her. The two men whisper something to each other, back and forth and intense, but Erin is nowhere near close enough to pick up on any of it.

Beside them, Tommy keeps pacing, muttering to himself. Charlie eventually looks over at him and asks him something, to which Tommy emphatically responds, "No, I'm not sure! But you didn't hear her—him—*it!*"

Aiden starts snickering.

Tommy walks up and shoves him. "Screw you, asshole!"

"Both of you, shut up," Charlie snaps, getting between them. "What *exactly* did she say?"

"She—that he was born a boy. That—" Tommy suddenly stops. "He said neither of us."

"Neither of us?"

"He said *neither of us are*. Like, the friend he was with."

Charlie points at him, the eureka moment. "There we go. Aiden, I need your phone."

Erin watches Aiden toss his cell to Charlie before the three of them hurry back to the house. It's only once the end of the broom in Charlie's hands disappears that Erin pushes herself to her feet and starts running again. A sob pushes out from within her chest, but no tears come. She just keeps making this frantic, near-screaming sound.

What has she done? *What has she done?*

Dread leaks in at the edges of her otherwise adrenaline-numbed mind. If she can find the road, there will be *somebody*. Surely there will be somebody. She can get help. She can get back to the Impala, and—

Something. She doesn't know what yet. She just runs and prays to whoever's listening that Max survives long enough for her to figure it out.

22

MAX COMES OUT OF HIS head when the car jostles over a pothole. A stress headache has its pulsating grip on his skull, although the pain in his knuckles has since faded into a dull throb.

It's hard to say how much time has gone by, although the radio has thankfully moved on from Restless Heart. Max sits up and rubs his eyes. Turns out it's possible to have an adrenaline crash even when you're the furthest thing in the world from *calm*. His throat is raw. But mostly he's just tired. He sits sideways, his back to the door, and pulls his knees into his chest, staring at the blur of trees through the opposite window.

Max wonders if Erin is still waiting for him in the car, or if she finally grew tired and went after him. Worse yet, he wonders if those two creeps came across her. His only source of incredibly minimal comfort is that he left her with the knife, and he knows she will use it if she has to. Erin used to go shooting with her dad. She's not a pansy.

Still. Max doesn't realize he's crying until he starts tasting salt. He has no idea if Erin is okay. All he *does* know is that if anything happened to her, it's his fault. This whole thing is his fault. He repeats this to himself over and over again, like he's picking at a wound. His fault. *His fault.*

Up front, a default ringtone cuts through the violin playing this last song out. Max bristles at the sound but then goes right back to numbly staring out the window.

Chief Laster turns down the radio and picks up the phone. "Yeah?"

Max wipes roughly at his eyes. It's been a few months since he's felt *scared* like this, and since he's felt it so openly. Crying is weak, and *boys don't cry*.

"What?"

Chief Laster slams on the brakes. The car jolts to a stop, right there in the middle of the road. Max barely has the reflex to catch himself on the seat and avoid a concussion. But it's enough to finally shake the fog of self-pity from around his brain.

Max looks up. Chief Laster is staring at him through the rearview. It's hard to put a name to the expression. But it's not exactly confidence-inspiring.

"No, stay there," Chief Laster says into the phone. "I'll call you back in a minute."

He hangs up and puts the car into park. And then he sits there for a moment, eyes blazing in the reflection. Max stares back, confused and a little scared.

Without warning, Chief Laster punches the wheel. The

horn squeaks more than it honks, and Max jumps. As the man turns off the car and steps out, Max nervously starts to feel around for the flashlight. He's so concerned with keeping his eyes on the man that, by the time he finds it on the floor and Chief Laster opens the door, he completely forgets to swing.

So instead of making an incredible escape, he's just grabbed by the arm and roughly yanked from the car. Chief Laster drags him onto the side of the road before letting him go with a shove. Max stumbles, which puts a few more feet of distance between them. But, although his first instinct tells him to *run*, he refrains. It's flashlight versus gun. If he wants to live, his best hope is the element of surprise.

Chief Laster rests his hands on his belt. For a moment, he just stares. Max watches him back, only increasingly unsettled the longer he watches the man's eyes shift up and down, looking over every inch of him.

At last, he sighs. "All right, kid. What are you?"

Max frowns. "What?"

"Are you a boy, or are you a girl?"

The question immediately makes Max freeze up. Why the hell does Chief Laster suddenly care? But he maintains eye contact with the man and sets his shoulders back. A move he hopes will do something to compensate for the rest of him.

"I'm a *man*, asshole," he answers.

Chief Laster is quiet. Then he starts to chuckle. "Yeah? You're a man?"

"Yeah, I'm a *man*."

Chief Laster nods. "Prove it."

Max scoffs. "Fuck you."

"Prove it, or else I'm gonna have to come over there and—"

"Go ahead," Max snaps. "Try and make me, pervert, and I'll kick your head in."

Chief Laster sighs. Then, sure enough, he starts walking up. His hand drops away from the gun on his hip.

Max waits, and he waits, until the man is close enough, and he finally swings the flashlight at his head as hard as he can.

Chief Laster throws his hand up and stops it, only inches away from his face, with little more than a grimace of exertion. Max panics and tries to yank it back.

That's when the man punches him in the stomach and pushes him down, with such mechanical efficiency that Max might as well wake up on the ground. He lets go of the flashlight on his way down; empty hands curl into the grass. It's a terrifying few seconds where he can't take a breath. It's worse when he finally manages to inhale and he can hear Chief Laster throw the flashlight somewhere out into the brush.

Max manages to scramble forward a couple of feet before Chief Laster grabs him by the shoulder and yanks him onto his back. He gets down on the ground with him, one knee on either side of Max's chest, and starts to grab at Max's shirt.

Max starts screaming. He can feel the burning at the back of his throat that tells him as much, though whether he's forming words or just *screaming* is a mystery. It doesn't sound like he's forming words. He swings and he kicks, but it's hard to get power behind anything when he's still gasping like a beached fish.

So even though it feels like it's a scene that drags for lifetimes, it probably doesn't take long at all for Chief Laster to get Max's shirt pulled up to his armpits.

Max's binder is a slightly off-color flesh tone. It's about half a size too small, but it's also his fourth binder and he was just desperate to have one again. He bought it from a website that he knew had discreet packaging, and one that wouldn't immediately sound the alarm when the transaction showed up on his bank statements. He intends to buy something better once he's in California. His old binders fit right; snug but not constrictive. This one pinches at his armpits and makes it hard to breathe when he *hasn't* been punched in the stomach. He has been wearing it for probably twenty-four hours now.

This is the binder that Chief Laster gets a full, unobstructed view of.

He almost seems confused by it for a second. But then his face shifts to an expression of *Yeah, that's what I thought*.

Max has gone rigid. In his head, he's still screaming. He's killing this guy for putting his hands on him, beating Chief Laster's head so hard against the asphalt that skull fragments will rain down for hours afterward. But in reality, he hasn't moved an inch. He doesn't even realize he's crying again until the tears roll down his face and hit the insides of his ears.

Chief Laster, at last, sighs and lets go of Max's shirt. It stays bunched up at his collarbone. "All right, honey. Come on."

He takes Max by the arm, as if to pull him to his feet, and

it's this movement that knocks Max's fight-or-flight response back into gear. The fear becomes secondary. It has never been easier to latch onto the anger rising up in his throat, and he's been doing that his entire life.

The two men lock eyes. Whatever Chief Laster sees in Max's glare makes him pause, if only for a moment. Never one to snub the easy shot, Max whips his head forward. He hears the *clack* of bone against bone, and he's distantly aware that it should hurt a whole lot more than it actually does. It's not any worse than the nausea still rolling around in his guts.

For good measure, he kicks Chief Laster hard in the stomach.

Max scrambles to his feet while Chief Laster falls back onto the ground. He runs. The only time he looks back, he sees the cop going up onto a knee, with one hand reaching for his gun. But for whatever reason, he never hears it fire.

Max has already gone too far by the time he realizes he has no idea where he's running to. But it doesn't matter. It doesn't matter that he can't hear Chief Laster behind him, nor does it matter that he still can't breathe. His brain is broken beyond one thought: *just run*.

So, he runs, and he runs, until his head is spinning and his lungs feel like they're expanding up into his throat. He has to catch himself on a tree to keep from collapsing onto his face. His body is practically in spasm and he still *can't breathe*.

He throws up. It's gross. But it's also a decent distraction. For a few minutes, he's focused on the taste of bile in the back of his mouth, which makes him dry heave once he's out of things to expel. He's focused on the lingering nausea and the cold sweat that clings to the back of his neck. It's over far too quickly. And then he just starts sobbing. The sobbing is how he knows that Chief Laster hasn't followed him. Even if he lost Max in the dark, the way he's wailing would be a pretty clear beacon to where he's kneeling beside his own sickness in the dead leaves.

Somewhere, in the back of his mind, Max is home again. An open, ugly secret. The curse of girlhood on his face, in his voice, on his chest and between his legs. A horrible slime that clings to him no matter how violently he tries to tear it off.

What burns is how unfamiliar this all is. People found out he was trans all the time. This is practically how October went down. Except that ended with Max in the hospital. And now, Max is forcing himself to breathe, wiping his eyes before he finally wipes his mouth clean. He's still shaking like a leaf. But as soon as he's sure that he's not going to be sick again, he uses the tree to pull himself up, and he staggers forward.

He's already survived himself once. He doesn't want to die. After struggling for so many years, he's finally figured that much out. He wants to *live*.

Behind him, something slides against the leaves. Max whirls around, raising a fist in the air. His eyes dart from the ground to the treetops, waiting for the first sign to start swinging.

He can't see it, but he can hear it. Sloshing against the leaves, like water against the rocks. His skin prickles with a wave of hot dread. He's waiting to feel those sweaty, fat hands clamp down on his shoulders again. He looks at the moon, hanging low and deeply yellow in the open space between a cluster of branches, and prays to whatever's listening that that doesn't happen.

Max shuts his eyes. After a moment, the leaves finally still. He takes a nervous step back, exhaling as the dead grass crunches underfoot. When he opens his eyes again, he looks up.

The moon hangs high in the sky, near-white and only partially full.

Max frowns and looks back to the spot where he thought he saw the moon for the first time, only to find darkness again. Undisturbed, unoccupied darkness. For a moment, Max doesn't move, just listens. The woods around him remain silent. Whatever he may or may not have seen, it's no longer *there*.

Slowly, Max faces forward again and continues on. He counts each step in his head, matching up the sound of his shoes against the dirt, until he is positive that he walks alone.

He has no concept of where the road is, the direction he's walking in, or what he's *supposed* to do in this kind of situation. He doesn't have the survival guide for handsy transphobic cops. But the only thing that matters to him is movement. Getting farther and farther away from Chief Laster's hands. He has not gotten this far just to be stopped now by some sonofabitch in a goddamn cowboy hat. And he will not be stopped by noises in the woods.

23

IN *BOYS DON'T CRY*, when the killers wanted to out Brandon, they dragged him into the bathroom, pulled his clothes down, and held him there, forcing his girlfriend to look at the fact that he was not anatomically male. It was a gritty, "real" scene where the camera was shaking and everybody was screaming. Except for this one moment. Right in the middle of the sequence, the angle changed. A soft, heavenly light cast itself over Brandon. He looked up and saw himself standing in the bathroom doorway; saw himself staring back at him. Max didn't understand exactly what the film was trying to say with that. Was it supposed to be a split? The "male" Brandon watching the exposure of the true, "female" Brandon? Was it just a literalization of a traumatic, dissociative moment?

Max didn't know if it meant anything at all, or if it was just a stupid shot in a stupid movie, but when he thought about the concept of *a split,* it almost made sense. Even though he wasn't a girl, he had to pretend to be sometimes. People still saw him as one. Sometimes Max was Max, and sometimes he wasn't; it all depended on who was around and what he could get away with. All depended on who was around to tell everybody that he wasn't really a boy. Whatever that was supposed to mean.

He tried to start something with Alex, in the last few weeks of summer before their senior year started, but that went absolutely nowhere. And maybe Max shouldn't have been surprised. His transness had never been a secret to Alex or that whole group of guys. There was no need for anybody to try and out him to them. It was probably a level of affirming for Alex to get a weird case of the Not Gays over him. But Max didn't need affirmations. He knew what he was. And so the rejection embedded itself within him.

"I mean—you're cool, dude. Really. But I'm not into—you know, whatever you are."

Christopher came next. He did not meet Max, the guy who once chipped the tooth of the varsity team's right fielder in a fight spurred by using *the wrong bathroom*. Christopher met Max the tomboy, dragged along by her parents to a friend's birthday dinner and stuck with the only other teenager there. It was early September, and Max was looking for something to keep Erin off his mind since things had gotten kinda weird with Alex. So he put on his best *girl voice* and smiled so much that it felt like he was going to pull a muscle. And that's how he found out that straight men are easier to hook than fish.

Christopher hung around for less than a month. It ended because he finally found out about the whole transgender thing, and, in his infinite wisdom, thought that meant that

Max had transitioned from male to female. Which would've been hilarious if there had been anybody for Max to laugh about it with.

"I wasn't—*born* a boy," Max tried to explain, as if that made it better. "But I *am* a guy."

Christopher's response was: "I don't care *what* you are, get out of my car."

Last and briefest of them all was Heather. Heather did not go to his school, did not know anything about him, and didn't look a thing like Erin, which was why Max talked to her in the first place. She was nothing like Erin. When she spat *dyke* at him, Max punched her in the face so fast that the *-yke* was barely even past her fat, pouty lips.

That night, that house party, was probably the closest Max had ever gotten to understanding that stupid *Boys Don't Cry* scene. He never left his body to get an aerial view of his own ass-kicking, but he felt *loss*. That was the only term that seemed to fit. Loss. He didn't know if he was supposed to call it his *identity* or just his *self*, but the Maxness of him was so real and tangible that having it denied was like dying.

Even with all of that piling up and up, Max had not been actively suicidal.

He hadn't been. Honest.

But that night, after taking him home, Brian had struck him hard enough to make his ears ring. When he couldn't find the grip to tear the binder off of him, he'd just grabbed scissors and sheared it off alongside Max's shirt. And while Brian turned his room inside out, looking for more freakish paraphernalia, Max's mother had begged him through tears to just *please*, stop embarrassing them. Standing there, half-drunk and battered, literally holding his torn-up shirt against his chest, it had honestly felt pretty reasonable to want to hit *eject*. If such a level of pain was inevitable, why drag it out any longer than he already had?

It was panic. That was how Max later rationalized it. Desperation and panic. Because as soon as he stormed into the kitchen and actually took a knife to himself, his brain kicked back on. And he realized what stupid logic that was. This wasn't inevitable. It never had been. This suffering was not his fault.

Still, that kind of thinking put him in the hospital and resulted in a social detransition that was its own kind of slow, torturous death. Having to look all those people in the eyes and act like they'd been right about him all along. But as soon as he was given the ultimatum, a clock started ticking in his brain. He knew what he had to do.

Max was not a stranger to being outed. But he swore to himself that as soon as he could manage it, he was gone. No more split. And the split idea was bullshit, anyway, because Brandon was not some fictional character that somebody could go and neatly analyze. These murdered trans people were real and they were not *split* by anybody but their killers. Max refused to be detransitioned by death. No matter what it took, even if it meant dying, he was going to do it as Max.

24

ERIN THINKS ABOUT HER DAD as she runs. The image she has constructed over the last few years is a grim one. Found by strangers. Eyes open, perhaps betraying that singular instant where he was capable of being afraid. Still warm to the touch. As she sprints through the trees, Erin wonders if it would be considered prophetic if she wound up being found that exact same way.

Here lies Erin Arlos, torn to pieces by a monster.

This time, when she can see the edge of the tree line up ahead, she has the foresight to pump the brakes early. She slows to a stop in front of the highway, with absolutely no idea how she got there. Her lungs burn. There's no way to know if she's going to be walking toward the car, or farther from it. It all looks the same out here. Having found the road does not make her any less lost.

So she sticks close to the tree line and just keeps hurrying forward.

Hayley does not know that their dad is dead. Her mom *must* know, but they've never sat down and talked about it. Nobody talks about him because there's nothing to say. Dad is just an awful feeling in Erin's gut, acknowledged only when passing through the front door. Beyond that first day without him, on the couch with her mom, Erin has never cried about it. Not even after learning he was dead.

She wonders if maybe she should have.

Behind her, a familiar bellowing *scream* echoes through the trees.

Erin freezes. Then, quickly, she hurries behind the trunk of the closest sourwood, whose body splits at the base and rises up into the dark above. She lowers herself to the ground, her back pressed into the wood, and puts her hands over her mouth. She's been trying to ignore how hard she's been breathing; she refuses to die because she got *tired*. But now that she's finally stopped, her chest is punishing her for it. Her lungs can't expand enough to get all the air that she needs. It takes ages for her to even get close.

The urge to cry comes in waves. Every time she thinks about how quickly she threw her womanhood on a pike. And Max—

She does not cry. Crying would be a waste of time and energy. Shame is for survivors, and she has not survived nearly enough to get to think about *what this means* in the long term.

On the thought of survival, though, the woods have gone quiet and stayed quiet since she dropped down behind the tree. Nothing to indicate that she's being followed. Erin slides her head into her hands and sighs. Her shoulders sag. She's *exhausted*.

In the dark space between her eyes and the palms of her hands, it almost seems like it's a good idea to fall asleep. After all, no one is following her. Her body wilts a little further under the allure. Even the silence of the woods becomes gentle rather than unsettling. Everything around her is asleep, why does she alone resist the urge?

Erin sighs and presses her palms into her face. Then she brings her head back up to keep on going.

She is no longer beside the road.

Her back remains pressed against *a* tree, but it's not *the* sourwood erupting from the dead weeds. It's not just her tree, either, but *all* of the trees around her, different kinds sprouting from different points in the ground. All of it is different. Erin looks around, disbelieving, before she scrambles to her feet.

Surely she would know if she was drugged. Right? Charlie drank from the same glass as she did. But she closed her eyes just feet away from the highway, and she's opened them somewhere completely different. It's all completely wrong. There's no other rational explanation, other than she might be insane, or tripping the worst kind of balls.

Erin starts running again. She tells herself that she's just gotten herself disoriented. It's dark, and she's exhausted. She's been in survival mode for a long time. And now, on top of all that, she's hearing—

That scream, which echoes out from somewhere behind

her. It starts low, guttural, before rising and rising into a *squeal*. The only thing she can compare it to is the way Hayley used to scream as a baby, raw and hysterical. The sound makes Erin stop for a moment before it makes her start running again, terrified by whatever inhuman thing is capable of making that noise.

She's barely gone anywhere when she suddenly bursts out into an open field. The moonlight offers little real visibility, but it's better than being under the oppressive shadow of the trees. She looks around, long enough to orient herself, before she keeps going. Her eyes lock on the next tree line, a decent length away.

She hates running, but she's out in the open. It doesn't feel like she has any other choice. She feels exposed.

Her brain is a loop: *not a girl not a girl not a girl not a girl not a girl not a girl*.

Halfway across, Erin's foot comes down on empty air. She inhales—gasps—but that's the only noise she gets out before she goes tumbling down the ravine. She lands on her shoulder, and the entire right side of her body lights up with pain. Then she hits water. Stagnant, but freezing. It feels like every last drop of it rushes up her nose before she bolts upright, sputtering and coughing.

Erin pushes the hair out of her eyes. Her shoulder aches. She's fallen into a shallow river, nestled where the ground slopes into steep embankments on either side. It's not hidden, exactly, but it's sure as hell not obvious when you're trying to run for your life.

The cuts on her hands and face have started to burn again. She grimaces and forces herself to stand.

She pulls herself up the embankment, fingers clawing at the dirt as it crumbles beneath her. For some reason, this feels familiar. At the top of the embankment, she frowns and looks back in the direction she came from. The sky is black and starless, but she can envision where the sunset would be. Where it *was*, several hours ago.

Erin looks down at the river again. What are the odds of her being wrong?

Only one way to find out. Erin turns on her heel and hurries on, toward the new tree line that might not be all that new. She quickly comes upon an all-too-familiar dirt path. A hysterical laugh bubbles up in the back of her throat. Her shoes squish with each step.

The Impala is slightly askew. Its back tires have been pushed completely off the road, and one of the front tires isn't even touching the ground anymore. But it is otherwise exactly where Erin left it. She doesn't pause to look over the damage. She throws open the door and climbs inside, grabbing the keys from the dashboard and shoving them into the ignition switch.

It's not surprising when the engine doesn't even croak, but it's still devastating.

"Come on," she begs out loud, voice shaking as she pumps the pedal and tries the keys again and again into failure. "Come *on*!"

In the corner of her vision, Erin swears she catches

movement in the rearview. But when she whips her head up to look, all she gets are her own horribly crazed eyes. One of them is already beginning to bruise. She stares at herself for a moment, a horrible reflection, before she looks back over her shoulder. As far as she can see, there's nothing outside. The door behind her has crumpled inward, and chunks of glass from the shattered window cover the back seat.

Erin turns around and stares at the wheel. She twists the keys as far as they will go, as if that'll create the magic spark to make the engine viable. Her eyes shut. A sob blocks up her throat.

Here lies Erin Arlos. She died because of a stupid little piece of plastic. Or whatever a spark plug is made from.

Please, she thinks, squeezing her eyes even more tightly shut.

Something suddenly slams into her door. Erin screams and is already halfway out of her seat before she gets a look.

It's Max.

"Oh my God," she exhales.

Max barely gets clear of the door before Erin pushes it open. She grabs him, and Max collapses into her. It's only then that Erin absorbs that he's *here*. Hugging her so tight that it's a little hard to breathe. Her own hands are sweaty, gripping fistfuls of Max's jacket until the joints in her knuckles ache. That sob makes its way out of her throat, mixed with relieved laughter.

"What the hell is *happening*?" Max gasps, muffled and breathless.

Erin shakes her head. Her chin comes to rest on Max's shoulder. "I can't explain it," she whispers. "But we've gotta get out of here. *Now*."

Max requires no explanation.

He nods, steps back—and then seems to notice the scratches on Erin's face for the first time. He stops. It's a steady pair of hands that comes to her face. "Who did this to you?"

The gentleness almost shocks Erin into her own state of calm. She stares up at him. Max is bleeding from a scratch along his cheek, a miniaturization of the road rash on Erin's.

His thumb traces the edge of her wound.

Then the urgency washes back into her mouth. "We've gotta get out of here."

"Who?"

"*Max.*"

He flinches, then nods and lets go of her face. Erin is surprised by how quickly the warmth leaves with him. She watches him walk to the front of the car, glimmering with sweat as he pulls out and breaks open a box of spark plugs. He's covered in dirt stains, skin so white he looks sick.

"What happened to *you*?" Erin stands, although she finds herself unable to actually walk up to him.

Max shakes his head. "Doesn't matter. Help, please?"

Erin moves mindlessly and holds up the hood. "Are you okay?"

He leans down. It takes a moment, but he gets two plugs out and pushes them both into place. "I will be, soon as we're out of here."

His voice warbles. He walks around to the driver's side and Erin shuts the hood. She lingers there at the front of the car, overwhelmed with a thousand different thoughts. What did they do to him?

Max turns the keys, and the engine wakes from the dead with a sharp, ugly gasp.

He looks up at Erin. "Hey. *Now*."

She finally remembers how to work her legs.

As soon as she's closed the passenger door, Max guns it. The car jerks, and then it's on the road again, flying forward. Erin finds a fleeting moment of amusement at imagining what they must look like, bloody and wide-eyed as they tear through the night. It's not long before they bounce, hitting the paved asphalt of the main highway. Max never slows down.

Erin peels off her hoodie and throws it into the back. She glances at the radio. Dots and lines seem to blink in and out at random, as if the whole system were glitching. No time. Just night. Just dark.

The woods flying by outside no longer seem tangible. If she stuck her hand out, she's not sure that she would feel the swipe of leaves as they passed through her fingers.

Erin swallows and finally pulls herself away from the clock. "Max?"

He continues to watch the road, knuckles white at ten and two. "Yeah?"

"Do you remember what we talked about earlier? About monsters and gender?"

"Why?"

"Because we might be about to find out."

Max turns to her with a bewildered frown.

Somehow, Erin didn't think about how stupid this whole thing sounded until now, now that she has to verbalize it. "That cop wasn't messing with us. That Beast thing is real, and there are these guys who give it—human sacrifices. Girls. Uh, very specifically girls. They were going to try it with me, but—"

"Oh."

The car goes quiet. Max sits with this for a minute.

"So they—?"

He looks over at her. He doesn't finish the question, but he doesn't need to.

Erin nods.

Max absorbs this, too. "We need to get out of here," he says quietly.

Without a trace of humor, Erin laughs. "Yeah."

It goes silent again. It's in this silence that she knows she's doomed them both. What haunts her is how she never even thought twice about it. It just came out of her. As if being trans has ever saved anybody before.

Erin wipes her eyes and turns again to the back seat. She brushes the glass off her bag before pulling it closer. She tosses a few things out haphazardly—one of her books, the Kentucky postcard, a purple-striped sock—and tugs a clean T-shirt from the mess. Now if she dies, it'll be a Garfield comic strip across her chest.

Here lies Erin Arlos. Daughter. Sister. Hates Mondays.

Max presses down harder on the gas, and the engine hums. The needle on the speedometer ticks closer to ninety. Erin eyes it nervously.

"Max?"

"Yeah?"

"You should probably slow down."

He laughs. "Er, I don't give a shit who tries to pull us over, I'm not stopping—"

Before he can finish that thought, he sees something in the rearview mirror that makes his face go slack.

Erin has just started to look back when the car suddenly *jolts,* as if they've been rear-ended. They lurch forward, and Max slams on the brakes. The air is flooded with the sound of metal scraping, screeching, *ripping.*

When they stop, Erin's head snaps back against the seat, and her skull hums with an almost instantaneous headache. She grimaces. The CD booklet and a few chunks of glass have slid forward from the back and now rest at her feet. Then she looks up and finds herself eye to eye with that smirking cardinal teetering on the edge of the dashboard. It sits there for only a moment before it slips off and lands on the floor.

Erin looks over at Max, and finds him staring at it, too. His expression is unreadable.

Then he puts the car into park and gets out, and Erin follows after him without a second thought. Without really having a *first* thought, besides, perhaps: *shit.*

She's right on Max's heels as he marches up to the bumper, which lies in a mangled heap in the middle of the road. One end of it is bent, its paint scraped off in long, jagged lines. Erin's memories supply the image of that black hole of a mouth she saw before. The sound of metal is still fresh in her ears as she imagines those teeth ripping into the car like butter.

Max stares at it for a very long moment, hands visibly trembling at his sides. Then he finally shakes his head. "Screw this. C'mon."

He spins around and stalks back toward the car. Erin watches him go, but lingers at the bumper. She takes a tentative step closer. Her reflection in the metal is distorted. The giant gash on her cheek makes it look like a whole chunk of her face is missing. Over her shoulder, the moon glistens like a big yellow eye.

It wants girls. Does that mean Erin is a threat to Max, or the other way around?

"*Hey*—"

A hand comes down on her arm. Erin turns.

"Come on," Max bites, as if he's repeating himself. Was he talking before? He shakes her arm. "Let's *go*."

He walks toward the car again, but Erin still doesn't follow. She looks back at the bumper, mind reeling. Goose bumps break out across her arms as she begins to quiver, though she's not even cold.

"Erin!"

She turns. Max is standing at the back of the car, glaring at her.

Erin shakes her head. "I'm not getting in that car again."

He stares at her like she's crazy. "We have to keep going!"

"Why, Max? So we can die tired? If that *thing* doesn't get us, any one of those cultist hicks will!"

"Bullshit! We got away from them!"

"For five minutes! And then what? They have *guns*!"

Max shakes his head and starts walking closer. "All we've gotta do is keep driving—"

Erin laughs. It's a horrible, angry sound, even to her. "You seriously think we ever had any chance of making it to Berkeley?"

"We *will* if you get back in the car!"

"Max, goddammit, I didn't sign up to die for you! I didn't sign up for *any* of this!"

"Well, I'm sorry I didn't plan for the cryptid and the human sacrifice bullshit!" he snaps.

"We're both going to die because you couldn't just take a plane like a normal person!"

Max stops. Erin does, too, and although she immediately regrets the venom that dripped from her mouth, there's nothing she can do to scrape it back inside of her. She's angry. There's a strange exhilaration in finally venting this.

An expression of hurt briefly shadows Max's face. "Don't you dare blame me for this."

Before Erin can respond, Max spins around and stomps toward the car. He flings open the door, and Erin follows him. If he tries to get in, she'll drag him back out by the hair.

But instead of getting inside and driving away, Max emerges with the postcard in his fist. Erin stops dead in her tracks. She is wholly unprepared for the wall of shame that slams into her, watching Max read over her scribblings. Then he crumples it.

For a long, almost unbearable moment, it's just quiet.

"Do you know what my mom writes about me on Facebook?" Max suddenly asks.

Erin frowns and slowly shakes her head.

"She's, like, *really* active in this mom's group for trans kids. Or something. Gender-critical old hags." His voice shakes. "Anyway, like a month ago, I had to use her phone for something, and she got a notification from it, and I just started scrolling through . . . *all* of it. She posts *my face*. She talks about how she *saved me* from the transgender death cult. And there are, like, literally hundreds of people cheering her on for doing the *right thing*."

Erin is still frozen to the spot when Max surges forward and shoves the postcard into her chest with such force that it knocks her back a step.

"Being selfish is one thing, being *stupid* is one thing," he seethes, "but I am not letting you ruin my life."

"Max—"

"If you thought this whole thing was *psychotic*, then you should've just stayed home."

Max turns, but Erin grabs him by the shoulder and whirls him back around. "I'm not trying to ruin your life, I'm trying to save it, asshole!"

"Yeah?"

"*Yeah!*"

"Then how did that cop know I'm trans?" He draws out each word of this question, slow and deliberate.

Erin falters. She can feel her heartbeat throughout her whole rib cage. She's not going to lie, and it seems like Max has already come to something close to the right conclusion. In the silence, Max just nods. His face continues to turn an even darker shade of pink.

"Maybe this *is* my fault," he mutters. "You have no idea what I've been going through—"

"Of course I don't!" Erin butts in. "You cut me off!"

"So? You did what everybody else does, and you got away from me as soon as you had the chance."

"*I* got away from *you*?" Erin's laugh is a tense, ugly thing. "Is that what you tell yourself? *I* didn't leave. Why the hell would you ask me to do this if that's what you think of me?"

"That's not—" Max pushes his hair out of his face, visibly frustrated by it. He takes a deep breath. "I already told you why. Columbus is a hellhole. I wasn't just gonna bail on you. Not without trying first."

Laughter is the wrong response, but it continues to come out of her mouth. Erin can't help it.

"What?" Now Max frowns.

"What?" Erin echoes him. "Don't act like this was for *us*. That's never what this was about."

"We used to talk about—"

"Yeah, and then I *stopped being sixteen*, Max! Did you not?"

His mouth snaps shut.

"You tell me to give you space, and *I do*, and you hate me," Erin goes on. "I *try* to talk to you, and you either ignore me or you push me away again. I'm *trying* to do the right thing, even though apparently everything I do is wrong. And I don't know why everything has to be such a fight with you! Why won't you just talk to me? What do you even *want*?"

In response to all of this, Max just stands there. The echoing silence that follows makes Erin's voice sound unbearably shrill.

"If you didn't want to come," Max finally says, "you didn't have to."

Erin comes very close to screaming, but she somehow manages to swallow it. "Yeah, I'm sure it would be that easy for you, but it's not for me," she mutters, shaking her head and finally starting to cry a little. "I mean, was I supposed to just let you go and kill yourself out here?"

"I'm not gonna kill myself if you take your eyes off me for two seconds!" Max snaps.

Erin throws her arms out. "Did you not already try?"

Low blow. Max looks murderous.

"Tell me I'm wrong," she says. Almost pleads.

Max does not. "If I wanted to die, I wouldn't be going through all of this, okay? I have *never* wanted to live more than I do right now!"

"So you don't tell me *any* of this, and it's my fault for not putting it all together?"

"It doesn't matter. We're gonna die because *you* made this all about *you* again!"

"*Everything* I have done since we left has been for you!" Erin snaps back. "I *wanted* you back in my life and I wanted to be your friend again because I care about you! For whatever reason, no matter how much of a *dick* you are, I still care about you!"

It might only be because she's crying, but Erin feels sick to her stomach.

"I'm sorry, for whatever that's worth," she continues before Max can start up again. "I'm sorry I didn't reach out. I'm sorry I didn't try hard enough—"

Max shakes his head. "Don't. Don't do that."

"—and I'm sorry I *still* don't know how to help you, but— goddammit, you used to be my best friend, I *loved* you—"

"Okay, and I love you, too, but that doesn't help us right now, does it?"

Erin opens her mouth to keep going, but the words crash into each other at the back of her throat. The silence is a crash in and of itself.

It goes quiet.

It goes *very* quiet as the malice abruptly drains from the air between them like it's seeping from an open wound. She shuts her mouth. Even the way Max stands goes from guarded and angry to exhausted.

Like a puppet cut from its strings, he drops back against the car door and exhales. He rubs his eyes with the heels of his palms. His face is red and blotchy. He looks even younger than he normally does; he looks as young as he *is*.

"I hate you so much." His voice comes out quiet and shaking. "And I love you. I don't know how to make sense of that. I don't know how to make any of this make sense. You have *no* idea what this has been like."

"Max—"

"No, shut up." He gestures between them. "Look at me and look at you."

Erin frowns. "That's not my fault, Max. The world isn't fair—"

"I *know* that!" he snaps. "Jesus Christ, you think I haven't picked up on that? Breaking news, the world isn't fair to the freaks, thank you!"

Erin says nothing.

Max shakes his head and scoffs. "Of course you don't wanna go. Your life's perfect. It's always been perfect."

Erin stares at him. "Are you kidding?"

"You wanted to transition and you did! All of the shit you had to go through, at least you did it in a *girl's* body!"

"That's not how that works! My life wasn't—*isn't* perfect just because *yours* isn't!"

"You got to be a woman from the *second* you came out," Max continues to press. "It's great that you got to stop being sixteen, but I'm still stuck there! You said you were a woman, and everybody just went, *Oh, cool! Erin's a girl now. Good for her.*"

"Max, you have no idea what you're talking about," Erin says tightly.

"Probably not!" he admits, laughing before he sniffles and wipes roughly at his eyes. "No, I *know* I don't. That's the problem, okay? That's just what it feels like. I just see how everyone decided that they loved you enough to learn about trans stuff for you, how they protected you when people tried to be assholes, and *I'm* just—"

He takes a deep breath. "I've been stuck inside this stupid body my whole life. I *know* the world isn't fair."

Erin wants to keep fighting. To keep telling Max he's wrong. But her throat blocks up, and her words get lost behind the barrier.

"I don't want you to be stuck the way I am," Max continues, "but—how was I supposed to feel? You used to get mad at your mom for trying to protect you, and that just drove me *crazy*, because you have no idea what it's like to have a mom who *actually* hates what you are. And that started to be all I could think about when I was with you—how lucky you were, how unfair it was. And I—I realized I couldn't keep doing that." He takes a deep breath. "Because I just started hating *so much*. I hated you. I figured getting out of each other's lives would make us both happier, y'know?"

The block at the back of Erin's throat has started to burn.

"But all that did was make it worse, because you have no idea what I'm going through, but also you're the *only* one who knows what I'm going through." He laughs weakly. "I know you don't believe me, but I meant everything I said when we were together. I promised that I'd get you out of there. I *promised* that. I thought that if I could get us both out, and if I could be in a body I didn't despise, then we could just . . . pick up where we left off."

It goes quiet again. Nausea rumbles at the back of Erin's mouth. This is all her fault, and she had nothing to do with any of it. She wants to hug Max just as badly as she wants to continue screaming at him.

Max takes a deep breath. It seems like he's calmed down some, although he has yet to look Erin in the eyes for more than half a second. "I'm not just going to lie down here and wait to die. Because I have spent my whole life fighting for this. I don't expect you to understand that because you've never fought for any of it, but I *have* to. Or I will die trying. So, please, for the love of God, *get back in the car.*"

He turns again for the door. Erin impulsively grabs his wrist.

Max freezes, but he doesn't rip his arm away. He stares at her hand for a long while. Then, slowly, he looks up at her, eyes puffy and bloodshot and devastatingly vulnerable.

Erin knows she should say something. Anything. But everything she can come up with dies in her throat, childish or stupid or unhelpful. None of this is fair. None of it is Max's fault. None of it is her fault. And yet regret burns away within her.

"Are you coming with me, or are you just gonna stay here?" Max asks, voice flat.

Erin continues to stand there. More than anything, she

wants to get back in the car, and she doesn't want to stop until their tires hit sand. She wants this all to be a nightmare that she can just forget about. She wants to know that if she gets into this car, she still has a chance to fix this.

But she remembers what Charlie said: *it likes the chase*.

Every time they've tried to get out of this horrible stretch of highway, something has happened. Something has stopped them, pulled them off course, or sent them in completely opposite directions. It's like fighting against a riptide that they can't see.

"I don't think we can run from this," she answers at last.

Max closes his eyes as if he's in pain. "Why not? Why can't we just keep going—"

"Because where does the running *stop*, Max?"

He stares at her, bewildered.

"Even if *we* get away, they're just gonna keep killing people. Maybe they keep coming after us. Maybe we find people just like them in California, and we have to run away again—"

"Somewhere," Max cuts her off. "That's a stupid question. The answer to *where does it end?* is always *somewhere*."

He pulls his hand out of her grasp, and Erin lets him.

"They've killed so many women, Max," she breathes.

His eyes are glued to the ground between them. "I'm not dying for strangers I won't ever know."

The coldness of this statement surprises Erin more than anything else he's said. She straightens and stares at him.

"We get out of here," he continues, "and we can go to the cops—"

"*Now* you want to trust the cops?"

"—and the cops can handle this, but it's not *our* problem!"

"How is it not our problem? What if the next person they kill is trans, too, huh? Would it be our problem then?"

"No, because it wouldn't be me!" Max's voice breaks.

Erin's tongue sits heavy inside her mouth. It's a disgustingly selfish thing to say. She understands exactly why he's said it.

"This is bigger than us, Max," she whispers.

He doesn't answer her. He only continues to stand there, unmoving, staring at the ground.

Finally, Erin opens the back door. A few pieces of glass sprinkle onto the asphalt. She rifles through the back seat until she comes up with the knife that Max gave her, that she forgot about in her moment of terror. She grabs it with one hand and takes the disposable camera with the other. Then she walks back up to Max and pushes the knife into his hands.

He looks down at it and frowns. "What—?"

"Go, then." Erin's voice is thick from the tears she's managed to swallow down, although they're dangerously close to pushing through again. "Don't let me hold you back."

Max stares at her. Erin knows she's being as cruel as he is. But she doesn't waver.

"Erin," Max begins, a whisper.

"I'm not asking. I'm saying that if you go right now, you're going alone."

"Please don't make me have to choose."

Her heart twists itself into knots. Because she knows the

answer. Erin is asking Max to consciously, willingly turn around and walk back into the mouth of the beast. She is asking him to take the freedom he has spent *years* clawing toward, and she is asking him to fall back. She isn't surprised. But it still hurts.

"I'm not making you choose," she answers.

And then she leaves him. With a familiar weight of dread pulling at her stomach, she marches back in the direction they were driving away from.

When Erin turns around, the Impala is already little more than distant red dots. Then the taillights disappear completely as the car drives on, into the dark ahead.

25

MAX DOES NOT LOOK BACK. He keeps his hands at ten and two and his eyes on the road, and he drives, ignoring the burn between his shoulders that tells him he's holding too much tension there. It takes a long time for him to realize that the ugly, choked keening sound is coming from his own throat.

26

ERIN DOES NOT HAVE A PLAN. Once she stops crying, she realizes she's probably walking in the wrong direction. But she's given up on trying to force the woods to make any geographical sense. Either she ends up where she needs to be, or maybe she finds a way out of here.

Down one knife and lacking in other weapons, she ends up taking a baseball-sized rock from the side of the road and carrying it with her. Her knee burns. Everything sucks. She does not have a plan, nor is she in much shape to fight, but she figures she might stand at least half a chance against some of these men. She has this new rock, after all.

No, it's that *thing* that concerns her. The Beast.

If she can survive long enough to get back to the house, she wants to try and grab that rifle. The one she saw Aiden carrying. That might give her an edge.

Erin passes the rock into her right hand and looks at the palm of her left. The skin is raw and bloody. She can't immediately find any part of her body that *doesn't* hurt. She sighs and presses her palm to her mouth. She can feel the gentle throb against her lips.

Surviving the night is not her end goal. Getting back to Max is. That should require her to form a plan that'll return her to that barely functional Impala, but she can come up with little more than *just do it*. She doesn't know how she'll kill any of these men. She doesn't even know if she'll be *able* to when it comes down to it. The details are all *yada yada yada*.

Erin sighs and passes the rock back and forth and back and forth in her hands.

You've never fought for any of it.

It was a dickish thing to say. Fundamentally wrong. But it also wasn't *wrong*, necessarily.

It's complicated. Every trans person faces an uphill battle of skeptics, bigots, and apathetic cruelty at the hands of all the folks who would rather forget that transness exists than actually deal with it. No trans person has it easy. Any ease is conditional. But Erin has never had to fight as long and hard as Max has for basic recognition. That much is more true than it isn't.

For Max, there's never been a time in which his transness wasn't actively making his life harder. This distant, forever-unattainable goal. For Erin, it's been more of a given. As frustrating as her mother can be, she has never tried to shove Erin back into that male-shaped box she previously occupied. Nobody has.

It's not fair. None of it is. Neither of them can help that.

Erin also realizes she might owe her mom an apology when she sees her again.

A harsh wind suddenly comes whipping through the trees, drudging an exhausted groan from the branches hanging overhead. Erin comes to a stop and looks up at the sky. It's unsettling to see such a clear sky and yet only be able to see the moon. As if something went and smothered out the stars. She tries to remember anything of what Chief Laster said about their Beast.

Maybe it brought floods. Maybe it's a creature that thrives on suffering.

Or maybe it's like Mothman: just trying to warn people away from the water. Although Erin doubts this. Whatever warning she was supposed to get from watching its jaws snap toward her has gone completely over her head.

Erin turns to the woods on her right. She already has no idea where she's going. It's not that the woods seem *safer*, exactly, but she'll be less exposed. The last thing she wants is for Aiden to see her coming down the road and to end this whole thing with one shot.

So she steps off the road, sneakers crunching against the dirt, and trudges into the woods.

As she walks, Erin looks up again at the sky. She wonders if her perception of time is really so bad, or if the night has been going by especially slowly. The moon hangs high overhead, still nowhere near the horizon line. It provides just enough light that Erin can navigate the path she's forging for herself without immediately twisting an ankle.

Something moves behind her. Erin spins around and raises the rock, but she raises it to empty air.

It surely is nothing more than a breeze, but Erin still slowly stalks backward, just in case. She watches the leaves shudder, listens to the crunch of grass underfoot, until she's sure that nobody is about to jump out at her. It's a good reminder to keep her focus on moving ahead.

Max is far away, going in the opposite direction. If something's behind her now, it won't be Max.

That thought only makes her feel worse. Erin shakes her head and continues on.

She soon decides that the moon *must* be moving, because it has suddenly gotten significantly harder to keep her feet clear of the branches underfoot since she last looked up. It's getting darker. It's only then that the rhythmic swinging of the disposable camera hanging from her wrist worms its way to the front of her mind. Erin sighs and catches it.

Then she keeps thinking about it, and ideas begin to blossom.

It's only a temporary solution, but Max didn't come back with the flashlight, and Erin doubts she would've thought to grab it even if he had. So, this is all she's got. She stops and fumbles with the camera for a minute. Once she's sure it's on, she pushes down on the shutter.

Click. No flash.

Shit. Erin feels around until she finds the switch for the flash and tries again.

This time, the flash lights up the woods in front of her.

Erin smiles, confidently walks forward about twenty feet, and then does it again.

This continues for six photos worth of flashes. After the sixth time, some light lingers in the distance while the rest of the flash fades out, and Erin surges toward it.

FROM THE RELATIVE SAFETY of the trees, she looks upon the old house. It is unquestionably a one-story building, covered in sun-faded white slats. The lights inside are on. There are no second-story windows.

Erin knows she is not crazy. But there is no time to go back and forth, no time to doubt if this is real or if it's only real to *her*. There is only what's in front of her and what isn't.

The stretch of flat grass between her and the house is a no-man's-land. The windows might be empty now, though Aiden could easily appear and put a slug between her eyes before she even gets halfway across. But that's a risk she has to take. Otherwise she and Max will continue to have danger burning at their heels. Until these men kill them. Or until Erin does something to stop them.

Erin puts her foot out and takes a step forward, ready to bolt, when headlights suddenly break through the trees to her left. She immediately ducks back and holds herself up against the tree closest to her until she's positive that she hasn't been seen. She can hear the sound of the car rolling to a stop. After a moment, she pokes her head out.

Chief Laster steps out of his patrol car and lumbers up to

the front door of the house. Charlie *did* mention his name, didn't he? Was Erin so freaked out by everything else that this detail failed to register until now?

Nevertheless, she waits until the front door opens. Chief Laster steps through. Then Erin sprints toward the house.

Twenty feet out, she drops to the ground. She doesn't slide as much as she was hoping to, but she manages to keep her momentum going, crawling forward on her arms like she's in boot camp, until she gets up to the house. Her heartbeat bangs in her ears. When no men come running out after her, she carefully presses herself up against the wall, underneath the closest window, which has been left cracked open. Erin twists herself around, peering in through the corner of the window, trying to see as much as she can without sticking her entire head into view.

Charlie is standing the closest, his back turned to the window. The sight of him makes something cold wrap around Erin's chest. But there's no indication that he's aware of her at all. Chief Laster and Tommy enter the room a moment later. Aiden is seated in an old wooden rocking chair, methodically wiping his rifle down as gravity sways him lazily back and forth.

"Glad to see you're taking this seriously," Chief Laster deadpans.

Aiden calmly gives him the finger, without even looking at him, and continues to polish.

Erin shrinks back under the window ledge and listens.

"Okay, so, they *both* got away," Tommy laments. "What are we supposed to do?"

"I'm sorry, Tom, is this the first time we've ever had somebody get away? Are you out past your bedtime right now?" Chief Laster's voice is sharp with agitation.

Tommy doesn't respond. Rhetorical questions.

The next thing Chief Laster says is directed at Charlie: "Any reason you think they'd turn around, try and go back the way they were coming from?"

Charlie answers, "Doubt it. If not both of them, then at least not Max."

"Perfect. Tommy, you're gonna come with me."

"What do you want us to do, then?" Charlie asks.

"You and Aiden are gonna wait here. If they *do* backtrack, you'll have to be ready to intercept 'em. One of you should wait near the road, and the other should stay here."

"And I'll shoot the girl," Aiden calmly adds.

Chief Laster has to think about this for a moment. "The blond one. Whatever. You shoot the blond, and you take the short kid alive."

"And you'll be doing . . . ?" Charlie prods.

"I've got Jesse and Colton on the road, a few miles up. Tommy and I'll go up there to check in, then we'll go back and clear the roads ourselves."

"If they're smart, they're probably not gonna be on the main road anymore."

"Probably not. But they'll be running, and the Beast'll be hungry."

Suddenly, the window above her is pushed farther open with an awful screech.

Erin goes rigid and presses herself closer to the house, as if there's anywhere for her to go. A moment later, a snuffed-out cigarette falls to the dirt in front of her. A spark lands on the toe of her sneaker, then fizzles out.

Chief Laster shuts the window.

"Come on," his muffled voice instructs. "Let's finish it. This is getting ridiculous."

Erin remains perfectly, unflinchingly still until she hears the car engine roar to life on the other side of the building. Only once she hears the tires peel out does she collapse back against the wall and take several shaking breaths. Her head spins.

It doesn't make her feel any better knowing that her killing will be the quick one. Sure, either way, it seems like the plan was always for them both to die; the only changes are about *why* and *how*. But now Max is going to die because of the one thing that has been haunting him for nearly his entire life. And that just cannot continue to play out any more than it already has.

Erin crawls from under the window and tiptoes to the back of the house. Now would be a pretty good time to formulate that ingenious plan, the thing that'll save both of their lives. At least now there are only two guys to worry about in the house. But one of them has a gun, and she does not.

She would do well to get another weapon. She considers the rock for a moment, then tosses it. There will be better options inside. She knows there will.

She slips the camera off her wrist and sets it on the ground, where it will hopefully remain safe. Then she approaches the door and carefully wraps her hand around the knob. When she twists and pulls, the door comes with her, slowly. By the time it's open enough for her to step through, the hinges have not made so much as one little creak.

Entering the house again makes Erin's heart beat so hard that she starts to worry it just might stop. A small, cowardly voice in the back of her mind tells her to *run*. It tells her that there must be a way to survive this that doesn't require her putting her life on the line.

She's her father's daughter, right? *So, run*.

Erin takes a deep breath, holds Max's face in her mind, and tells the voice to *shut up*.

She eases the door shut behind her. There's some noise coming from the front of the house, so she is especially careful as she tiptoes into the kitchen.

When nobody comes running after her, Erin allows herself to move a little faster. She walks up to the table and crouches in front of the glass shards that are still scattered on the floor. Most of them are too small or fragile to be useful, breaking apart in her fingers as soon as she picks them up. But one shard—a curved piece of the bottom of the glass—does not immediately crumble. One is all she needs.

A slight smile crosses her face because maybe she has half a chance to do some damage. Even if survival is not guaranteed.

She stands up and turns around. Aiden is standing in the entryway.

The rifle glistens in one hand, reflecting the harsh kitchen light. Erin freezes. For a moment, they both just stare at each other in mutual surprise.

Aiden moves first. He slowly steps into the room, setting the rifle down in the far corner before he comes up to the opposite end of the table. Erin takes a step back and tightens her grip on the shard of glass, wincing as the jagged edge digs into her palm. Aiden's eyes linger on her. It's not quite *leering*, but something closer to curiosity.

His eyes finally land on her face. "You want the first swing?"

Erin frowns. "What?"

He shrugs. "Never hit a *girl* before. Figured it'd be rude to just, y'know, go at it."

Abruptly, Aiden picks up the chair closest to him and hurls it at her. Erin has no idea how she ducks fast enough to dodge it, but she can feel the breeze of its *weight* as it passes over her. It slams into the wall and breaks into a dozen pieces.

She pops back up just in time to watch Aiden sprint around the table toward her. She bolts for the doorway.

To be exact, she has only *just* gotten to the end of the table when Aiden is suddenly on top of her. Erin hits the floor hard, pinned down by probably two hundred pounds of murderous maniac. The glass slices into her palm again, but Erin keeps her grip on it.

Aiden grabs her by the shoulder and pulls her onto her back. Erin takes what might be her only chance and slashes at him.

She misses.

Aiden jerks his head out of the way, despite the fact that Erin's arc would've probably only grazed his chin if he'd stayed still. He grabs her by the wrist and slams it into the ground with such ease, it's like he's been waiting his whole life to do something like this. He *squeezes*.

Erin clenches her fist, but she just doesn't have the strength to counteract Aiden's grip. Another slam into the floor and she lets go, gasping in pain. She can hear the glass bounce around on the wood for a moment before it settles somewhere above her head.

For a guy who claimed to believe it was rude to hit a girl *without warning*, he doesn't seem to actually have a problem with it. Aiden rears back and punches Erin in the mouth. The taste of blood is hot and suffocating when it explodes in the back of her throat.

Aiden lets go of her wrist, and then both hands wrap around her throat. Erin's eyes widen.

If he really wanted to, Aiden could break her hyoid bone with one well-placed push. It's a common result of strangulation. Erin doesn't remember exactly where she learned this, but it probably came from her mother. This should be a quick death.

But Aiden applies just enough pressure to cut off her breath and nothing else. He rests one knee on the floor while the other presses into Erin's chest. The tingling sensation of *pressure* intensifies on the sides of her face.

Erin tries to grab at his hands, and then uselessly hits at his arms. A ghost of a smile crosses Aiden's mouth. He leans a little harder into her. Erin gasps for a breath she cannot take, and the noise she makes in the process is this horrible croak.

Distantly, the floor shakes with incoming footsteps. Charlie stops in the entryway of the room a moment later, somewhere to Erin's right. She can't see him—her vision has started to get fuzzy, the browns of the room bleeding into Aiden's face—but she can hear him.

"Jesus, you couldn't just shoot her?"

Aiden's eyes do not leave Erin's face. "Didn't feel like it."

Erin croaks again. It feels like her body is trying to expel tears, but nothing comes. Something is ringing. The floor is rolling like waves. Nothing looks real. She blindly reaches out anyway. Her nails scratch against the linoleum.

She's such a nonthreat that she doesn't distract from their conversation by doing this.

Aiden turns away from Erin and glares at Charlie. "*You* want to do it?"

"No! Just shoot her!"

Erin's fingers brush against something smooth.

Above her, Aiden smirks. "Pussy."

Erin's fingers draw the glass shard into her palm. Charlie shouts something, but he sounds like he's a thousand miles away from her. Aiden is little more than a hazy blur.

With one last push, Erin throws her arm up, plunging the glass into Aiden's neck.

The shouting all stops at once. The grip on her throat loosens, and suddenly the only thing Erin can hear is her own gasp for breath, an inhale that almost becomes a scream of its own. Aiden's eyes are unfocused. Like a fish left to asphyxiate on the dock. Erin rips the glass out, long enough for one good squirt of blood to sputter from his neck, before she stabs him again in the same spot.

Then again. And again.

A deep, wet gurgling noise rises up in Aiden's throat as he starts to realize what's happening. Too late. He swats blindly at the air to his right, which is not even the side that he's being ripped apart from. As sensation comes back to Erin's extremities, she can finally feel the blood raining down onto her face.

She does not stop stabbing him until Aiden starts to sway, until he finally loses balance and falls over.

Erin's breathing is loud. She has enough awareness to know that she sounds hysterical. The back of her throat is still splattered with hot blood that tastes of copper, and she realizes that she must have had her mouth open the whole time. She wonders if she was screaming.

She pulls herself up to her knees and turns around.

Charlie is still in the entryway, watching all of this with wide eyes and his mouth shut. As Erin moves, his gaze shifts from Aiden's still-convulsing body and back to her.

Erin spits out the blood that has pooled in the back of her mouth.

Her eyes shift to the rifle that remains propped in the corner of the room. Charlie follows her gaze. They bolt for it at the same time. Erin drops her shard—she'll need both hands.

Charlie starts out about two or three steps closer than she does. Probably even closer, considering that the edges of

Erin's vision are still dark and hazy and she can't be moving *that* quickly. But Charlie has barely put his hand around the barrel of the rifle when Erin gets there, and, still lacking a plan, uses her momentum to slam him into the wall. This does not make him drop the gun, but it at least initiates a struggle.

He elbows her in the face, which sends Erin's head snapping back, but she manages to get her hand on the barrel before she can lose her balance. It descends into a tug-of-war. Erin's palms are slick with blood. She isn't even looking at the gun. She's staring at Charlie's face as he tries to fight her off without letting go of the rifle. His expression is warped with frustration and what might even be a bit of genuine fear.

Erin drops her legs out from underneath her, sending her full body weight to the ground. Charlie goes with her, still refusing to let go. This new angle isn't ideal, but survival instinct is one hell of a coach to have in her corner. She and Charlie share one very vital weak spot.

While they're still struggling with the increasingly slippery barrel, Erin slams her knee up between Charlie's legs. It's immediate on his face, the *rage* behind his eyes as his body responds of its own accord. He starts to crumple. Erin grips the gun with both hands and slams it up into Charlie's face, which is finally enough to knock him down.

She stumbles to her feet, and Charlie is fast enough in regaining his senses that he knows to back up and put his hands in the air. Erin flips the safety off and points the rifle at his face. The edge of the gun digs into her shoulder.

Her dad's hands are on her arms. *Crease of the shoulder. Breathe.*

Erin lets the butt slide into the groove of her arm as Charlie stands. Wisely, he keeps his hands up, bloody but impressively stable. He lifts his head to look at her. His chin is bleeding.

A grin spreads across his face. He even starts to laugh for a second before he suppresses it into a chuckle that makes his whole body shake. He gives her a slight bow, as if to indicate that Erin has earned some respect. As if this is a fight that can end with peaceful admissions of defeat before they both go their separate ways.

"All right, Erin, come on." Charlie nods at the gun. "How about you put that down before you kill yourself?"

Erin smiles back, points the rifle lower, and squeezes the trigger.

The sound of the shot seems like it should explode the house into pieces. And the kickback feels like getting punched in the chest. But Erin's still a half-decent shot. The bullet tears through Charlie's left thigh and buries itself somewhere in the wall behind him.

Charlie drops to his knees, barely able to catch himself on the doorframe and avoid hitting the ground. The pain registers a second later. He curls in on himself and *shouts* into the floor. Blood has already begun to soak through his jeans by the time he puts a hand over the wound.

Erin cycles the bolt and kicks the empty shell aside.

"I think I'm good," she answers, "but thanks for worrying."

Charlie's eyes are squeezed shut, one hand keeping him braced against the doorframe. After a few shallow breaths, he starts to laugh again.

It's an unsettling sound, but Erin holds herself still. She could kill him right now if he tried to lunge for her. Or even if he didn't. She doesn't know why she doesn't. After all that's happened to her, to Max, she thinks she might have every right to unload the whole thing into Charlie's face.

"Where do you keep the ammo?" Erin asks.

Charlie scoffs and looks up at her. His eyes are still hot and raging. That pretense of respect is gone, just as quickly as it came. "Find it yourself, Rambo."

Wrong answer. Erin raises the rifle and fires again, this time into the wall closest to Charlie's head. He flinches away and then immediately seems like he hates himself for doing so. Erin cycles the bolt.

"Living room," he finally answers. "Table. Top drawer."

Erin nods and then gestures toward the table with her rifle. Charlie sighs, but he doesn't make much of a fuss. He sits down and uses his hands to lift and pull himself away from the entryway. Lift, scoot, drop, repeat. Erin keeps the gun trained on him for as long as it takes, until she decides that he's far enough back.

Erin walks to the living room as quickly as her feet will take her. By the time she gets there, her hands have started to shake. She has just enough foresight to put the safety on before she tosses the rifle onto the couch and drops to the floor.

Her tongue bumps against a welt forming on her lip. She

looks down at herself. Garfield is pretty hard to distinguish now, what with all the blood drying over him. She can't imagine what the rest of her face must look like, but she can feel even more blood drying there, and she can envision the bruises that will form on her neck. If she survives that long. The force of the two shots is still reverberating in her shoulder. The inside of her mouth tastes like blood. And there's just no time for her to tend to any of these things.

Erin sighs and finally takes a real look around. Much like the hallway, there isn't a lot to see. There's the couch, which Erin is resting against; the rocking chair she saw earlier, with Aiden's cloth left behind in the seat; and the coffee table in front of her. It has two small drawers on its front.

She leans forward and pulls open the drawer farthest from her. There's a brick of a phone inside that looks like it's from 2001, and some empty gum wrappers. Erin opens the second drawer. Boxes and boxes of bullets.

Erin takes the rifle and sets it on her lap. She finds an inscription near the end of the barrel. Made in Kalispell, Montana. *AJW* is carved into the stock beneath it, in what must be Aiden's tight, jagged lettering.

Erin opens up the chamber and grabs a handful of bullets from the drawer. She loads two of them in before she closes the chamber again and double-checks the safety.

As she does this, Charlie's voice comes in from the kitchen. "You're not gonna be able to shoot your way out of this, you know."

Erin ignores him. She's going to need at least five bullets:

one for every surviving man (Tommy, Chief Laster, the two boys mentioned earlier who she has yet to meet), and one for that thing in the woods. That's assuming she's a perfect shot, which she isn't. She'll need the spares. So she grabs two small boxes of bullets and shoves them into her pockets.

She attaches the strap to the rifle before she slings it over her head and tightens it on her shoulder. The weight of the gun is strange, but something of a comfort.

In the meantime, Charlie's pulled himself onto one of the remaining chairs. His shirt is tied off around the gunshot wound. Aside from that, and the pale hand clamped down on the makeshift bandage, he seems almost calm. He's not bleeding heavily, as he would be if Erin nicked an artery. If he doesn't do anything stupid, it's likely he'll live to get help.

Aiden, on the other hand, has already turned a strange shade of gray. Definitely dead.

"You can't shoot your way out of this," Charlie says again.

Erin turns back to him. "I heard you the first time."

"I mean you can't shoot the thing."

"Can't, or shouldn't?"

"Shooting it won't kill it."

Erin sighs. She grabs one of the chairs and pulls it out, sitting down a safe distance across from him. "Guess I'll find out. Where are they going to take Max?"

Charlie stares at her. His gaze is slightly less manic now. If she had to put a word to it, Erin would say that he looks almost *disappointed*. It's creepier.

"Where," she repeats, "are they taking Max?"

The last time she saw Max, he was driving away. Yet there isn't a bone in Erin's body that believes he's managed to get out of here. She *wants* to believe it, but she can't. Not the way tonight's been going.

"What makes you think you'd be able to find him even if I told you?" Charlie finally returns, as if he were reading her mind.

Erin frowns. "Same way I found you again," she answers flatly. "It seems to keep working out that way."

At this, Charlie smiles. "Smart girl. You've noticed it."

Her frown deepens. "Noticed what?"

"The—" Charlie fails to find the word and sighs. "It's the hardest thing to try and explain. Dennis believes it's *God's wrath*, or somethin' to that effect. He thinks all of this ties back to God somehow."

"That what you believe, too?"

He switches out the hand applying pressure to his wound, failing to mask a grimace. "I don't think it's of this Earth. Whatever that might mean to you. Don't know if that means God or if it's . . . just something with this town. Something in the woods that draws a thing like *that* out from its world and into ours."

"Your cop friend said something like that," Erin recalls. "That they built a town where a town wasn't supposed to be."

"Yeah? What else did he tell you?"

Erin shrugs. "There used to be floods. There was a girl—"

"He told you about her?"

She nods.

"He mention that was his wife?"

Oh. Erin doesn't say anything, although two scenarios quickly form in her mind.

Had Chief Laster known? Had he dragged his wife into the woods with the intent to sacrifice her to this thing, after perhaps decades of suspicion about the Beast? She imagines being in the position of his wife, imagines living through flood after flood only to be wiped out by a husband who hated her. She imagines marrying the kind of person who thinks *Maybe killing you will create a better world for me.*

There's also the possibility it was accidental. That Chief Laster *intended* to kill her because he's a violent man, but the Beast happened upon them first somewhere out in these twisted woods, and it was all one strange, horrible coincidence. A coincidence that gave him an excuse to keep killing women, because he thought he was saving the world.

"I didn't figure he would've." Charlie sighs. "Hard thing to bring up."

Erin fixes her eyes back on him. The disgust she's feeling must come through in her expression as Charlie keeps on talking.

"Anyway. Point is, once that sun goes down, once it's got a scent to follow, that's it. The woods close in. Time stops. Or, it *stretches*, maybe, I don't know. Few winters back, another girl got loose, and I swear on my daddy's grave, we spent half a day chasing her from one end of the woods to the other. That sun did not come up until after that Beast fed. And not a damn soul seemed to notice. It was like—the world didn't stop, just us. If you aren't involved, you'll never know it was there, but if you're involved . . ."

He sighs and slumps in the chair. "I don't know. But I'll tell you what I do know."

Suddenly he leans forward. Erin nervously leans back, despite the fact that they're still several feet apart.

"Blood calls it," he says, "so if you get tired of running around out there, give yourself another paper cut. It'll be easier than trying to turn that gun on yourself."

Erin just stares back at him. As if the task ahead of her weren't insurmountable enough already. Although she doesn't quite believe that she's going to be running after the literal wrath of God with nothing more than a bolt-action rifle, it's still a tall order to be going up against something that wants to *eat her*. Something that can make this night go for as long as it wants to, until it finally gets fed.

There must be something about pain that draws words out of a man. As the silence drags, Charlie starts talking again. "You know, I like you, Erin. I really do. If things were just—a little different, y'know?"

Oh, sure. If things were just a little different. If Charlie weren't actively trying to kill her and Max, and if she weren't trans, and if she hadn't just shot him in the leg.

"If you had just told me," he goes on, "we'd be having a real different conversation right now. Really. Nobody woulda laid a hand on you."

Erin doesn't understand exactly what he's trying to imply, but she knows she doesn't like it. "Because you only kill girls."

He gives her a funny look. "Because you don't need to die."

Erin *really* doesn't like this conversation. She shakes her head and looks away from him.

It's a scary feeling, to know she just has to trust that her feet will lead her in the right direction. That she can only hope that Max doesn't get himself killed first. Or that *she* doesn't get herself killed.

"Who's Cassie?" she tries again.

She imagines that if Charlie could manage it, he would lunge at her again. There's a noticeable difference in his anger when Erin says that name. Pressing her heel against that exposed nerve fascinates her. All this talk of death and torture and the world bending around the need to feed this Beast, and the only time she's seen him emotionally respond to something is when she says that name. *Cassie*.

The grind of his teeth is audible. Erin watches blood dribble between his fingers and onto the floor. The bloated silence stretches on.

"My sister," he finally answers.

Oh.

Erin takes a moment. "Younger?"

"By thirty minutes." Charlie laughs a little, in a way that Erin has before. In an effort to keep from crying. "Twins."

Tears of a sniveling coward.

"Why?" she asks.

His eyes meet hers. There might be tears welling up, but

if there are, none come falling down. He doesn't give her an answer.

Once it's apparent that he's clammed up, Erin sets her jaw. Then, with one hand keeping the rifle steady, she stands and marches out the back door. She picks up her disposable camera from the ground and reenters the house, taking the steps to the second story as quickly as she can.

27

SHE FINDS THE SKELETON in the room farthest from the stairs, on the right side of the hallway. It is sprawled on its back, staring up at the ceiling. There's a hole in its head, right between its eyes, which indicates that it was watching the person who shot them. There's nothing left of it but bones, although the room still smells of mold, something rotting in the carpet, and that is when Erin finally realizes that's the smell permeating the whole floor—rot.

It's hard to identify a skeleton, even harder to gender one, although Erin has to assume that this is what happens to the men who are unlucky enough to get caught in this warpath. They're killed—without prejudice, without torture, just shot cleanly in the head—and left up here to decompose. The other rooms she checks, though empty, all share the smell of decay.

Erin catches her breath in the hallway. Her face itches where the blood has begun to dry.

Looking out through the window, she can see the sky, still

empty besides the moon. Like somebody upstairs turned off the lights. Nobody home. She thinks about what Charlie said: that time *stretches* here, until the Beast is fed, and then it seems to just snap back into place. Time stretches, the bugs go quiet, the stars go out, and with every death, the rot extends farther and farther out from the house.

Once Erin can breathe again, she walks into the room with the bare bed frame and rips the drawer of wallets out from the dresser. She turns it over and dumps everything onto the floor. There's a part of her brain that's just screaming at her to grab them all and run for the hills.

Except she can't carry them all with her. Probably couldn't even manage half of them.

Erin checks the top of her camera. The little number next to the shutter reads *20*. It'd be stupid to waste them all here, but it'd be worse to use none of them. So, as quickly as she can, she clumps the driver's licenses and passports together and uses half of her remaining photos to catalog the girls who came before her. It's the least she can do. She can only hope that when it's time to develop this film, half of these names and faces will still be legible.

When she goes back downstairs, Charlie remains seated at the table. Erin nearly passes right by him, but something makes her linger in the entryway.

"Anything else I should know about that thing?" she asks.

Charlie looks up at her. A humorless smile tugs at his mouth. "If it sees you, run."

So, nothing she didn't already assume. No matter who the

right sacrifice is, that thing in the woods is still after them. After *her*.

Erin nods.

As she turns to leave, Charlie speaks again. "Can I ask why you don't just kill me?"

Erin stops and looks at him. For a moment, she seriously considers the question.

She can come up with a few different answers. The guilt of killing Aiden is already heavy in her chest, even though she knows one of them *had* to die in that situation. The power of survival she felt in the moment hasn't lasted. There'd be nothing brave about shooting a guy who's just sitting there.

And, even though she knows it's an act, in much the same way that poison dart frogs lure in their prey with their pretty colors, he's shown her flashes of kindness. Even if it was only false kindness. It's a stupid thing to rationalize her hesitation with, but that's what she's got.

"Don't feel like wasting the bullet" is the answer she gives him before she walks back into the living room and out through the front door. Out into the night that only seems to grow darker and darker as time crawls on.

28

MAX DRIVES FOR FIVE MINUTES before he stops.

Despite the caterwaul that keeps building up in his throat, he never starts crying again. That surprises him. Although he isn't feeling too much of anything, really, beyond the need to *go*. All the while, the car strains to keep itself from rattling to pieces. Wind pours in through the broken back window. The engine is a pair of pneumatic lungs: alive, but struggling for breath.

Eventually, Max takes his foot off the gas. The car continues forward for a bit before it finally slows to an imperceptible crawl. Only then does Max brake and put the car into park. Then he sits there.

The first coherent thought that comes to his mind is this: he doesn't know how to live if not constantly on his guard. He doesn't know how to move around a house without cringing at the sound of floorboards creaking underfoot. He doesn't know how to tame a fire that's been burning out of control since before he knew how to speak of it.

Max has been burning bridges practically since he was old enough to understand the concept. He doesn't know if he's ever been anything but *reactive*. It was simple: he didn't get hurt if people weren't around to hurt him. Bite the hand that's stupid enough to reach out, and people stop reaching out. It's gotten him this far. He's managed to leave an entire life behind him; he is finally almost stringless.

Max stares at the road ahead. He superimposes the jagged California skyline over the mostly flat smattering of rural shrubbery. He imagines the light pollution burning out all of the stars, the incessant sound of big-city traffic. He is so close he can taste the salt air on his tongue. But instead of putting the car back into drive and gunning it, he just sits there.

The lingering string still wrapped around his ankle is Erin. Maybe the only person who's gotten a real good look at whatever evil, ugly little monster lives at the center of Max and hasn't recoiled with disgust. It's always felt like a cruel joke. She's literally everything that Max wants to be and can't achieve. A better man, a better woman, better at being trans, better at *everything*.

None of that's her fault; half of that isn't even really accurate. Logically, he *knows* this. Erin can't control Max's mom, or Brian, or their stupid little high school, or the broken state of health care for thousands of other miserable trans kids just like him. Max knows he isn't special. He's seen himself posted across a dozen different websites, in hundreds of message boards, from kids who will asphyxiate in the bodies they are locked inside of. Erin is not responsible for the hundreds of years of systemic oppression that has led them to this moment.

But Erin was right there. Tangible. It was easier than constantly being angry at a bunch of abstract institutions and untouchable figures who seemed to multiply by the hour. Erin was right there, completely oblivious to the salt she was grinding into his wounds. Even now, she buys postcards to send home, which flies in the whole face of *everything* he thought they agreed upon. She knows *far* too much about the kind of person Max is, and yet—

Max takes a deep breath and sinks into his seat.

And yet Erin agreed to do this with him. She still worried about him. Cared about him. Left him with a weapon and told him to *go*.

It had really seemed perfectly logical back when he broke up with her. He just wanted to stop feeling so miserable and hopeless every time he looked at Erin. The solution should have been to stop keeping her company. Stop looking at her, stop comparing his transness to hers.

But in this plan's execution, it had been like trying to rip fishhooks out of his skin. Erin had already embedded herself in so much of Max's life—his thoughts, his music, even the way he dressed—that he just kept losing chunks of himself the more he tried to rid himself of her. He kept ripping until he was little more than a constant, open wound, and even now he still feels tethered to her. He can feel the wire cutting into his skin.

Max wonders where the proverbial scissors are in this metaphor; what's he missing that makes him unable to cut this final string and just *go*?

He rubs his eyes, grinding his knuckles into the bone of his brow as if he were going to twist the answer out of his skull. Is it still a haunting when the ghost isn't dead and when Max has explicitly asked her to come along? Why did he ask her to do this if he was just going to drive away from her?

He looks over at the empty seat to his right. That stupid homecoming photo still hangs in the sunshade. He is alone, in an empty car, on an empty road. Emotions cannibalize themselves in the back of his throat, grief and anger consuming each other.

Max prays that he isn't stuck like this forever. He hopes that whatever's inside of him hasn't stewed for too long and warped into something unfixable. He hopes because for whatever reason, Erin hasn't cut the string yet, either.

And he's just driven away from her.

What are you doing, Max?

Max, suddenly crawling with horrible nervous energy all the way down to the bone, pulls his jacket off and throws it into the back. He looks down at his chest—

Nope. Binder stays on.

He puts the car into reverse and slams the gas. The car jerks and shudders with the sharp change in direction, but it whips around nevertheless. Back into drive, straighten the wheel, gun it. He takes off in the direction he was just driving away from.

Max doesn't want to arrive in California alone. He does not want to become a man alone. As badly as he wants this manhood, he cannot stomach the idea of choosing this loneliness again. Even if he can't make things right with Erin, he can do *something*. He can make the effort. He can go back for her. He can apologize for the last several years of being a total prick, and then they can go and beat sparks off a bunch of transphobic hicks. Because, Jesus, he's gotta make up for this somehow. For the fact that he's done this to them. If he's lucky, maybe he can reach out in time to catch Erin's hand before it's gone forever, and he can figure out all the rest later.

29

ERIN ATTEMPTS TO FOLLOW the dirt road back to the highway. But she has barely put the house behind her when the beaten path suddenly peters out, overgrown with weeds and dead brush until there is no tangible way forward. Charlie's words, fresh on her mind, do nothing but make her miserable. The world is literally conspiring against her.

She keeps walking, listening for a road she knows she's not going to be able to hear. There hasn't been a sign of real life in hours. Her plans are little more than trying and hoping and wishing, which are not exactly solid means of survival. It doesn't make her feel great about her chances.

Erin sighs and rubs her eyes. The rifle hangs from one shoulder, and she's tied the camera's wrist strap around her belt loop. She tries to focus on what is certain.

Certainty: the monster eats girls.

Whether Erin qualifies isn't clear, but safe to say she's in danger either way.

Certainty: she is trapped in this place, at this time, for the foreseeable future.

She doesn't know if there's a way to break out of this that doesn't involve dying. She doesn't know how to even approach the subject of escape now.

Certainty: she has a weapon.

She doesn't know how effective it will be.

She doesn't even know if Max is still alive.

The thought makes Erin suddenly, deeply nauseous. She tries to force it out of her mind but it clings to her like Saran Wrap. He *has* to be alive.

But does she know that for a fact? No. That terrifies her.

Even on the rest of that list of certainties, there's a whole lot of *but*s and addendums because she just *doesn't know*. She has so many questions, needs so many answers, and it's unlikely she'll get any of them. There's a lump in her chest, pressure that isn't from any physical injury. It's something deeper.

Erin finally stops and sits down, her back against what she's pretty sure is a beech tree. It's all starting to blur together out here. She looks down at her hands, closely, for the first time. It's hard to discern color in the moonlight, but her palms are a muddy hue, somewhere between red and brown.

She killed somebody.

She knows how this would look written out on paper: a guy tried to strangle her, and she stabbed him until he let her go. It's not *murder* so much as *self-defense*, but—she still killed somebody. The weight of this presses on her and presses on her until she realizes she's hyperventilating. Her heart is pounding at the back of her mouth, as if it were trying to escape her body. It is the knowledge that she is capable of such a thing, and it is the knowledge that she's going to have to do it again.

If she could get out of this without killing anyone else, she would. She wants to. She would rather leave them all as she left Charlie, wounded but alive. Like Max said: leave them for someone else, *not our problem*.

But this *is* their problem. Even if by some miracle Erin can find a way to set time back into motion, these men aren't just going to let them go. She told Charlie they were going to California. They can't leave these men behind, not to keep coming after her and Max and not to begin anew with some other girl.

Out in the distance, that *thing* starts screaming again.

Erin winces and puts her hands over her ears. The sound cuts through her like ice, a wail that just keeps pitching up until it might as well be a shrieking whistle. It only lasts a couple of seconds before it cuts out again, but Erin remains curled up on herself, hands on her ears and eyes squeezed shut.

Slowly, Erin pushes her hands back and curls them, pulling at fistfuls of hair until the little bursts of pain bring her back down to earth. She has half a mind to just start screaming back. If memory serves, that's what you're supposed to do with bears: make yourself big and scream and convince them that you are too much trouble to eat. Erin wants to scream just for the relief of it. She is tired of being so afraid of this. Of everything. Trapped in a purgatory, faced with questions she cannot answer and people she cannot save.

She takes a deep breath and looks up.

At first, it's quiet. That type of total silence that fills the space within an idling car or an empty classroom. Silence that shouldn't exist in a forest, no matter how large. Then the smell comes wafting in, and Erin knows she's not alone before she finds the two scorching aureolin lights burning between the trees.

Erin freezes. It isn't a gentle glow; it's like fire. Brighter than a flashlight. Her stomach falls into her feet.

As she stares at it—as it stares at her—she slowly pulls the rifle into her arms. There's a distant voice in her head that tells her she's almost guaranteed to miss if she tries shooting it. But she might not get another chance at this. She's taking the first shot while she can.

Erin sits up straighter and squints, pulling the bolt out and only looking away long enough to check her rounds.

For a moment, she hesitates. *Bad idea.*

Then she pushes the bolt back in with an audible *kuh-clack*.

As soon as she does, a third light expands from below the Beast's two eyes. Just as Erin realizes that's its *mouth,* that scream pierces the space between them.

If not for the strap, Erin would've dropped the gun. She's brainless with fear when she scrambles to her feet and starts running, rifle and camera swinging from her waist like dumbbells. She doesn't make it more than a couple of feet before the weight makes her stumble and she falls right back down again.

She whips around, and, for the first time, beholds the Beast in its unobstructed entirety.

Its eyes, far and away the most striking part of it, appear to be floating amid its seemingly shapeless body. It towers above her, with one haggard limb propping its body up against the tree. Its hand is *almost* a paw. It's a thick, clumpy thing, but its fingers have an almost human curl to them, wrapped around the side of the trunk. It's hard to distinguish the Beast from the darkness around it until its eyes suddenly drop, and the ground *thunk*s with the weight of its front limbs planting back on the ground. Erin can hear the thud of saliva dripping to the earth. Her whole body suddenly feels numb.

If she were to try and bring the gun into her hands, she would be dead before getting her finger anywhere near the trigger. Some stupid part of her still wants to go for it. At least she would go out *trying* to protect herself.

But instead, Erin pushes herself backward, blindly crawling away until her back suddenly bumps into the base of another oak. And then she's frozen, watching those long, thick legs stalking closer to her.

The hopelessness that hits her is overwhelming. What chance did she *ever* have? The woods have warped around her, trapping her inside a maze with no rules and no clear exit point. The woods have been trapping them all day, breaking their car down piece by piece. Breaking *them* down piece by piece, exactly for this purpose.

She thought the only way out was through, but *through* immediately proved itself to be just as impossible as everything else they tried. Running has failed them every time, in every direction.

Charlie is going to get his rifle back without a single shot fired.

The Beast takes a slow, almost contemplative step closer, and Erin shuts her eyes.

She remembers, distantly, that if the screaming thing fails, you're supposed to play dead in the event of a bear attack. Her brain does not offer up any advice for how to survive *this thing*.

Erin shuts her eyes tighter when the pad of footsteps comes down even closer. Its paws crunch against the dead leaves, and Erin realizes just how close it is when she can feel the heat radiating from its belly. It's like being sat in front of an incinerator.

She feels a huff of breath against her face, and a sob wrenches itself from her throat. If Erin opened her eyes now, the last thing she would see is a void of death. A black hole of serrated edges to separate her face from her skull with the ease of peeling an orange. She remembers how Chief Laster described that myth, the girls who would meet their fate in these woods. There would be no eyes for the birds to pick at; those would be the first things to be punctured.

Another huff of air, hot and thick, and Erin flinches violently. The creature's breath reeks of something rotten. Perhaps the source of that pervasive smell. How many bodies are preserved in chunks between those teeth?

The trunk crunches, on either side of her head, with the weight of something pressing against it.

She thinks frantically of Max. She hopes he—

Suddenly, something large and *wet* smacks Erin in the face. It's a hot, disgusting feeling, and she would scream if it didn't mean opening her mouth. For a second, Erin thinks: *that's it.*
That's it. You're dead.
Except. She isn't.
Erin sits there for a minute, waiting to hear the sound of her own skull splintering. For the rush of sudden and unbearable pain. But nothing comes.
The Beast hasn't left. She can still feel the heat of it, standing over her, but it is just standing there. It has not ripped her head off.
Erin slowly brings her hands up and wipes away at the substance clinging to her face like warm, congealing snot. She takes a gasping breath, heaving like she's just survived something. Like she's not still in the mouth of the Beast.
After a moment, the sound of her own breathing suddenly amplifies. When Erin opens her eyes, she is staring the Beast in the face. There is no longer any glowing, open mouth; the jaw hanging open before her is as black as the rest of it. But she realizes that the sound is coming from this thing.
It is mirroring her exactly, half-sobbing alongside her.
Then, a secondary thought: it licked her.
Erin swallows and wipes off her face again, and finds herself unable to look away. The Beast stares back at her. As if it is just as curious about her as she is about it.
It does not look human. Up so close, Erin would say this with certainty. There is barely *a face*, let alone anything identifiably human about it. But she struggles to come up with

any other creature against which to compare it. Wolflike, perhaps, in its movement. Bearlike in its height and the way it goes from standing on two limbs to four. But wolves and bears probably don't warp in and out of space and time, here one second and gone the next.

Erin can acknowledge she might be wrong about that. She's not an expert.

The most humanity Erin can assign to this creature comes through its eyes. There are no pupils, no irises, just a blazing yellow heat through which there are no emotions. But they're human-shaped. Its eyes gaze upon her, round and down-turned, and creased with focus. It doesn't have a noticeable nose. Erin doesn't know how it's breathing. Even its mouth is hard to parse out. One moment, there is blackness, and the next there is just *teeth*.

"Okay," Erin breathes. "I'm gonna get up now. Nice and slow."

She puts her hands on her knees. The Beast brings its arms down, detaching from the tree trunk with an audible *crack*. A moment later, loose leaves rain down from above.

"Cool. Okay. Just gonna get up." She nods to herself, then pauses. "Don't know why I'm narrating this to you. Please don't start talking."

Erin pushes herself to her feet. The Beast watches her, laser-focused but not hostile. She thinks. She hopes.

Erin moves the rifle to her other shoulder. It's not until she makes a too-quick turn to keep walking that she hears its breathing shift from near-silent to an audible *growl*.

Her knees lock and she freezes. Waits to feel the full weight of its claws tearing into her back. But then the seconds tick uneventfully by, and the growl tapers off into nothing, and Erin tells herself she needs to calm down a little. She lets herself breathe and looks back.

The Beast stalks around, almost brushing against her as it passes by. Without thinking, Erin reaches a hand out and lets her fingertips drag against its skin. Or, to her surprise, fur. It's *hot*. Like she were reaching into the air immediately above a lit candle. Hot, but not all that painful to touch. Erin flinches her hand away, nevertheless, as if it might still burn her.

The Beast circles around the tree, jarringly fluid despite the clear weight of each step. It titters. The sound is like loose teeth clacking against a tabletop. Then it starts to walk away. Off in a new direction. Erin *thinks* it's new, at least; hard to tell which is where anymore.

Erin remains still. She could always run. Or sling the gun into her arms and take her best shot. There's a chance that she gets lucky and ends this whole thing right here, right now. Or she can do the thing least likely to end in her demise.

She adjusts the rifle where it rests between her shoulder blades and tries to breathe with some normality. Her heart is still beating too fast, too erratically. Somehow, this thing *not* trying to eat her is the hardest pill to swallow, in a night of very large, unswallowable pills. Is there a reason it's not trying to kill her? Was it *ever* trying to kill her?

Is this confirmation of some weird transmisogynistic logic within nature? Maybe. That would explain why her relief at still being alive is tinged with something much less pleasant. But it also might be something else. Something Erin has yet to crack. Charlie might know a whole lot, but he also seems to think that this thing is an extension of God.

The Beast stops and looks at her. Not too far away, and yet it's already back to being only eyes floating in the dark. Beacons. Erin finds herself walking after it.

They must be an odd sight. It feels even stranger to be walking alongside this creature as if it were any other animal. But the Beast *hasn't killed her*. So, one foot in front of the other. For now. If she suddenly has the time to formulate a plan stronger than *shoot* or *run* she will utilize it. But until then, she might just tentatively consider herself safe.

As she walks, narrowly dodging the roots and rocks underfoot, she has a thought that makes her start to laugh: Max is going to be so pissed that she got to see a cryptid before he did.

30

MAX DIDN'T THINK HE WOULD have to go far before finding Erin again. After all, she's *walking*. He also left his bumper in the middle of the road, like a progress marker. It's a straight road: nowhere to get off and nowhere to get on. But after Max has been speeding down the highway for a good while, he realizes something is wrong. Something he can't put words to.

His right headlight starts to flicker. Max takes the cue to finally slow to a hair below sixty. He can still see the road, but he's had enough surprises out here to make him immediately anxious.

Actually, driving fast is probably a really stupid thing to be doing. He drops to forty.

He scans the trees. He looks for a flash of blond, a hint of that horrible purple T-shirt standing out in the dark. But he never even passes his own bumper. The curves of the road feel unfamiliar. These woods aren't . . . right.

A similar thought briefly crossed his mind earlier, but

he didn't give it much consideration. He was far more concerned with getting to safety than anything else. He had just been running, and walking, and running some more, his legs throbbing the whole time. He'd been almost certain he would never even see Erin or the Impala again, and that he'd end up walking to some small, unincorporated township of thirteen and a half people and wind up clawing his way to California from there.

And yet he found the Impala. And Erin. As if the woods just opened up and placed him there, without rhyme and without reason.

He knows that's impossible. Obviously. Max found Erin through blind luck he'll never be able to replicate. But as he drives on and still fails to recognize any of his surroundings, he can't help but wonder if it really was something more than that.

Max wonders how crazy it is that he's even considering it. If the woods are alive, he should just pull over and give up, right? Because how is he supposed to fight *that*?

The radio, which has been silent this whole time, suddenly flickers to life.

Max instinctively slams on the brakes. The car skids to a stop and the ache in his neck quickly flares back to life. It takes a moment to register that the sound of music is not an attack. Max frowns, until he recognizes the tune.

Boys don't cry

Great. So if the woods are alive, they also have a really lame sense of humor.

Max sighs, waiting until he's caught his breath before he

puts his foot back on the gas. He doesn't turn the radio off. He doesn't care. If Robert Smith wants to score the drive so badly, let him.

I would tell you that I loved you
If I thought that you would stay

Up ahead, the road swells over a hill. At the crest, reflective traffic cones are lined in a row, blocking the way. Absolutely none of this was here before. The car slows to a crawl as Max curls his fingers tightly around the wheel.

It's that giant maroon truck parked in front of the cones. A panicked numbness creeps in through the tips of his fingers. It's the same feeling that paralyzed him before with Chief Laster.

Max glances down at the radio. The clock was broken at some point, little dots and dashes blinking in and out sporadically. Not only does he not know *where* he is, *when* is also a bit of a fuzzy question, too.

For a moment, he considers flooring it. He figures he could at least try to take them out completely, if not do some significant damage. But then he does some math, sizes up his sedan against this jacked-up white-trash truck, and decides there are plenty of less painful ways to kill himself.

So instead, he takes the knife from the empty passenger seat where he tossed it and tucks it between his thigh and the seat. The angle has the handle sticking out, just enough that he can grab it at a moment's notice. He puts his foot on the gas and keeps driving, right up to the top of the hill. He comes to a stop just a few feet away from the truck's front bumper.

Boys don't cry

Star-Spangled Wifebeater and Overalls stare down at him from inside the cab. Max stares back. He's sure it would be easy and painless to be a good little human sacrifice and get out of the car of his own volition. It would also not nearly be as much fun.

Max raises his hand in the air so they can see it before he presses down the button that locks the doors. He then sits back and crosses his arms over his chest.

The guy in the wifebeater says something to his buddy, then gets out of the truck and meanders over to Max's window. He taps against the glass with his knuckle. Max quietly rolls the window down and looks up at him, innocent as the day he was born.

If Star-Spangled were smart, he'd punch or grab Max the second he became exposed. That's what Max would do, if the tables were turned. But the man just leans against the door, and his smile drips with malice. There's already a bruise on his face.

"You want ice for that?" Max asks conversationally.

Star-Spangled's expression doesn't change. He brings a hand up to the window's edge and reveals his clunky little handgun again. It looks oddly out of place here, in his grasp. The fear that pangs in Max's ribs is hollow, although some of that may be just how little he takes this guy seriously.

"Sweetheart," Star-Spangled begins, raising the gun, "if

it were up to me, you'd be full of so many holes, whatever you got between your legs would be the least of your problems."

Max's jaw clenches. Star-Spangled seems to notice, and his grin curls at the ends. His thumb fiddles with the hammer, like he's debating whether he should just shoot Max anyway.

But then he shrugs. "Well, it's not up to me, but if you try anything cute again, I'm allowed to do just about anything *but* kill you. So be a good girl and come out nice and slow."

Self-restraint has never come naturally to Max. He has to think through every muscle that goes into his tight, twitchy smile while white-hot fire starts to roar behind his ears. The safety pin in his grenade is the element of surprise. He can't blow it prematurely.

"I'm gonna take my seat belt off, all right?" Max shifts his voice up a little.

In his head, he sounds so unbelievably fake. A prepubescent boy's idea of how a girl is supposed to talk. But whether this faux girlishness is off-putting to Star-Spangled or not isn't apparent. He just silently nods his approval. Max doesn't break eye contact with him, crossing his hand over his body. On his way to the buckle, his fingers graze the handle of the knife, cold and unyielding.

He presses the buckle and pulls the seat belt off with his other hand.

"You wanna open the door, or you want me to do it?" Max asks.

Star-Spangled has to think about it for a second. Max

almost smiles. Which option puts him at the greatest risk of having something thrown at his face again?

"Turn the car off first," he answers.

Max pulls the keys from the ignition. The radio cuts out. Goodbye, Robert.

"Hand 'em over."

Max looks up at Star-Spangled again, and pretends to think about it. Just to be a dick. He can feel the cold air on the back of his neck where he's been sweating. He moves the keys to his left hand and turns slightly, holding them out for the man to take. His right hand falls down to his side, down to the handle. His heart is seconds from bursting through his rib cage.

As soon as Star-Spangled reaches for the keys, Max pulls the pin. Knife in his fist, he swings. He can feel the blade puncturing the skin. It connects with the man's cheek with a thick, wet *pop*. It sounds almost like a slap.

It's horrible, and there's not even a moment for Max to be perversely giddy about it. He stabs him, and then the gun goes off.

It misses, because Star-Spangled is thrown into a panic by the knife suddenly in his cheek, but the gun still goes off right next to Max's face. It's an explosion of heat. For a moment, Max thinks maybe he *was* shot. But the burning feeling quickly recedes, even when the sharp ringing in his ears does not.

The man's mouth is moving. Max isn't waiting around to figure out what he's saying.

He pulls his arm back, before the guy can take a real shot at him, and stabs down. He misses the intersection of the neck and shoulder he's aiming for, but he still hits his shoulder, and that's better than nothing. Max rips the knife out and scrambles for the passenger door.

The plan, loosely, is to try and lose them in the woods. However, he fails to consider that he's not playing cat and mouse with just one guy. Max has barely gotten through the door when Overalls tackles him from the side like a linebacker. They're both on the ground before his brain even registers the impact.

By some miracle, he doesn't stab himself. But that might only be because the knife goes clattering across the asphalt several feet away.

Max still tries to scramble for it. He can visualize the scene in his head, even as it plays out: his arms straining for the handle he has no chance of reaching, just as Overalls grabs him by the hair and drags him back. It's over in a matter of seconds. Max still struggles a little, but he knows his window of opportunity is shut.

"Colton? You good, man?" Overalls stops at the hood of the car, still holding Max by the roots of his hair.

Max can't see Colton, but he can hear the man shout back something unintelligible. And distinctly *wet*.

Max starts to laugh. The sound just bubbles up in his throat and spills out. A hysterical, childish giggle. It would be even funnier if the danger weren't so real, if he weren't grabbing at Overalls's hand and trying to loosen his grip.

"Is she *laughing*?" Colton's incredulous voice gets closer as he stomps over.

Max starts laughing even harder.

The image comes to his mind easily. This guy, this *asshole*, walking around with the scar that's going to form on his cheek, puckered and horrible-looking. He won't be able to hide it. Colton is going to spend the whole rest of his life with Max carved into his face. Even if nobody else ever knows that, *he* is going to know.

Max stops laughing when Colton grabs him by the collar and punches him, so hard that it feels like his head should be spinning. The ringing in his ears goes up to full intensity again. Nausea rises up into his throat.

"We should just kill her now." Colton's voice is far away and fuzzy, like he's coming through on a bad connection.

Colton suddenly lets him go. Max takes the opportunity to sink to the ground, his back to the front bumper of the Impala, hand to his jaw. He realizes that Overalls must've pulled Colton off him.

"Are you that goddamn stupid?" Overalls hisses.

"What does it even matter? It's gonna eat her alive or dead, and I'm sick of—"

"It *won't* eat her, dead or alive, 'cause it don't eat what it don't kill!"

As they argue, Max's eyes turn again to the trees. Very slowly, he puts his hands onto the ground. He starts to crawl forward.

Overalls suddenly brings his foot down on Max's hand. He

puts his entire weight onto it, pinning Max to the spot. Max doesn't scream, though he does make a squeak of pain that he's not too proud of.

"That another one of his bullshit rules?" Colton asks, like Max isn't even there.

Overalls shifts his weight, grinds his heel down, and Max has to start breathing through his mouth. "You know what, man? When you've been doin' this as long as Dennis has, *you* can make the rules. Or maybe I'll take you serious when you don't get stabbed by a *girl*."

Colton shoves him, and Max pulls his hand into his chest before Overalls can put his foot down again. He rolls onto his back and tries to catch his breath. Neither man seems to care. He's not going anywhere.

Max looks down at his arm. His hand is already turning red, around splotches of white where the blood has yet to return. A few inches farther down, along his forearm, his eyes catch on the strip of raised scar tissue. Its ache is a phantom one, and yet Max swears he can feel a twinge of pain pulse throughout the nerves.

"I'm trying here! You're supposed to be teaching me all this shit!"

"Okay, first rule: don't let them stab you in the face!"

Max starts to laugh again. When he opens his eyes, both men are staring down at him; Colton seems slightly more baffled, and Overalls looks like he wants to kill them both.

"Is this your first time doing this?" Max asks, once he can

catch his breath. "Oh my God, that's so cute. I thought you were both just *really* stupid."

As he starts to laugh again at the absurdity of this—not just the fact that he's being attacked by a bunch of idiots, but *newbies* at that—Colton rears back and kicks him in the ribs. Max stops laughing and starts wheezing.

"Are they always this irritating?" Colton asks.

"No," Overalls answers, "usually it's just a whole lotta screaming."

Max presses his forehead into the road and focuses on breathing. Before he can start to worry about things like *what happens next*, he opens his eyes and watches as a new pair of headlights joins them on the hill. He doesn't bother to sit up. He just waits for the sound of pebbles crunching underfoot to get closer until the boots come to a stop beside his head.

Max hopes he never sees another cowboy hat in his life.

"What in the *world*," Chief Laster sighs, "happened to your face?"

Max breathlessly grins.

Overalls grabs Max by the collar and yanks him to his feet. He locks his arms around Max's, like a reverse backpack. Max resists the urge to try and struggle. He doesn't want to know what it feels like to have his shoulder ripped from its socket.

"You know, if we didn't have to kill her, I think she'd be pretty fun to keep around," Overalls says, like that's supposed to be a compliment.

His voice is right in Max's ear, which makes him grimace.

He tries to twist away, and Overalls just tightens his hold on him. His chainsaw laugh revs into Max's brain. To the side, Colton mutters something about his friend being a "total dickweed."

Chief Laster sighs and looks at Max in a way that tells him he's just as flabbergasted with the Wet Bandits as Max is. "Thank you for your opinion, Jesse. I'm glad you were able to do *one thing* right tonight."

Max can't see Jesse's face, but the man has enough of a handle not to snap the way Colton so easily does. The giddiness drains out of his voice. "Right, boss. Sorry it took so long."

Jesse abruptly shoves Max forward into Chief Laster, and something ignites under Max's skin. It feels like he's on fire. For all his laughing, he can't stand to be touched by this man again.

He thrashes against the cop's grip, as if he has any chance of brute-forcing his way out of it. Chief Laster grumbles something under his breath before he shoves Max up against the side of the Impala. The handcuffs that go around his wrists aren't surprising, but they send a cold chill across Max's skin.

"My face *hurts*, man," Colton whines, still pacing on the other side of the car. "I need stitches!"

"You need to go take care of the blond," Chief Laster answers. "And when that's done, I will stitch you up myself."

"What if I bleed out!?"

"You won't!" Chief Laster snaps, and yanks Max off the car and nearly off his feet.

Apparently, there's been a *fourth* guy here this whole time, and Max only figures this out when Chief Laster abruptly shoves him into the man. Max cranes his head to get a look, but the man seems little more than another pair of hands with a mullet attached. He's got enough of a grip that Max can't immediately wriggle out of it, either.

"Tommy, put her in the car." Chief Laster then gestures to Jesse and Colton. "And you two: find the blond. Kill it. No more screwups. We should've been done with this hours ago."

Tommy starts to drag him back, but Max digs his heels in. "Hey, Colton!" Max yells.

All three men turn to look at him.

Max grins, adrenaline-crazed. "We're gonna put so many holes in you, that shit on your face'll be the *least* of your problems!"

If Jesse and Chief Laster weren't there to intercept Colton as he surged forward, that probably would've been the last thing Max ever said.

"Real mature," Tommy mutters, just loud enough for him to hear.

Max doesn't respond. As Tommy drags him toward the cruiser, his gaze remains fixed on Chief Laster. He watches the cop start talking to the two knuckleheads. He can't hear any of it, right up until the end, when Chief Laster shouts something, and then Jesse whoops and slaps Colton on the back, and then they're running back to their truck like the smallest, dumbest lynch mob ever conceived.

Goofy as it is, the sound of the engine roaring and revving

makes something pull at Max's stomach. But they have guns and trucks and brute strength. Last he saw, Erin had a disposable camera. It's a rigged fight.

There's barely a chance to duck his head before Tommy shoves him into the back of the car, familiar territory now. In the couple of seconds where he's alone, he lies back across the seats and shuts his eyes. He should maybe be screaming, or crying, but his tank is running on empty. His hand is still throbbing. He just wants to catch his breath.

Sure, gun to his head, he'll probably find the strength to freak out when it matters. But until then, it's all familiar to the point of banality.

Max keeps his eyes shut as both men enter the car. He feels the car turn and drive away from the roadblock. He strains ever so slightly against the handcuffs, until he can feel the burn of breaking skin, and until he doesn't have the strength to shake anymore.

31

THE BEAST DISAPPEARS AGAIN WHEN Erin catches sight of the highway.

Already, the novelty of that has started to wear pretty thin. Erin sighs and trudges up to the roadside and takes a real look around. Once again, she's alone and directionless. Only able to *hope* she's where she's supposed to be.

She flips a mental coin—*tails*—and continues to her right. Not on the road, but beside it, close enough that she can hide if she needs to. Close enough that she can flag down a car, should the universe decide to give her one.

She wonders what that must be like: driving through the dead of night and hitting the boundary line of this time stretch. Because there *must* be boundary lines. There must be a place where the edge of the untouched world meets this endless night. If she and Max drove through here, would they just pop out on the other side, none the wiser?

That must be the case. Otherwise, people would be

flocking to this place in droves, trying to figure out the Bermuda Triangle of the rural American South. The Kentucky Triangle.

Erin looks down at herself. She wonders who in their right mind would even stop for her, looking the way she does now. Monster drool has joined with the blood on her shirt and jeans, and even the camera is starting to pick up a few stains of its own. Her shoes are tight, still damp after her tumble into the river.

The feeling of lingering spit on her skin makes her grimace. She wrinkles her face in an attempt to break up the hardening bits, and glances back every couple of seconds like clockwork. Every time, no Beast and no car.

Running would be faster, but Erin only walks. Whatever the Beast is, it doesn't seem to like sudden movement.

A steady breeze comes rumbling through the trees. Goose bumps rise up Erin's arms. Paranoia nags at the back of her mind, and it's harder and harder to have to constantly knock those thoughts away. The dark terrifies her. Not for its own sake, but for whatever might come out of it next. What it might still hold.

Suddenly, Erin stops, looking down at her feet. There's light. Fast approaching.

She looks up. In the far distance, she can see a pair of headlights cutting through the inky blackness of night. For a very brief moment, her heart jumps. But then the lights get closer, and she realizes that it is not the Impala.

The sight becomes simultaneously relieving and terrifying. It's a new car, one she hasn't seen before, and yet she knows that it can't possibly be anyone coming to help.

She remains still as the truck cruises closer. It's not the dirty white one that Aiden was driving. This one is maroon, and runs with an audible rumble. Its wheels are raised, elevating it easily another foot into the air.

It's apparent when the driver finally notices her. The truck slows, and it drifts so that it's coming down the middle of the road. Erin, distantly, thinks that now should be the moment to move. Or, at least, to be ready to do so. Surely there's no way this is someone who will help her.

But something weighs her down, sluggish and uncertain, and she just watches it come.

The sound of the truck's acceleration is first. Then the vehicle suddenly veers toward her, and finally, Erin's brain kicks into gear.

Run.

Erin throws herself toward the tree line and feels the breeze of several thousand pounds of metal as it rips through the dirt where she was just standing. She hits the ground hard, hands and knees burning from the impact, but her adrenaline has her on her feet again in a matter of seconds.

The truck's engine roars as it swerves back onto the road, tires spitting out dirt and rocks behind it. Trying to think rationally and run for her life aren't the easiest things to manage simultaneously, but Erin tries as she hurries onto the road and sprints in the opposite direction. The last thing she wants is for this to turn into a foot chase through the trees. She doesn't trust these woods as far as she can see into them.

She looks back over her shoulder and watches as the truck curves wide. Coming back.

Erin doesn't realize she's shaking until she stops, turns, and pulls the rifle into her hands. Whether it's nerves or just good, simple fear doesn't especially matter. It only matters insofar as it makes readying the gun take longer, and she doesn't have all the time in the world to begin with.

She flicks the safety off. A few hundred feet out, the truck fully spins around, and then stops. The bolt almost slips in Erin's sweaty hands when she pulls it back to check the rounds. Her heart twists in her stomach. She can't afford to keep scaring herself and messing up.

The truck revs. Erin looks up.

It revs again, but the truck doesn't move. They're just taunting her.

Erin stops for a moment. The cuts on her hands are bleeding again, but the world has narrowed down to what she sees in front of her: the rifle, and the truck. The fear melts into something angrier, desperate but grounded. Like when Aiden's hands were around her throat. She does not have options outside of survival or death.

Erin forces herself to take a deep breath, feels it in her lungs before she pushes the bolt back into place.

The tires spin, squeal, and then jolt the truck forward. It's as close to a starter pistol as they'll get. Erin hefts the butt of the gun to her shoulder and fires.

It's impossible to tell where the bullet goes, only that it doesn't change the trajectory of the truck hurtling toward her. Erin cycles the bolt, nudges the butt away from the bruise forming on her shoulder, and fires again.

This time, the vehicle swerves but doesn't slow. Three rounds left.

Erin cycles the bolt. Fires. A headlight goes out.

Even as she reloads for the third time, her mind's eye grabs at details, the specifics of which she will only be able to recall later: namely, the outline of the driver. The glint of what might be blond hair.

There's a target. Erin exhales, adjusts, and squeezes the trigger.

This time, the truck snaps to the side. Not enough to send it off course. But enough that Erin almost forgets she's staring down a pickup coming *right at her.*

Just as Erin starts to backpedal—it will not be fast enough, it will not save her—the truck suddenly rips diagonally across the road, still coming close enough that it sends Erin's stomach lurching. She continues to take a few delayed steps backward, even after it's missed her. Just like that, it's over.

Erin flinches at the sound of the front bumper crunching against the tree that it collides with. A clump of leaves is knocked loose with the impact and is still falling when a few branches also rain down onto the roof of the truck. Even after that, though, it's not a silent aftermath. She can hear the creak of metal as it attempts to settle into its new, broken position.

Smoke billows out from under the hood. Erin just stands there for a moment, shoulder throbbing and adrenaline still zipping its way through her veins. Inside the truck, nobody moves.

And yet she doesn't quite believe that the driver can be dead. As she tries to keep her eyes on the truck, Erin pops the bolt and digs in her pockets for a few loose bullets. The longer she stands still, the more her heart starts to beat its way into the back of her throat. If that driver is not dead—

Her head snaps up at the sound of the truck door opening.

To her surprise, it's not the driver's door. For a moment, she thinks he might be trying to crawl through the other side, as if to escape unseen. But she can see the outline of that body has not moved from behind the wheel.

Oh, she is going to be so beyond pissed if she has to start dealing with *ghosts*.

Erin pushes the bolt back into place and raises the rifle, keeping careful mind of where she rests her fingers. She doesn't want to develop an itchy trigger finger now, not when Max is still running around out here somewhere. Slowly, she walks around the back of the truck, though keeping herself at a bit of a distance.

The man who stumbles out seems dazed and definitely injured. He's covered in blood. It takes Erin a moment to realize that a majority of it is his own, and not just splatter. It seems to be coming from a wound on his cheek. There's something like a napkin or a tissue taped to it, completely soaked through. This is not the man she just shot.

He holds himself against the bed of the truck, wincing in pain. Then, for the first time, he seems to realize that Erin is standing just a few feet away, pointing a gun at his face.

"Jesus Christ," he mutters. His voice is thick and clunky. He spits a glob of blood into the weeds at his feet. "Why can't you freaks just die?"

Erin takes one step closer. "How about you sit down?"

She points to the ground with the barrel. In the same way she did not want to kill Charlie, she does not want to kill this guy if she doesn't have to. She won't shoot him just standing there.

The man makes a noise, a scoff that turns into a laugh. "How about I gut you, like I did your girlfriend?"

Erin doesn't for a moment believe him. Not for a second. But she can't stop the imagery from painting itself on the backs of her eyelids.

He is covered in blood. She wonders if Max did that to his face. And then she wonders what this guy could have done to Max subsequently.

Never mind, the little voice in the back of her head decides. She wants this man dead.

The thought has only just crossed her mind when the man suddenly stumbles backward. His eyes are wide with terror. No sooner has Erin opened her mouth—to tell him *Sit down, or I'll make that face a whole lot worse*—than he turns and starts to run.

As soon as he does, something dark and fast flies past Erin and slams into the man so hard it knocks the truck askew.

Erin's finger reflexively pulls the trigger when she startles, and the gunshot sends the butt slamming back into her collarbone. The pain is worse than the explosive *crack* of the shot itself. She has no idea if she even hits anything. She just drops the gun and clutches at her chest, where she can feel how hard her heart is pounding.

She can't see exactly what happens. It's dark. And it's over rather fast. But the sounds are worse than anything she might be able to imagine. The man's screams just keep going.

Erin tries to swallow back her nausea, but her stomach decides to finally stop listening to her. As well it probably should. Even as she's sick, off into the bushes near the roadside, she can still hear the squelch of flesh with horrible clarity. The Beast continues to rip at him long after the man has gone quiet. His wet, gurgling death rattle is the last thing to fade away.

Thankfully, by the time Erin stops losing what little remained in her stomach, the creature seems to have finished as well. Erin wipes her mouth dry and looks up.

There's nothing left for her to throw up, but she retches again, anyway.

The man still looks... *vaguely* human. Enough that she can make out where the bloody tissue has impossibly remained attached to the side of his face. Or, at least, she thinks it has. The moonlight reflects off a chunk of visible jawbone. A shimmering trail of loose teeth decorates the carnage all the way to the ground. All the rest is just meat, blood, and chewed-up flesh.

A long, fat tongue extends from the Beast's mouth, lapping after the taste as the moonlight reflects off the blood staining its face.

Well. So much for *It won't eat a man*.

Really, Erin doesn't know why this isn't more surprising, or why it isn't more of a relief. This should be huge. But it doesn't mean she's not at risk. It just means that *everybody* is.

Of course everybody is.

Grief blocks up the back of Erin's throat. These men are all idiots who convinced themselves that they had control over a monster they, in actuality, knew nothing about. They just wanted to kill girls.

It still doesn't explain why the Beast seemingly has no interest in hunting down Erin, but she puts a pin in that. One mystery at a time.

The Beast plants its front legs on the truck bed and crawls over the top of the car, slinking to the front. Despite the heft it clearly requires to move, the car doesn't buckle. It barely seems to register the weight on top of it at all. Erin spits, even though it does little to help the taste of bile still lingering in her mouth. Her stomach continues to roll as she forces herself forward, around the *other* side of the truck.

In comparison, the corpse in the driver's seat is prettier. This may only be because most of his face is hidden where it's slumped against the wheel. If the hole in the windshield is any indication, it was a head shot. Indeed, there's an exit wound in the back of the guy's head, vibrant crimson standing out against blond hair.

Erin also notices a handgun left in the passenger seat. For a moment, she considers taking it. But as much as the rifle is destroying her shoulder, it's already becoming familiar. She's only ever held a handgun before, never tried to shoot something with one.

She takes a deep breath and spits into the grass again. That taste isn't going anywhere. The Beast slinks around her side. For a moment, it seems like it might be interested in the corpse inside, but then it turns away and lumbers toward the road with little more than a sniff and a *huff*.

Erin doesn't give it much thought. If it gets her away from this scene, fine. She has nothing left to throw up, and these men are beyond saving. She moves the rifle back over her shoulder, and she follows the creature down the road. Her feet throb with every step. But when Erin looks up at the sky, she comes to a sudden stop.

The moon brushes up against the spiked tops of the tallest trees. It's getting *lower*.

A hysterical little laugh builds up in her chest. She doesn't know when the moon began to move, but it moved. It's no longer hanging in the sky, untouchable. It still might not be sunrise for a long time yet, but progress is progress. And it's enough to put some energy back in Erin's stride, to push her forward with a renewed sense of hope.

Time is moving. She isn't dead.

That might mean that Max isn't, either.

32

THE FIRST GUNSHOT COMES ONLY moments after Max is dragged out of the car.

It's a sharp, sudden little *pop*. Max almost doesn't even take note of it. But then it's followed in rapid succession by one, two, three more. By the third shot, even Chief Laster has stopped and turned in the direction of the sound.

Max swallows. He wants to tell himself that the sound of gunfire is a good thing. That it means the beginning of the end of this horrible, *endless* night. But he's also seen several guns over the last few hours, and Erin never once had her hands on any of them. And so the fading echo of the final shot only makes something icy run under his skin.

"That was Aiden, right?" Tommy asks, taking Max's arm from Chief Laster.

The cop nods, even though his face is vacant. "That was his gun."

"Four's a *lot* for—"

"Yeah. I know."

Max comes back to himself when Tommy starts to drag him away from the roadside, away from the sound of gunfire and farther into the woods. He kind of struggles, but his heart isn't in it.

Which is almost ridiculous. But it feels like he's been awake for days. His feet hurt. His stomach hurts. His hand has yet to stop throbbing, and that's to say nothing of his chest, where it feels like his binder might crush his rib cage at any moment. He at least got his hands to the front of his body while he was in the car, but it's not much of an improvement. He's still in *handcuffs*.

He has half a mind to stop, lie down, and quietly ask the cop to shoot him and get it over with. Erin might've been onto something about not wanting to die tired. This is the *worst*.

"Did I already tell you that your goons suck at this?" Max looks back over his shoulder, where Chief Laster is bringing up the rear. Gun in one hand, flashlight in the other.

The man grunts, like he's irritated that he's chosen to acknowledge Max at all.

"Because I think your goons really suck at this," Max continues. "I mean, clearly you've got a system. And I know you didn't ask for notes, but, maybe next time, if you don't want to get run around by a couple of trannies, I *do* have some notes."

Now his mouth is going, and he can't stop. He doesn't know why. But the longer he talks, the further away he feels from the nausea bubbling inside him.

"Do you think that was Erin killing all of your guys? Or

do you wanna keep pretending like that didn't totally freak you out—"

"You need to shut up," Chief Laster snaps, warning him.

"Why?" Max gets shoved forward by Tommy, but he just looks over his other shoulder. "What, *are you gonna kill me?* You didn't go through all this trouble to shoot me *now*."

Faster than Max can react, Chief Laster comes up, grabs him by the arm, and nearly lifts him off his feet as he rips him from Tommy's hold. As if Max is going anywhere. But the feeling of Chief Laster's fingers, digging into his skin, makes that nausea wrap around his throat again.

Max almost wishes to hear another gunshot somewhere out in the distance. Some proof that a fight is still going. That there's still some chance—

Some chance of *what?*

Max has no idea. He can't think. He's too focused on staying on his feet and trying not to cry. The cop still has hold of him, and that suffocating panic spreads through his chest.

Abruptly, Chief Laster pushes him and lets go, sending Max flailing forward. He catches himself on his palms. Bolts of pain shoot through both wrists, and Max grimaces. Now his right hand aches, but his left has been *burning* from somewhere deep within, deeper than he realized he could even feel. He wonders if Jesse broke his hand.

"All right, Tommy," Chief Laster's voice floats in, too far away and too close all at once. "You keep an eye out. Just in case."

"Yessir," Tommy responds, completely unaffected.

Max rests back on his haunches and opens his eyes. The trees have cleared into a small field, overgrown with weeds that brush against his stomach. He pushes a few strands of hair from his face and looks at the sky. It's still dark, although it has seemingly started to lighten with the promise of sunrise. One way or another, the night is almost at its end.

Before his brain can move to its next train of thought, a hand grabs him by the hair and yanks him fully upright. Max clamps his mouth shut and grimaces.

Chief Laster is on his level, close behind him. "Now, you and I are gonna sit here. Just for a minute. You behave, and I'll make sure this next part goes fast."

He lets go of Max's hair, and Max quietly takes a breath.

The relief is short-lived. The next thing he feels is the bottom of a boot pressing against his calf. Not stepping down, not yet painful, but the threat of it is there. Max goes still, resisting the urge to turn around and shoot Chief Laster a look. He's not *going anywhere*.

Still, he's trying to avoid getting punched in the head again, so he holds his tongue. Even when Chief Laster reaches down and takes him by the left arm. He winces and shuts his eyes and tries to ignore the way his whole body wants to recoil. The man's fingers dig into the scar that runs along the inside of his forearm. Max wasn't aware of how much he could still *feel* there. It's like being touched with a live wire, sharp and too much.

He waits for Chief Laster to comment on it. He braces himself for whatever cartoonishly evil thing the man's got up his sleeve, just to rub salt into the wound. *See? We're just helping you get what you've clearly always wanted.*

But he doesn't. Chief Laster just switches his grip, takes Max's right arm, and turns it so his palm is facing upward. Max doesn't even realize what's about to happen, let alone have time to stop it. He opens his eyes just in time to watch a knife drag across his wrist, almost in slow motion.

"Jesus!" Max attempts to jerk away, but he barely manages to shake the grip on him.

Instead, he watches as Chief Laster turns his arm back over and *squeezes*. Blood wells up along the cut. It's a steady drip onto the ground in front of him, but not a heavy one, and Max quickly realizes that this isn't meant to kill him. Nevertheless, by the time Chief Laster finally lets him go, his whole body is shuddering. It's probably not a great sign that he's covered in goose bumps.

In the interest of total honesty, Max wasn't on board with Erin's *human sacrifice* explanation when she brought it up earlier. Was there something in the woods? Oh, definitely. It ripped off his entire bumper. Hard to dispute that kind of evidence. And it's not like Max doesn't believe in things like that. But it was also far easier to believe that this was some weird sex trafficking thing. Or a run-of-the-mill hate crime. Or a thrill kill, where the thrills just happened to come from murdering girls instead of boys. Rational shit. Way more rational than genuine, archaic human sacrifice.

But. Max sort of doubts that ritualistic bleeding is a common part of most sex rings. This feels a whole lot more like

The Wicker Man. Or—well, his brain isn't super focused on remembering weird horror movies that Erin made him watch once during spring break. It's a little more concentrated on the blood seeping through his fingers where he clutches his wrist.

In the back of his mind, he adds *slowly bleeding out* underneath *suffocating inside of my binder* to his list of really stupid ways he could still end up dying, even if he manages to survive the whole human sacrifice thing.

33

ERIN WALKS DOWN THE MIDDLE of the road, following the Beast for what seems like ages until, suddenly, it stops. Erin stops as well.

The Beast stares into the trees as if it's heard something. Then, inexplicably, the thing scampers off into the woods. Erin stares at the branches that don't so much as sway in its wake. She hesitates to follow, but only until she looks back at the road ahead of her.

Not far away, a patrol car is parked halfway off the road.

Erin promptly pulls the rifle into her hands and returns to the woods.

She doesn't immediately regain sight of the Beast, but she's used to that by now. It seems better used as a guardrail than an active guide. It won't bring her to the exit, but she realizes that this thing has an agenda, too. Following it will bring them closer to something that gets it fed.

So long as it keeps her going toward Max, and as long as it

doesn't suddenly try to eat her face, Erin's happy to let it keep doing whatever it wants.

As she checks the rounds in the bolt, Erin tries to tell herself that she's past doubting whether she's capable of this. She knows she can do this. That's part of the problem.

The image of Aiden flashes through her mind.

The man in the truck.

The *squelch* of punctured flesh.

Her stomach turns.

Suddenly, the Beast stalks across her path, from left to right. Erin startles and stops, finger itching toward the trigger. There's nothing to hear or see, but she curves her path anyway, and continues forward at that angle. She hopes she's avoiding whatever the thing is warning her away from. She hopes it's not warning her away from Max.

As if triggered by the thought, something in the distance catches Erin's eye. Movement.

She freezes. Raises the gun. Her finger moves over the safety. Every part of her brain focuses on her next step forward, so painstakingly slow that the leaves on the ground don't even crunch when she puts weight on them.

The figure of the guy only becomes recognizable when Erin has crept within a few feet of him. His mullet is outlined in the moonlit shadow of dusk; he's just beginning to unzip his pants. Erin figures she must be lucky. Aiden or Charlie would've already sensed her with whatever serial-killer sixth sense they've been using throughout the night. Tommy clearly doesn't have it. *Good*.

She glances around, as if this could be a trap. Farther out, to her right, the trees open up into a meadow of some sort. She takes note of the sky: finally, a lighter shade of indigo. The promise of daybreak is only something of a relief until Erin considers the implications of it. If time is moving again, and moving quickly at that, then that means something has happened. Or something is *about* to happen. Something is certain to happen.

The thought makes the hair on the back of her neck stand on end. She takes the deepest breath she can, trying to hype herself up for this. Tommy's back is to her; she has the advantage.

But then her eyes dart to movement beyond the tree line, in the meadow.

Max.

Her plan completely shifts.

She doesn't have a great view of him through the trees, but Erin knows what Max looks like out of the corner of her eye better than *anything*. She spent two years perfecting the habit. Process of elimination tells her that the figure behind him is probably Chief Laster.

Erin exhales and returns her focus to Tommy. He looks down to tuck himself back into his pants. Out of time.

She flips the safety off. *Click.*

34

THE SIGHT OF TOMMY COMING into the clearing is not immediately an alarming one. But Max has barely processed his presence, the sight of his hands held up in the air, when Chief Laster suddenly grabs Max by the shirt and yanks him upright.

He was slouching before, as the terror of being a human sacrifice had quickly slipped back into the banal *twiddling his thumbs just waiting around to die* thing he was already really, really sick of. He is mostly just picking at the grass around him, waiting for the chance to do something brave or stupid, when Tommy starts coming toward them.

Max is confused by the whole thing until Erin emerges from the trees, just a couple of steps behind Tommy. She's holding the barrel of a rifle between his shoulder blades. Then Max feels something hard press into the back of his own head, and suddenly they're one gun shy of a true deadlock.

Max has to give the moment credit: it's the first time in a *minute* he's been this genuinely scared. He doesn't move a muscle. Hardly even takes a breath.

Erin plants her feet, and Tommy stops in turn, several steps ahead of her. Max stares at her—because she's *covered* in blood and looks like she just crawled through hell and back, and he can't begin to imagine what's happened since he last saw her—but Erin is only looking at Chief Laster.

"Shooting him would defeat the point, wouldn't it?" she asks.

A beat goes by. Chief Laster chuckles. "Do you want to find out?"

Erin slowly takes a step to the right, just barely out from behind Tommy. Chief Laster takes a similar step to the left and brings Max with him. Max awkwardly tries to twist his body to keep within orbit.

Tommy and Max briefly lock eyes. Max figures they aren't the most sympathetic hostages. Nothing passes between them beyond some acknowledgment of the situation. Like, *Yeah, this does suck, doesn't it?* Max looks down at himself; the blood from the cut on his wrist has continued to softly pool into his hand and onto his leg, where it creates a slight puddle. It makes his knee cold.

"You know there's a fifty-fifty chance that you got the wrong one," Erin goes on.

"Are you trying to explain how this works? To *me*?" Max can feel the way Chief Laster's grip tightens on his shirt.

"I'm saying you should think long and hard about which one of us you need before you do something really, really stupid."

Chief Laster doesn't say anything right away. In the silence, with the cold barrel pressed into his head, Max actually wonders what is the likelihood of him being killed right now.

Erin looks over at Max.

"You okay?" she asks, a little softer.

Max tries to nod, even though he barely moves his head. He's very aware of the cold metal still pressing into the back of his skull. "I've been worse. I think."

It's not even much of a joke, but it makes Erin smile.

Between them, Tommy sighs. "Look—"

The gunshot is sudden and deafeningly sharp. Max watches a halo of blood explode out from the back of Tommy's head. He jerks, and then he drops. Somebody screams.

35

WHEN CHIEF LASTER SHOOTS, Erin almost returns fire. She does not know how she has the self-control to hold back. Because with anything less than perfect accuracy . . . well, at *best*, she misses both Chief Laster and Max completely. At worst? Unthinkable.

Either way, it's the sign of a bad night when it's not the first time that blood splatter has covered her. It's sudden and almost feels like needles. She startles back and jerks the gun up, at Chief Laster, finger on the trigger but unable to pull it.

Lucky for her, the man does not use her hesitation to also shoot her. He puts the gun back against Max, and here they are again. Rotating in orbit. Minus Tommy.

"I am very, *very* tired of this, sweetheart." Chief Laster's voice seems almost as loud as the gunshot. "So, unless you want your girlfriend to be the next one, I—"

"You want that?" Erin cuts him off. Her voice sounds too high, warbling with adrenaline. "I told you, fifty-fifty. You hurt either one of us and this could all be for nothing. How sure are you that you've got the right one?"

She stops and plants her feet. Chief Laster is silent, though he never stops staring at her. Erin spares a glance at Max. His eyes are glued to Tommy's body, wide with terror and virtually unblinking.

Erin glances down at the body herself. She can still feel the blood on her cheeks. And she is thankful that she cannot see Tommy's face.

Back up to Chief Laster. Something in his expression has shifted. Erin can't quite put a name to it. She doesn't have the time to name it, either. Her index finger twitches again.

Every second that goes by makes the anxious knot in her chest tighten, notch by notch. She needs to be quicker than this guy. *Has* to be.

Every disaster scenario plays in her head on a loop. The sound of gunfire is still fresh in her ears. She knows what blood looks like under the fading moonlight. Her mind imagines everything: the gun jams, or someone panics, or that *thing* in the woods finally decides it's coming for her.

She has no reason not to shoot him now. She *should* just shoot him now.

When Chief Laster lets Max go, Erin almost does.

By some miracle, she keeps her cool. Her exhale is heavy. Relief.

Chief Laster smiles at her, as if a secret has passed between them. His gun dangles uselessly from his thumb. Max hasn't moved, although he seems to be vibrating with the urge to do so. Erin points her rifle down at the ground before bringing it back up.

The cop doesn't need to be told. He tosses the gun. It doesn't go nearly as far as Erin would like, but it's acceptable. He nods down to Max, checking Erin's reaction to every action before he fully commits to it.

Weird. Erin wonders why he's going so slowly, but she nods and plays along. She still has a gun on him. Even if she can't protect herself, she can protect Max.

She follows him with the rifle as he kneels down, takes the key to the handcuffs out of his pocket, and unlocks the cuffs.

As soon as his hands are free, Max scrambles out of reach. But he doesn't go much farther. He stays on the ground and rubs at his wrists, paying particular attention to his left hand. He looks between the other two, and then lingers on Erin expectantly, as if her inaction is not intentional. As if she should be doing something right now.

Maybe she should be. But if she shoots—if she *misses*—this all goes to hell in a handbasket. For as long as she has Chief Laster at barrel's length, she holds control over the situation. Whatever kind of control there can be. Control means she can figure out how to get them both out of this without getting shot in the back.

"Max," she begins, still laser-focused on Chief Laster, who has just been standing there this whole time, which is just freaking her out more and more, "if you go straight, my right—your left—you'll be back at the road."

His response is immediate: "I'm not *leaving you*!"

"I'm not saying leave me! I'm saying wait for me there!"

"I'm not doing that, either!"

Erin clenches her jaw and turns to him, preparing to snap. She does not have the time nor the patience to explain why she just needs him *out of here*. Out of harm's way from Chief Laster; from the guns; from a creature she knows she cannot truly control.

"You got a plan for what you're doing next, kid?" Chief Laster's voice cuts through the noise inside her head.

Erin jolts. The rifle has dipped, and she quickly brings it back up again. She wasn't paying attention. *Stupid*.

"Shut up," she answers. Her voice warbles. "Toss him the keys to your car."

Chief Laster does not. "How many of the boys did you kill?"

Erin falters. Guilt and a bizarre grief clash in the back of her throat. "Charlie's still alive."

A tense silence passes between them. Erin wonders how he brought each of the boys into the fold in the first place. She wonders if any of them meant anything to him at all.

Judging by Tommy, she guesses probably not.

Chief Laster's smile is tight, as if he expected her answer. "Miserable little idiots, weren't they? Girls get away from us all the time. But suddenly they act like they ain't never had to think on their feet before."

"Yeah," Erin flatly responds. Her arms ache. "Toss him the keys."

Chief Laster still doesn't.

Erin exhales hard, trying to beat back the exhaustion that keeps flooding in the longer she's just standing there. It's as if she were full of holes, and she's running out of things to plug them with, and the adrenaline is cascading out of her body by the bucketfuls. "I'm not gonna ask again—"

"Do you want to die?" Chief Laster cuts her off.

She stops. Frowns. "What?"

He takes a step forward and Erin takes a step back.

"I don't think you want to die."

"You think?"

Chief Laster chuckles. "Yeah. You're a smart kid. You proved that enough tonight. Tellin' the boys about your . . . *condition*. You bought yourself a lot of time with that."

It suddenly hurts to breathe. Her teeth hurt, too, and she realizes she's been clenching them this whole time. She can't look at Max.

"I don't know what you think your plan is, but even if you shoot me, you're gonna have bigger problems on your plate. Real soon."

Another step back as Chief Laster takes another forward, like the world's slowest tango.

"I think you see where this is going," he continues. "Your girlfriend—she's necessary. You know that. I *know* you know. And if you really don't want to die tonight, you don't have to die tonight."

Erin's feet stick to the ground, as if they are suddenly weighted. It's a very bold lie. A small part of her almost respects the audacity. "You really think I'm gonna believe that?"

Chief Laster puts his hands up a little, as if to say *why not?* "You, me, and Charlie? We can all put the guns down, and we can have a nice, long chat about it."

What an image. Her letting Max die for the sake of her own survival, as if she hasn't spent this whole night committed to keeping him alive. As if she does not have a gun pointed at Chief Laster for this very reason.

She's seen what they do to the *men* they catch.

Then she remembers something eerily similar that Charlie said earlier. Something about how Erin did not need to die. She thinks of Cassie. Is that what happened to her? Did they ultimately turn on her because she was, at the end of the day, just a girl?

Maybe Erin is the one woman who can make it in their death cult because they don't view her as a woman at all.

Horrible thought.

"Toss Max the keys," she says.

She has a hard time believing that Chief Laster can be genuinely surprised, but something in his expression twists anyway. His smile is tight and warped.

She holds her ground.

"You know what it likes, Erin?" he asks suddenly. "More than girls?"

Step forward. Step back. The dance resumes.

"It *loves* fear. It loves people like her—like *you*." Chief Laster gestures toward her wildly, and the next step he takes is a little faster.

Erin's finger twitches against the rifle, but she doesn't return to the trigger. Not yet.

"More than anything, it flocks to fear." He chuckles. "Charlie had no idea what he stumbled upon when he picked you two out. You *came here* afraid. Wondering what was gonna happen when we found you out."

Max bristles. "Erin—"

"I don't want to shoot you, but I will," Erin warns Chief Laster.

Either he doesn't believe her, or he just doesn't care. He keeps talking like Erin hasn't said a word. "Romans 1:22—*Professing themselves to be wise, they became fools.* You and your girlfriend did this to yourselves. Desecrate God's image, and God will chew you up and spit you *right* back out again. You want to make a fucking mockery of man and woman—"

Max shoots to his feet. *"Erin—"*

"—then *this* is what happens to you."

Erin doesn't even know what Max could possibly be freaking out about. She takes another step, just trying to be fast enough to keep Chief Laster from getting within lunging distance.

And she walks back into something. Something heavy but lacking solidity. It's like standing under a heat lamp cranked up as hard and hot as it can go.

Erin wavers. For a moment, she's afraid to turn around. Chief Laster grins at her. His eyes are like fire pits. He grins at her like he's won.

She looks back.

Those aureolin eyes are glimmering at her, shoulder-level. They prove Erin's previous metaphor about Chief Laster's eyes to be incredibly nonliteral. *These* are fire pit eyes. These are eyes that could reach out, lick at your skin, and melt you down to the marrow. It's right there, pressed up against her, practically curled around her.

A few hours ago, Erin might've collapsed from fright. She might've even tried to shoot it. She watches the Beast's jaw unhinge, teeth upon teeth upon teeth crowding on top of one another. Its tongue drags along the edges of its canines.

It's certainly focused on Erin, but there's an element of control to its gaze. It's not doing anything more than just staring at her. Hungry. Waiting.

By the time Erin turns back to Chief Laster, the weight of *something wrong* has fallen over his face. It's not obvious; he's not freaking out. But there's something. Realization, maybe.

Erin's heart pounds in her ears. She brings down the rifle a little. In pushing her back, the man has walked forward, away from his own gun.

She stares at him. "Fear, right?"

Chief Laster takes a step back. His fingers twitch near his belt, for a weapon that isn't there.

He whips around. He's going to run for it.

The weight of the Beast blowing past almost knocks Erin off her feet. It lunges forward, as if spurred on by an unheard shot, faster than Erin can see or otherwise comprehend. She tenses up, hair flying wildly in front of her face, but there's a part of her that was expecting it.

Chief Laster never stands a chance. By the time Erin has reached up to push the hair out of her eyes, the only thing left to see is a tail, all the way at the farthest tree line, before it whips to the side and vanishes. Chief Laster screams only once. An echoing, bellowing shout that seems more frustrated than fearful. Betrayed.

Erin is thankful she does not have to see it.

She lets go of the rifle so it dangles from her neck. It all gets uneasily quiet. The tall grass continues to sway in the path of those two cursed bodies. Something heavy settles in Erin's stomach. Not quite nausea, but something that still makes her want to start dry-heaving again.

She doesn't, though. If only barely. She looks at Max.

He's still standing, frozen in the same spot, not even turned around to look after that creature. Then, slowly, he sits down, and Erin finally remembers how her legs work. She rushes forward in long strides until she's close enough to get down onto her knees in front of him.

"Hey." Erin pushes the hair out of his face and gets a good look at him. There's a new bruise blooming on his cheek. "Are you okay?"

Max nods. An automated response. He's still looking out somewhere in the middle distance, between Erin and himself.

"Sure?" She looks him over.

There's blood on him, though most of it doesn't seem to

be his own. A gash on his wrist is already starting to congeal. After a moment, Max nods again, a little more self-assured.

He finally looks up at Erin's face. His eyebrows knit together. "Yeah. Are *you*?"

A lot of things hit Erin at once. The fact that they're both alive. The fact that they just survived *that*. The fact that the sky is brighter now, in the east, than it has been all night. The fact that she found her way back to Max, just like she'd hoped. For what might be the hundredth time in her life, she's been led back to him. She can't get away from him. And she can't help but start to laugh.

She might be a little hysterical. Mostly, though, she's just happy.

Slowly, Max starts to laugh, too, even though it's a lot more nervous and shaky. "I almost hit that? With the car?"

Erin nods. Her hands linger on Max's face. She holds the curve of his jaw.

"Oh my God." Max's laugh becomes a little more genuine. "Are you kidding me? That was so big!"

"I *know*, right?"

Her face has started to ache. Then their laughter slowly fades out as the unbelievability of the situation seems to clash with its horror, and Max suddenly kisses her.

Erin is too surprised to do anything but sit there. It's the strangest thing in the world. Max's smiling mouth against her own was something she told herself she'd never experience again.

Then it's over, and Max's expression is one of palpable worry.

"Was that stupid?" he asks.

Erin shakes her head.

Instead of kissing him, she hugs him. The rifle hangs awkwardly between their chests. She can feel every breath that Max takes as it becomes heavy and shaking. Then she can feel him cry before she hears it.

"I'm sorry," he gasps, muffled and almost inaudible. "I tried to turn around. I *tried*—I'm so sorry—"

Erin nods, even as Max continues to blindly stumble through an apology. She just keeps her arms around him, methodically stroking up and down the center of his back. She doesn't try to say anything. He's sorry. She knows. Erin lets him get it out.

She imagines they could spend a lifetime here, just sitting in the grass and grabbing at each other like lost sailors who found one another in the storm-whipped surf. She would like to. The moment still feels so fragile, like it might break at any second. But although a part of her wants to cling to this for as long as she can, they're also overdue to *get out of here*.

Erin winces when she finally moves to stand, as her body seems to suddenly remember all the scrapes and bruises she's accumulated over the night. She gets to her feet before she reaches down and helps Max to his. Around them, the trees shudder with a new gust of wind, a chorus of hushed, childish giggles.

Erin looks up. In the gentle purple of the almost-dawn, it seems a little less daunting. A little more solid, more *real*.

The trees shudder again, harshly this time. Goose bumps form on her arms. She looks back to Max. He's looking at her, too. His mouth is poised like he might say something, but nothing comes. Instead, his lips form a tight smile.

Then his eyes land on something behind her. "Erin—"

It's almost scary how fast she moves. Her hands have already grabbed the rifle before her brain even has the chance to catch up. Though that may be a good thing; she doesn't waste any time being scared or confused. She just whirls around and raises the rifle into position.

She registers a human form, having come out of the trees, and her body does the rest. She squeezes the trigger. It's only after she's done it that her brain finally comes back online. Only then does Erin recognize Charlie, right before he crumples like a house of cards.

That cold feeling lands in her stomach again. Hard. And suddenly, she couldn't move if she wanted to. The silence that follows the gunshot is deafening.

Even Max remains silent. After a moment, she feels his hand on her arm, but the touch is muted, as if coming in through layers upon layers of plastic. Everything else just feels numb.

Erin's still not sure if *sympathy* is the right word for what clogs her throat, even as she forces herself forward, step by step, up to where Charlie lies. There's a chord of frustration to the pity. *All you had to do was nothing*, she wants to scream, *and you would have lived.*

I was going to let you live.

His shirt is still tied off around his thigh. A new yellow-and-white checkered flannel is what soaks up the blood where she has shot him for a second time. It blooms out from his gut, just beneath the bottom curve of his rib cage. Erin forces herself not to grimace. That is a painful death, and it's a slow one.

Charlie's mouth briefly gapes, like a fish suddenly beached. He might be trying to say something, but nothing leaves him except for short, punched-out little breaths. He stares up at her. Erin stares back, wondering if she should say something. Wondering if *sorry* would mean anything.

Her eyes drift. A handgun lies discarded in the grass, its weight making an exceedingly obvious outline for itself. If Charlie were to stretch for it, his fingers might only be able to brush against the barrel.

He would have shot her in the back. Erin has all the reason in the world to return the favor. To put him out of his misery. But something wet gargles in the back of Charlie's throat, and Erin finally recoils. Her feet keep wheeling her backward until she's finally able to turn herself around and keep going as far away from Charlie as she can get.

"What are you doing?" Max hasn't moved.

Erin pauses in front of him and realizes that she's gripping the rifle with both hands. The barrel is still hot. She looks at herself before she looks at Max. "I can't."

"Can't—?" Max starts to ask, but Erin speeds past him before he can finish.

She stops at the tree line. The strap around her neck suddenly feels like it's made of sandpaper, and Erin can't rip it off fast enough. She hurls the rifle into the woods. It clatters to the ground somewhere she can't see, and she hopes the earth grows over it.

Erin swallows and feels the burn at the back of her throat. Charlie would have killed her without hesitation, and yet guilt rots inside her mouth. She hates all of them. She hates their self-righteousness. She hates how they *don't stop* until they're dead. She hates that they've forced her to do this.

But maybe her guilt is good. She doesn't want to feel like she did something *righteous* here.

When a gunshot rings out behind her, Erin screams.

Her first thought is that Charlie might have had enough left in him to finish the job. But it takes no time at all to realize that nothing has hit her. She's clean.

That leaves one other option, which is instantly and infinitely worse. But when she whips around, Max is upright. He seems totally fine. At some point, he walked up to Charlie, where he's still standing now, holding the gun.

As if the sight was not enough, Max fires again. And again.

Erin finally runs for him. By the time she gets there, Max has already emptied the clip. But he continues to pull the trigger, quiet little *click*s echoing one after the other. As if it will make Charlie any more dead.

Erin grabs him in a hug from behind, arms wrapping tightly around him and pinning his arms to his sides. A few more empty *click*s. Then Erin hears the gun fall back to the grass.

"He's dead," she exhales, just as much to herself as to Max. She does not dare look.

Max is breathing like he just finished a hard sprint. A moment passes. He swallows, sniffles, and puts his hands over Erin's. Holding her there.

"Just making sure," he replies.

Max's hands are cold. Paradoxically sweaty. Bits of dirt rub between their hands.

"Well." His voice shakes, and he clears his throat. "Guess we're both gonna have rap sheets after this."

Erin swallows a laugh, even though it's not funny, and even though Max is still shaking. She rests her head against the back of his neck.

Max suddenly stiffens. "Erin."

She looks up right as Max starts to try and rip himself out of her arms.

Those fireball eyes have emerged at the tree line, just a few feet away. The Beast is up on its back legs, paw-hands clinging to a branch above its head before it drops down onto all fours. Erin can feel it through the ground. It stalks forward, eyes locked on the both of them. It's not stalking them, necessarily, but it seems like they've got its attention.

Erin locks her arms and drags Max back in until he's up against her chest. "Don't move."

"What—"

"Don't."

For once in his life, Max listens. And Erin is pretty sure that saves them both.

Max is deathly still as the Beast pulls itself closer. Once it's near enough to smell—that same pungent mix of *rot* and something like body odor—it seems to narrow in on Max. Erin can feel him tremble against her, but he remains still as the thing circles around them. Just like it did before with her.

Then, like before, it seems to lose interest in what it has determined to be Not Lunch.

Cautiously, Erin takes a step back. Max follows along. The Beast doesn't so much as glance in their direction. It sniffs around Charlie's body, the almost gentle clicking sounds of teeth filling the air. Erin takes a few more steps until they're no longer quite so close.

"I think as long as you don't run, it won't attack," Erin says, for the first time verbalizing her theory.

Max looks up at her, over his shoulder. "How do you know?"

"I don't. But—" Erin shakes her head.

She doesn't know how to explain it. Because there's certainly a logic to its behavior. Whether Erin has the right understanding of it or not is another question entirely. But when she ran, or when they were driving away, it went after them. When Erin did not otherwise flee, it didn't seem to register her as a possible meal. It didn't seem to mind her at all.

For a moment, they both watch the Beast consider Charlie's body. Erin wonders if just one human sacrifice would have ever been enough for this thing. She wonders how much it *could* eat, given the opportunity. She wonders a lot of things she'll probably never know the answers to.

"Max?" she asks.

"Uh-huh?"

"Remind me of what you said earlier about Mothman."

It's such a strange request that Max actually stops being scared for a moment. Long enough to turn and give her a look, anyway. Then he turns back to the Beast and watches it.

"That, um, some people think it brings disaster," he mumbles, "and some people think it's trying to warn people away from the disaster."

It's quiet for a second. Erin considers this.

Max turns away from the Beast again. "I feel like we should be doing something about—this."

Erin continues to watch, unable to look away. "Any suggestions?"

"Not really."

There hasn't been a flood around here in thirtysomething years. Maybe, she thinks, without anyone around to feed this creature, the floods will come back.

Or maybe the floods will never come back.

Either way, they can't do nothing. Can't leave things half-finished. She has to assume that they're the only people left alive who know about *this*. Otherwise, these nonexistent co-conspirators should've come out as soon as things started to go sideways for them.

"I don't think it's got, like, ideology." Erin finally lets Max out of her death grip. "I don't think it wants to hurt us. I think it's just hungry."

No sooner has she said this than the Beast locks its jaws around Charlie's ankle. There's the *pop* of teeth breaking through flesh.

"Jesus Christ." Max turns away and shivers.

But Erin watches the Beast drag the body into the trees, into the shadows. Its eyes, floating in the darkness, look into Erin's once more. And then they blink out like a candle.

Weird, she thinks. It didn't eat him.

As if reading her mind, Max suddenly speaks up. "One of 'em said it doesn't eat what it doesn't kill."

"Really?"

"Something like that, yeah. Otherwise, I don't know why they didn't just shoot us and be done with it."

Perhaps. That still leaves an unaddressed detail, which itself leads to an entire world of other questions: *Where did it just disappear to?*

Where does it go?

"Would anybody actually believe us if we told them about this?" Max asks her.

Erin is still staring at the trees. Who would believe them? Unless they saw everything Max and Erin saw, who would believe a single word of *any* of this?

Nobody would believe them. As soon as she thinks it, it's as clear as anything. If they ran into the nearest town screaming about human sacrifice and monsters in the woods, not a soul would take them seriously. Not unless they saw the Beast for themselves. Not unless they smelled the decades of decay inside its mouth.

The responsibility to *do something* has fallen pretty squarely on Max's and Erin's shoulders, but Erin doesn't know where to begin.

Some things can't be told. Only experienced.

"I think we can talk about it later," she finally says.

Neither one of them moves. The Beast does not reemerge.

It's only once Max steps out of her personal space that Erin starts to think about the details of what getting out of here really entails. She shuts her eyes and groans.

"What?" Max's voice comes from a little farther ahead, as if he's already started to walk away.

"He didn't give you his keys," Erin answers, dread weighing on each word.

Besides the cruiser, the closest vehicle is the truck that Erin shot full of holes and left smoking on the side of the road. She has no idea where the Impala is. That means they're probably going to have to *walk*, who knows *how* far, until—

"Oh. No, he didn't." Max goes quiet. "But your boyfriend got here somehow."

Erin frowns and opens her eyes.

Max dangles a set of keys between his fingers, smiling like a kid on Christmas. "You coming or what?"

In the distance, she can hear something chirp. A happy little warble as the sunrise breaks over the horizon.

"Yeah. Coming."

36

CHARLIE'S DIRTY TRUCK ROLLS TO its final resting place outside of a hospital, in what Max thinks is Evansville, Indiana. The whole map situation is kinda screwed, so he just tries to follow the highway exit signs. He looks at the clock as Erin puts the vehicle into park: 7:52 a.m. They've been running on fumes for the last hour. The engine sounds as ragged as he feels.

He slept for maybe forty minutes, not long after they got in the truck and gunned it out of there. When the adrenaline crash hit, it *hit*. But then Max woke up the first time the truck jostled over a pothole, and he remained awake for the whole rest of the drive, nervously watching for any signs of movement in the side mirror.

He observes his hand, which has settled into all the wrong colors, black and blue and noticeably puffy.

It's still early enough that the hospital parking lot is only half full. A few people shuffle to and from their cars, juggling paper coffee cups and folded-up wheelchairs. Two nurses are huddled together near a pair of exit doors, periodically bringing cigarettes up to their mouths. Even the nearby highway is surprisingly quiet.

Erin looks over at him. She has bruises under both of her eyes, and there are marks forming on her neck, too.

"You look awful," she says, mouth curling into a smile.

Max blows air out of his mouth. "Seriously? Dude, check yourself in the mirror. Right now."

They both start laughing at each other until Max's chest pinches and he grimaces, putting a hand over his ribs.

Erin sobers up quickly. "All right?"

He nods. He's definitely not, but he's fine. "Yeah. Just, y'know. The everything."

"Why didn't you take your binder off?"

Max doesn't immediately answer. He looks at Erin; she's raised her eyebrows.

"Okay, I thought about it earlier—"

"You are such an idiot."

"*You* try taking one of these things off in a hurry. It's like one of those Chinese finger traps."

Erin shakes her head and unlocks the doors. "You're gonna end up breaking your ribs doing stuff like that."

Max pulls the sun visor down. A bruise has bloomed on the right side of his cheek, already green and ugly around the edges. He pulls a face, feeling out which expressions make it the most sore. If he's totally honest, it's a little gnarly.

Max carefully opens his door and rolls onto his feet. He

puts his hands on his hips and stretches, which feels great and terrible at the same time. "That'd be kinda funny, though, wouldn't it? If this glorified sports bra did more damage than getting punched in the face?"

Erin does not give him a verbal response, even though she rolls her eyes. Max watches her put the keys down on the dashboard before she gets out of the truck, too. Fair enough; it's not even theirs. He trails slightly behind as they walk through the double doors of what the posted signage declares the West Entrance.

The smell of antiseptic is immediate; muted, but still somehow overwhelming. It makes Max instantly nauseous. For some reason, it's that very specific smell that sends him back home again. The SEX: FEMALE on his wristband and all the nurses calling him *hon* and how everyone who was supposed to care for him just sent him right back into that house again.

He wavers, but when Erin looks back at him, he shakes his head and puts his hand on his side, and he keeps walking forward.

The woman behind the information desk doesn't look up at the sound of either of the sliding doors as they open and shut. She seems kinda young, maybe only a year or two older than the both of them. She's doing something on her phone, smiling absently. Her eyes flick up once, take in Erin, and then go back to her phone.

Max practically watches her brain register the sight of them. Half a second doesn't go by before her head snaps back up. She looks between them, as if she isn't sure whether she should call a nurse or security. People looking like they do probably don't often walk in on their own feet. Max manages to swallow back his laughter.

Instead, he beelines for the adjacent waiting room, which is marked off with a bunch of tacky blue carpet and fat, square armchairs. He melts into the closest one and exhales with relief. It's not comfortable, really, but it's something. There's an older couple on the other end of the room, talking to each other, and one single guy several chairs down, but otherwise it's a very empty place. None of them even acknowledge that he's there.

Erin gets all the way to the information desk before she realizes that Max isn't with her; she looks back at him and freezes for a moment. Max lazily raises a thumbs-up into the air.

She smiles at him, and then turns back to the girl behind the desk, who has been staring at her with bugged-out eyes this entire time. Max can hear Erin's voice, gentle and sweet, as she asks, "Hi. Can we please borrow your phone?"

37

MOM IS IN EVANSVILLE BEFORE the sun has set on that very same day. Not that it's exactly far; they're only about six hours from home.

Erin tries to brace herself for whatever's coming. Whatever it is, she deserves it. It's all she can think about while she and Max are getting patched up. Broken hand. Bruised throat. Bruised ribs. Slight whiplash. Max requires a few stitches. The whole time, Erin is thinking: *Don't even bother with me because my mom is just going to come in here and kill me anyway.*

While they wait, they buy vending machine chips with some of Max's quarters.

"You know the one thing I can't figure out?" Max suddenly asks.

Erin frowns. "About what?"

"About—" He sighs and bends down to pick up his bag of Fritos. "The thing with spark plugs is that your car isn't supposed to start if they're really broken down. I don't know why I wasn't thinking about it earlier, but—well, yeah, I do. But we drove for, like, half an hour after we got the car back."

Erin thinks about this. She smiles. "*That's* what you can't stop thinking about?"

"I know, right?" He pops the bag open, stuffs a handful of chips into his mouth, and keeps talking. "Human sacrifice? Sure. Actual monster? Yeah, why not. But I *know* how cars work, and *that's* the part that doesn't make sense."

Erin agrees. She imagines that they could drive themselves crazy wondering about all the ways reality had to warp and twist and bend for the night to have gone exactly as it did. Erin can feel the edge of that cliff. It reminds her of staring at that picture of her father. A ghost years before he was ever actually dead. Staring up at her from the bottom of the cliff, as if she could get to the bottom and get her answers without jumping.

She can feel that familiar cliff's edge, but not the urge to go clamoring over it like she once did. Life does not stop for loose ends or closure. It just goes. It will leave her behind if she continues chasing after ghosts.

Before she can so much as look at the vending machine to figure out what she wants, Erin hears the sound of loud, heavy footsteps thudding down the hall, and somehow she knows it's her mother before she even looks up. In so many words, her mom looks frazzled. She's wearing pajama pants with little Santa Clauses on them. In June.

For a moment, they both just stare at each other. Erin is ready for the screaming to start. Having Max right there, trying to quietly pull his hand out of his bag of Fritos, makes it all the more embarrassing, but Erin quiets the voice in her head that tells her to *run*.

Her heart pounds, doubly so when her mom starts walking toward her again. Erin holds her ground. She's ready for it. She deserves it.

It is surprising enough when all Mom does is hug her.

Erin awkwardly stands there for a minute, arms sort of pinned to her sides. She realizes her mom is crying when she hears a wet, choked inhale. And then Erin's crying as it hits her all at once how much she needed this. A hug from her mom. Of all things.

Once she's squeezed the breath out of Erin, Mom turns to Max, who's just been leaning against the wall watching this whole thing play out. He awkwardly waves. Then Erin's mother walks up to Max and gives him the same desperately relieved hug. And although Max tries to appear disaffected by it, Erin can almost see the exact moment that the same emotional weight comes slamming into him, too.

Being hugged by a mom who cares about him with no caveats, no strings—simply as he is.

Epilogue

BERKELEY IS COLDER THAN COLUMBUS. Not entirely in the literal sense, although Max does find himself grateful for the jackets and hoodies he brought along. Berkeley is *bluer*, marked by gray concrete towers and small white houses with terra-cotta roofs and yards of rock and dirt. The buildings seem to grow from the sidewalks. When Max thinks back to Columbus, he thinks of orange, of old brick buildings and the fire of autumn leaves blowing along the cobblestone paths in German Village.

Maybe, then, it's apt that the room he and Erin get inside the Wilde House only has three white walls. The fourth wall, the one which Max's bed rests against, has been painted a beautiful, deep shade of autumn red. Sometimes the sunset hits it just right and it's like the whole room catches fire. Max will never go home again. In the orange glow of the West Coast sunset, he finds a sort of relief in this. He can find home anywhere.

The first night in Berkeley is a long one. Max and Erin stay awake out of what Max assumes is shared paranoia. He is now, for the first time in his life, made a little nervous by the dark. As the hours bleed into the early morning, however, they move from tense silence to quiet conversation. They talk about how much Ohio sucks; the House passed a bill banning teenage trans girls from school sports on the same day they flew into town. They talk about how the girl in the next room over, a strikingly beautiful trans girl named Nora, said she was from Denver. They talk about the idea of finding home anywhere.

The blue light of morning has just begun to come through the window when Erin tells Max that she can't stay in California. "I don't want to spend the rest of my life running away from things," she says. "And I think I have to start with this."

Max is tempted to fight with her, but he doesn't. The bruises on Erin's neck are a soft shade of yellow-green. The same color as the bruise on Max's cheek. Things might not be actively on fire anymore, but it's all still pretty scorched. He can't blame her for wanting to feel some kind of solid, familiar ground. He can't blame her, but it still hurts.

Erin doesn't jump on the first flight out of town, though, and for this, Max is quietly thankful. They've only been in Berkeley for four days when it's time for Max's consult appointment to start testosterone. Max and Erin are both still spectacles at this point: the Midwestern kids with bruises and scraped-up faces who give very few details on how they got them. Those brave enough to ask get more or less the same story as the cops got—a couple of transphobes in a pickup truck, a hate crime out in the middle of nowhere.

The house is full of nice, queer people. But nobody knows what Max went through like Erin does. Nobody knows what *she* went through like he does. There's nobody else Max wants at his side when it finally comes time to walk into that Planned Parenthood.

The first appointment is the most boring one. It's nothing but paperwork: the known side effects, the unknown side effects, the *theoretical* side effects. Confirming that Max is healthy, mentally sound, and explicitly aware that taking these hormones will result in a great number of physical changes.

After Max confirms all of this stuff (*yes, relatively, duh*), there comes a second appointment for blood work. Erin goes with him to make sure he doesn't freak himself out and pass out in the chair. By some miracle, he doesn't. After that, more waiting, this time to hear back from the clinic. By the time they get the call that confirms Max to be a healthy eighteen-year-old guy, the important appointment—*the one*—is scheduled for June 21. This is the day Erin is set to fly home.

Clarke volunteers to drive them both. Clarke is the first real *friend* that Max has found in the house. A nonbinary kid with pink and purple braids out of Boston, who's been teaching Max about what they plant in the garden and who has a giant poster for *The Lost Boys* on the inside of their door.

Anyway, their help is appreciated, because one of the first things Max did after *that night* was sell the Impala for what little it was worth. The Kentucky State Police had found it abandoned in the middle of the road, pretty much where Max had left it. He can still recall the slight frown on the face of the cop who explained the condition of the car to him—appearing as if something had rammed into it from the side—and how easy it was to lie and say, *Yeah, those guys hit us with their truck. They rammed us with their truck and we were scared and we just ran.*

Max is happy that he doesn't have to make the walk down to the closest Planned Parenthood, just as he's happy to be distracted from the fear rising up into his throat with every passing moment. Fear that something will go wrong. Fear that his appointment will get delayed or canceled. Fear that his body might just spontaneously combust, because a pile of flesh goop doesn't have much use for testosterone, does it?

It's a short drive. Clarke drops them off at the clinic and Max checks himself in at the front desk. Then he and Erin wait for what feels like ages. Long enough that Max almost manages to tire himself out of his anxiety. The incessant bouncing of his leg has slowed to near-stillness by the time a nurse sticks her head out into the waiting room and calls, "McCoy?"

Max has already shot out of his seat before he remembers himself. He takes a breath and very calmly (very normally) continues forward, with Erin following behind him. The nurse proceeds to weigh him, checks his blood pressure ("a little high, but that's not uncommon"), and asks the usual twenty health questions.

Then more waiting.

"Swear to God, if I ever have to wait for anything again in

my life, I'm gonna start biting people," Max mutters through his hands.

He feels Erin shake with a silent laugh. They're both sitting on the exam table, legs pressed up against each other. He didn't ask her to remain so close, but he's thankful that she has. Erin's presence grounds him in a way that little else does. He needs it. Clarke trimmed his hair a few days ago, so he can no longer grab at the ends of it and hope to hide behind it. Erin talked him out of a jacket—because it's, like, *still summer*—but sitting here in jeans and a baseball T-shirt doesn't do anything to make him feel calmer. It only makes him feel unnecessarily vulnerable.

Max moves his hand enough to look at Erin. Her hair hangs at her shoulders. She's wearing a forest-green blouse and a jean skirt she bought from one of the shops out here. None of it's her usual style, but she looks beautiful. As always.

At last, there's a knock at the door before the doctor lets herself in. A Black woman with short red braids smiles and introduces herself as Dr. Faye.

"Do either of you two have any questions before we get started?" she asks, leisurely sitting down in a rolling chair.

Max throws a nervous glance to Erin. "Uh, no?"

Dr. Faye nods and rolls herself over to the counter on the other side of the room. She sets her clipboard down and takes a white paper bag that's been sitting there. From it, she removes one small vial. Max's eyes linger on it, even as the doctor moves on, setting up everything else before she wheels herself back over.

"Are you ready to get started?"

Max frowns. "Just like that?"

Dr. Faye smiles and rolls back for her clipboard. "Says here that you're a perfectly healthy young man. My only concern would be your history of smoking, but it also says here that you've quit recently. So, yes, just like that. If you're ready."

Max quit smoking *the day of* his consult appointment, but sure. He holds his hands in his lap, gripping his fingers so hard that his knuckles start to ache, and he nods.

Then the doctor looks up at Erin. "Do you want to help with this next part?"

Erin sits up. "Really?"

"Of course! I can walk you right through it. Lots of people get their partner to help with their injections. But if you'd rather I do it, that's up to you, hon," she adds, nodding at Max as she screws the larger needle onto the syringe.

Erin and Max look at each other at the same time.

Erin speaks first. "I won't be offended if you say no."

Max gives her a funny look. "As if," he finally says before he turns back to the doctor. "Yeah, she can do it."

Dr. Faye nods and stands. "All right, where do you want it? We can do the thigh, stomach, butt, or arm. Whatever you're most comfortable with."

"Uh, arm. I guess," Max answers.

He sits there for a moment before he pushes his sleeve up on his right arm, all the way up to his shoulder. His throat is dry. It hurts to swallow.

"Now, you'll pull air into the syringe first, exactly the amount you're going to draw." Dr. Faye narrates each action as she does it. "Stick the needle in the bottle. Push the air out. Pull the testosterone in. Am I going too fast?"

Max shakes his head.

He's been reading about testosterone shots since he was in middle school. If he wanted to, he could have done all of this already. This doctor could've laid out everything in front of him and Max could've put everything together from muscle memory. He *knows all of this,* a fact that makes him more giddy than it does impatient.

Max and Erin watch on silently as Dr. Faye changes out the needle head. She wields the syringe in one hand and wipes down Max's right arm with an alcohol wipe in the other. Like this is nothing more than a flu shot. Like it's nothing at all.

"Scared of needles?" she asks conversationally.

A small laugh rattles in Max's chest. "Not really. I mean— scared in general, I guess."

"Ah, nothing to be scared of. You're in good hands." Dr. Faye gives him a friendly pat on the shoulder before her attention turns to Erin. "All *you* have to do is hold this at a ninety-degree angle, like this."

Max wonders if this doctor realizes that Erin is trans. He might tease her about that later. *You pass so well even the gender clinicians think you're cis. Retire from gender.* Erin is visibly fighting a smile as the doctor hands her the needle.

Then Dr. Faye takes Max's arm and feels around his

shoulder, and the humor of the moment fades out into the same garble of nerves and fear and *what if you survived all of that for it to go wrong now?*

Erin's hand is cold when she places it on Max's arm. Her hands are always cold. Max shuts his eyes and stretches his hands flat against his thighs before he closes them and digs his nails into his palms. His toes have curled inside his sneakers.

"Hey." Erin's voice comes as a gentle whisper. Max opens his eyes and looks over. "Just look at me. I'm not scary."

Max almost laughs. Then he almost starts crying.

Max is thirteen years old again, on top of a Ferris wheel with the most beautiful girl he's ever known. Even when Erin looks down to position the needle, Max doesn't take his eyes off her.

They also talked about this on their first night in Berkeley. Their feelings for each other are going into a box. They are going to be friends. If they can manage being friends again, only then will they revisit the box and reconsider what comes next. That's all well and good in theory, but Max doesn't think there's a box big enough to fit the feeling that swells against his ribs as he watches Erin's face. He still loves her more than anything.

It's slow at first, enough that Max can feel when the tip of the needle finally breaks the skin. It doesn't hurt, but the sensation is such a strange one that his breath hitches anyway. Then in one smooth, painless push, the needle goes in all the way until the base comes to rest against his arm. Max watches Erin's thumb push the flat end of the plunger until the syringe finally goes dry.

Done. Just like that.

"All right, hold it there for a second," Dr. Faye's voice floats in from somewhere far away.

Erin looks at him. Her expression is almost apprehensive—as if she might've done something wrong—before it seems to melt away when her eyes meet his. Only then does Max remember that he needs to breathe. He exhales, sharp and shaky.

"And, *out*." Dr. Faye places a cotton ball over the injection spot as Erin removes the needle. The Band-Aid she smooths over the spot has a yellow smiley face in the center of it. "There! That wasn't so bad, was it?"

She takes the needle from Erin and disposes of everything into the sharps container on the wall. Then Dr. Faye starts talking again, but it all sounds like white noise to Max. He fixates on the Band-Aid, slowly rubbing his thumb over the material.

It will be months before he starts to see any noticeable changes. Weeks, if he's lucky. Despite how he fought to get here as quickly as possible, Max is aware that this isn't a process that can be rushed through. Rebuilding a body is like rebuilding a house where you only have the foundation left. There's a lot of work to be done. But the first brick is still something. It's a start.

"—you'll pick them up from your normal pharmacy after today." Dr. Faye's voice is suddenly close again as she steps in front of them.

Max looks up sharply, startled out of his daze, before his

eyes fall to the white bag in the doctor's hands. She gives it to him, and Max takes it like he's just been handed the sun.

"Unless either of you have any questions, that should just about do it." Dr. Faye smiles and looks between them expectantly.

Max tears his eyes away from the bag. "That's it?"

She shrugs, still smiling. "Easy, right? Now, if there are no questions, I'll walk you two back up front to schedule your next visit, and you're free to go!"

By the time they step out into the parking lot, Max has already read over the label taped to the side of the bag twice over. Testosterone cypionate. Sarah Faye. Max McCoy. His name, even if it's not his legal one yet. It's warm outside and there's not a single cloud in the sky. The sky never seemed so blue and bright in Columbus.

"Hey." Erin taps his foot with her own.

Max looks up, wide-eyed, wondering what he missed. But she's just smiling at him, and Max relaxes. "Sorry." He digs into his pocket and pulls out a box of gum. It's recently become his new de-stressor in lieu of cigarettes. "Just—y'know."

It's kind of embarrassing that he can't find any way to articulate the emotions swirling in his chest besides *y'know*, but Erin is not judgmental company. "You did it," she whispers, grinning.

The excitement webs out as if it's the first time Max has ever felt it. It's an energy that spreads all the way down to his toes. Max bounces in place for a moment before he grabs Erin in a hug. "Sorry," he immediately says into her shoulder. "It's just—"

Again, he cannot find the words.

But Erin hugs him back, and the pressure to say anything melts away.

Short, excited little honks signal Clarke coming down the road for them. Max breaks away from the hug and runs ahead, grinning from ear to ear.

WHILE CLARKE AND MAX chatter up front, Erin pulls one of her suitcases closer and unzips it. The disposable camera is right on top, next to the still slightly discolored Garfield shirt. Erin picks it up and checks the number at the top.

"Hey." Erin wriggles her way between the front seats when they stop at the next red light. "Last one. We need to commemorate."

Before Max can protest, Clarke has already put the car into park and taken the camera for themselves. They don't allow any time to argue.

"Dude, we're on a time crunch, hurry up," Clarke says as Max messes with his hair. "Nobody cares that you look weird."

"Oh, thanks." Max laughs, tucking the edge of his binder back into his shirt.

"Hey, I had TERF bangs in high school. We look embarrassing now so being hot later feels better. Erin, scooch in, unless you wanna just be in the back, all awkward and shit."

Erin pretends not to notice the grin that Max aims at her and leans in, close enough that she can smell the spearmint on Max's breath.

Smile. *Click!*

Clarke grins and hands the camera back. "You both look gay as hell."

Erin accepts the compliment. The light turns green a second later.

Max and Clarke continue talking about TERF bangs, so they aren't paying attention to Erin as she puts the camera back into her bag. She pushes a few more shirts aside until she finds *Through the Looking-Glass*.

She opens it. Cassie's face greets her with the same frozen smile.

The Kentucky State Police, in their desaturated blue-gray uniforms, promised Erin that they would be in contact. Funny thing was, they did seem to believe the story Max and Erin had given them: that they had been attacked by a group of men who tried to kill them. That much was still true, even without mention of the monster and the time stretch. A random hate crime.

The police seemed to believe them, but there were no bodies. When they finally came upon the house of horrors, they found blood and broken glass and several shell casings, but no body. No second floor. No drawers filled with wallets and pepper spray. As if all of those things had been sucked up with the rising sun. The only proof that any of it was *real* is the crumpled photo Erin pulled out of her jeans several days after her last interview with the police.

She found a small page for Cassie on the Charley Project, which has given her only a few more facts. She knows that Cassie was last seen around June 5, 2014. She wasn't reported missing until six months later. She was seventeen years old.

Erin doesn't know where to begin. She only knows the overwhelming weight of responsibility that presses against her throat when she looks at this girl's face. The grief of knowing that when she turns nineteen in August, she'll be two years older than Cassie ever got to be.

Erin doesn't know what sort of power she has, if she has any power at all, but she has this photo. She has her camera, and all of the secrets it may or may not preserve in its tiny, plastic body. And she has a small white business card with the phone and email of the doughy cop who first interviewed her. The same cop who called her with the news about the house and promised that he'd be in touch as soon as they found those sons of bitches.

She isn't sure how much she trusts the cops. She isn't sure if she has evidence of the Beast at all. But she might. She supposes she has to give it a shot.

They park at Oakland International. Max makes Clarke swear that they'll send Erin photos of the lettuce they've planned to cultivate in the garden. Then Clarke gives Erin their final hug goodbye.

Inside, the anxiety starts to creep in. A pins and needles

sensation at the back of her neck. An omnipresent watcher. A sense of *wrong*. Erin thinks the problem is just how fast everything happens. In no time at all, her bags are checked, and then there they are, watching the midday line work its way through security.

She turns to Max. His arms are crossed over his chest, and it takes him a moment to tear his eyes from the security line and look at Erin.

"I kind of thought it'd take longer to get here," she admits.

Max cracks a smile. "Clarke drives like a maniac, don't they?"

Not what she meant, but sure. "Yeah, no wonder you two like each other."

They both stand there for a moment. Erin swallows.

"So," she sighs.

"So," Max echoes.

Erin has no idea what she's supposed to say. Or do. She holds the straps of her backpack like it's her first day of kindergarten.

"December," she blurts out. "Bucket list. Go."

Max grins. "Christmas on the beach. Give you your first tattoo—"

Erin gives him a look.

"—*obviously I'm gonna practice a whole bunch first,* Jesus. Uh, find a good bookstore for you. Either get a car or get an apartment, 'cause it can't be both. Oh! And I want to have one single hair of a mustache going."

Erin almost hunches over with how hard she laughs at this.

Their plans are tentative. Erin has yet to even buy the plane ticket. But it's something to look forward to. Something to keep them going and to make this right here feel less *permanent*.

"As long as you remember to shave, you'll have more than a hair," she promises him, glancing back at the security line.

It's not lengthy, and nobody is really paying any attention to them, even though they've just sorta stopped in the middle of the walkway.

Erin's smile fades. It feels almost wrong being here. She knows she's doing the right thing—she believes this with all her heart. Ohio may not always be home, but it's home *now*, and she will not be driven from it—but there's a voice in her head that raises doubt. It questions her certainty about where she wants to be. Where she needs to be. If those *are* two different places.

"You're not gonna pass out, are you?" Max's voice brings her back down to earth.

She shuts her eyes and smiles. "No, asshole, I'm just—"

Waiting to see if she gets cold feet? Hoping to figure out a way that makes this feel less definitive? She doesn't finish the thought. But Max nods, anyway.

"Yeah." He sticks his hands into his pockets. Then he takes a dramatic deep breath. "Okay. You'll text me when you get on board? And when you land? And when you're home?"

"Obviously. You'll text me when you get back to your room?"

He looks up at the ceiling, pretending to think about it.

"Max."

"Yeah, totally. As soon as I start to miss your big, stupid face, I'll let you know."

They smile at each other. Erin wants to do and say so much more, but they don't have time for even half of it.

It shouldn't be this hard, she thinks. It's *not* goodbye. She's coming back in the winter. She already has half a mind to come back next summer, too. But those things are all so far away, and the last time she was away from Max for that long—

"Hey." Max's foot knocks against hers. He's taken a step closer. "Seriously. You good?"

Erin nods, too quickly. "Yeah. Are you gonna give me a hug or what?"

Max rolls his eyes, but he opens his arms and wraps them around Erin's midsection so tightly that her heels lift off the ground. She hugs him back with equal intensity.

"Okay, now hurry up or else you're gonna be late, and you're gonna miss your flight, and then your mom's gonna kill me, and that's just gonna be a bummer for everybody," Max says, voice slightly stilted from having his chin pressed into Erin's shoulder.

"My flight's not for another hour."

"Exactly. You basically already missed it."

Erin snorts, and they separate. The weight of the unsaid continues to hang between them, but it feels . . . almost manageable. The way that normal people have plenty of unsaid things between them. Things that can wait until later.

She's stalling again. Lamely, she gives a little wave. Max's shoulders shake with laughter, but he mirrors her and waves back.

Finally, Erin's feet take control and start to move her away from him, toward the little metal dividers that mark the true beginning of the security line. It still doesn't feel right. But every step gets easier. Slowly but surely.

Halfway there, Erin takes out her phone to get her ticket ready. Two texts are waiting for her. The first is from her mom, wishing her a safe flight; she and Hayley will be waiting for her when she lands. The thought of seeing her sister again almost throws the whole plan for not crying out the window.

The second is from Max, so recent it doesn't even have a proper time stamp.

max:)
texting you

Erin stops. And frowns in confusion. But before she can even start to think of a response, another message joins the first.

max:)
u know. cuz i said i'd text you when i missed you.
just letting you know.

Erin laughs, sudden and startled. Her stomach twists into knots. It's not quite nausea, but something deeper, not so inherently bad. She looks back over her shoulder. Max is still holding his phone, looking as if he's considering a third text, before he glances up and finds Erin staring at him. He smiles and bashfully waves.

Something pulls within Erin's chest. Her hand waves back of its own accord. Then she slings her backpack off onto the ground and starts walking back.

Fact: this is not goodbye.

Another equally true fact: she is not doing another goodbye. She's not just *hoping* that things will work themselves out this time.

As soon as she's close enough, Erin grabs him in a bear hug. She can feel Max laugh more than she can actually hear it. That could just be because of how loud her heartbeat is thrumming in her ears. Then Max stops laughing, and Erin feels his hands bunch up in her shirt.

It feels like they stand there for the rest of their lives.

Then, in her ear, she hears his voice: "See you in December?"

Erin nods. "December."

Pulling away again should be harder than it was before, but, somehow, it isn't. It's almost easier. Erin makes it all the way to her backpack before she looks behind her again. Max, smiling and punch-drunk, watches her go.

Time has gone on normally ever since they left Kentucky. Several times since arriving in California, they've stayed awake all night to prove this to themselves. Erin has watched the clock as the moon sets and the sun rises. She does not fall asleep in one place only to inexplicably wake in another, nor does Max. But a part of her is still waiting for reality to slip up, for the curtain to drop just once and prove—*something*. That the night never really ended.

This has yet to happen. Erin hopes that it never does.

But, as she swerves through the minimaze of metal dividers up to the TSA agent sitting behind his podium, Erin gets that feeling of déjà vu again. That feeling of the earth moving around her feet. A feeling that once led her back to the Impala. Back to Max.

She's not walking away. It's a long and convoluted path, perhaps, but it's one she's confident will bring her back to Max, as it did before and as it hopefully will again.

Resources

If you are struggling with thoughts of self-harm or suicide, know that you are not alone. Please consider calling or texting 988 to get in contact with a counselor at the 988 Suicide & Crisis Lifeline.

988lifeline.org

For resources on transgender health care and support in your area, please go to:

transgendermap.com/resources/usa
or
glaad.org/transgender/resources/

Acknowledgments

Before I ever started writing this novel, I spent a lot of time watching horror films with transgender characters and writing about them online. Some of those movies are actually pretty good, a lot of them are bad, and all of them are the reason you are holding this book in your hands today. Ergo, the first thing I'm going to thank here is the power of spite.

The first *proper* and most heartfelt thanks must go to Chloe, my beloved agent. You believed in this story back when it was an incomprehensible 99,000-word behemoth, and I still cannot believe how easily you found this story's heart and guided us here. You are a goddamn superstar and I can't imagine where I would be without you. *Thank you*.

Similar thanks must go to Krista Marino, Lydia Gregovic, and Becky Walker, my phenomenal editors. I am so honored by the passion, expertise, and kindness you've brought to this book from day one. Thank you to Liz Dresner, Michelle

Crowe, Colleen Fellingham, Tamar Schwartz, Beverly Horowitz, Diane João, Kris Kam, and Kelly McGauley for your hard work. And thank you to Zoë van Dijk for your fantastic cover. I cannot fathom a better team for this book than you folks at Madeleine Milburn, Delacorte Press, and Usborne. You have given Max and Erin the greatest possible homes, and I am grateful to you all.

Thank you to Rory Power, Laura Steven, Amy Goldsmith, Kat Ellis, and Lex Croucher for lending your eyes, your beautiful words, and your kindness. It's an honor to be in your ranks.

Mom, Dad, and James. What can I say here that could ever be adequate for the amount of thanks you're owed? I would be nowhere without the unwavering support of this family. Thank you for supporting me, even if you didn't always understand what the hell I was doing. Thank you *especially* for your support in those moments. I love you more than words can touch.

Thank you to the rest of my family, the aunts and uncles and grandparents who have been propelling me forward since I was small and writing very bad stories. Thank you to my second family, my home away from home: Terra and Eric and the whole Hayes clan. I cannot thank you all enough for your support.

Thank you to Daithi and Coley. This book was basically written while sitting on your bed, and then rewritten a dozen more times after that. Thank you for your friendship; I love you both endlessly. Thank you, Dia, for your intense support and invaluable consultation on dead parents in fiction. Thank you to Cecil, Bahram, Lexa, and Riley for your early reads, art, and general support. Thank you to Maddie and Paige (I hope I've earned that "Future Best-Selling Author" mug you bought for me) and to all the friends I *know* I'm forgetting; I promise to get you in the next book!

Additional thanks to Micah Stack: without you, I would have never found a love for writing screenplays, which *Old Wounds* was initially conceptualized as. Thank you to Jill Franczak, who has been singing my praises since I was literally twelve years old. Thank you to Allison Halpin, one of the first teachers to ever call me Logan and easily the kindest and most supportive woman I have ever had the pleasure to know. Thank you all for the unique ways in which you've touched my life and my writing. I hope that I've made you proud.

Finally, I have come to feel that books are a place to put ghosts. A contained haunting where our loved ones can linger and exist in some state of happiness. In that vein, I want to thank more trans people than I could ever realistically name here. All of you will linger in the pages of this book and in the pages of everything I will ever write.

For Mattie Lucero, the first trans guy I ever knew.

For Lee, Billy, Isaac, Charlie, Louise, Carter, Drew, and Jenna. For all the Reno queers who took care of me through those first awkward years of my transhood.

And, finally, for you, Nora. I place you here praying to God that you have found peace. I will never forget you.

About the Author

LOGAN-ASHLEY KISNER was born in, raised in, and continues to blindly wander around in Las Vegas, Nevada. He graduated from UNLV with a bachelor's degree in creative writing and a minor in film studies. A transgender man and horror aficionado, he has spent the last few years as a historian, critic, and analyst of transgender characters and imagery often used in the horror genre. He has been published on several horror websites (including *Dread Central* and *Slay Away With Us*), and his reading of *The Evil Dead* as a trans narrative was published in *Hear Us Scream: The Voices of Horror Volume II*. *Old Wounds* is his first novel. You can find Logan-Ashley on social media at @transhorrors and online at loganashleykisner.com.